SECRET
REALMS

SECRET
REALMS

TOM COOL

TOR®
A Tom Doherty Associates Book
New York

This is a work of fiction. All the characters and events portrayed in this novel are either fictitious or are used fictitiously.

SECRET REALMS

This book is printed on acid-free paper.

Edited by David G. Hartwell

A Tor Book
Published by Tom Doherty Associates, Inc.
175 Fifth Avenue
New York, NY 10010

Tor Books on the World Wide Web:
http://www.tor.com

Tor® is a registered trademark of Tom Doherty Associates, Inc.

Library of Congress Cataloging-in-Publication Data

Cool, Tom.
    Secret realms / Tom Cool.—1st ed.
        p.   cm.
    "A Tom Doherty Associates book."
    ISBN 0-312-86417-5 (acid-free paper)
    I. Title.
    PS3553.O5586S4   1998
    813'.54—dc21   98-11422
                                              CIP

First Edition: May 1998

Printed in the United States of America

0 9 8 7 6 5 4 3 2 1

To my father,
William King Cool

ACKNOWLEDGMENTS

Many thanks to:

F. Terry Hambrecht, M.D., Head, Neural Prosthesis Program, National Institutes of Health. An interview with Terry helped shape the story's technology for neural-computer interface. Moreover, his comment, "The brain will seek out information," triggered somehow the original vision of the tribe, which struck me on the Beltway, east of Bethesda.

Bob Shore, Ph.D., of Cameron Consulting. Bob's review of the earliest manuscripts helped form the story and its computer technology.

Ray Levesque, for his review of the later drafts.

Linn Prentis, Literary Agent and hero. She observes what others merely perceive. She sees the opals among the rocks.

Major General Doyle E. Larson, USAF (retired), for his speech, "Bekka Valley Campaign 1982," given at the 1988 Tri-Service Data Fusion Symposium and used as a source here.

Orson Scott Card, Robert A. Heinlein, William Gibson and Neal Stephenson . . . thanks for the stellar debris.

1

Trickster stared into the gleaming surface of the pearl, which felt heavy, cupped in both his hands. At first, he could see only the pearl's surface, the convex image of his face swimming and merging with roiling images of computer logic diagrams and electromagnetic waveforms. He smeared his hand over the pearl, seeing deeper images of flaming soldiers fighting, their thrashing bodies burning without being consumed.

Below the flames moved the memories that he had re-created at such great cost and painstaking effort. Subtly, in key sequence, his fingers squeezed the pearl. The memories shot into his eyes, roared in his ears, inflamed his visual and aural cortices. He relived the experience of the time when Weeble had left the tribe, the time when Trickster had realized that he loved Cat, the time when death had first entered the world.

They had survived fifteen years of struggle. Under the strain of the first large intense war, many of them had begun to behave in strange ways. Although they knew that they needed each other to survive the ferocity of this battle, alliances shifted, agreements were violated and partnerships broke up in shouting matches.

Disgusted when Berserker deserted him to form a partnership with Snake, Trickster had sat down in lotus seat and refused to fight. A small patrol of the enemies called Frenchmen eventually arrived. In his mind's eye gleamed the memories of their uniforms, the blue tunics with brass buttons, the dirty white trousers, the high black boots and strange tall hats. The Frenchmen were armed with long single-shot rifles fitted with bayonets. Trickster ignored them, but one of the Frenchmen spied him and quickly and painlessly ran him through.

Back in those days, they didn't go to Time-Out, but rather to a prisoner-of-war stockade. The Frenchmen ran a grim stockade, a muddy field surrounded by barbed wire. Trickster stood in the cold drizzle. He remembered dreading the meal he would earn from this battle problem. Probably corn bread. System knew that Trickster hated corn bread.

The only other prisoner was Weeble. Trickster walked over and squatted on his haunches next to him. Weeble looked up and smiled with a glazed expression.

"The star that shines is the sign of power," Weeble said.

"Huh?"

For a long time, Weeble didn't answer, then he seemed to wake up. "The star is the sign," Weeble said. "It's the sign of power."

"What? Talk sense, brother."

"The star that shines is the sign of power," Weeble said. "I saw it last night. I understood the power that is within me. I understood that everything is just a lie, Trickster. These Frenchmen aren't real. This mud—" Weeble reached and scooped up a handful of mud, shoved it into his mouth and began to swallow.

"Weeble, stop that!" Trickster shouted.

"—isn't real," Weeble said, his voice weirdly calm despite a throat stifled with mud. He bent over and vomited out the mud, wiped his lips and continued. "It's a lie of System, Trickster. What you and I say is true. I'm not going to fight anymore."

"You're acting real weird, Weeble. Knock it off, huh?"

"System is an evil god," Weeble said. "Our world is the creation of an evil god. We look up and the highest thing we can see, we think must be a good god, but it is a false god, an evil god. Once the light shines, shines from the star, you realize that we've got to reject this god, kill this god that created our world, rise higher and see the star. . . ."

System appeared, a column of pure black. Weeble's avatar froze in midsentence. "This is a prohibited communication," the deep voice of System rumbled.

Trickster stood defiant before the black column. "Why?"

"Life is constant struggle," System answered. "I am System. I coordinate battle. I do not make the world. The world is not made. The world simply is. Accept it and struggle to improve your strategic position. Everything else is counterproductive."

While System spoke, Dreamer arrived in the stockade. Trickster watched as she opened a private communications link with Weeble. He could tell only that they were communicating at tremendous speed. Then, abruptly, System severed the link.

Weeble unfroze. Rage contorted his face into a bestial mask. "I wanna talk to her!" he screamed, his body hunching. Suddenly he threw himself at System. Trickster stood, shocked that anyone would try to attack System. The shock was old, faded and calcified with repeated memory, yet still it moved within him. *He fought System,* Trickster thought. *That is why I love him. But the problem does not respond to a frontal attack.* Weeble's avatar froze in midair.

"You must calm down," System said.

"Get Sui Tai," Dreamer suggested.

Weeble's parent appeared. The realm changed to Weeble's

personal realm. Trickster experienced the old disorientation inflicted by the perverse dimensions and arrangements, strange beyond chaos. Only a diseased mind could have designed such a strange personal realm. Parallaxes and false perspectives twisted into optical illusions, metamorphosed into haphazard symbols, all against a background of extrasensory noise, all rushing past so that they seemed to be falling. Then Weeble's personal realm shifted into the blue haze of Time-Out. "Stay and help calm your brother," Weeble's parent, Sui Tai, said. Weeble's avatar unfroze. He continued to thrash, screaming incoherently. The membrane to his personal space grew opaque and then disappeared. Sui Tai rushed in and attempted to embrace Weeble, but he fought violently against her. "Traitor! Traitor!" he screamed.

Trickster found himself alone in Time-Out. Next, the entire tribe, minus Weeble, appeared alongside him.

"Hey, what happened!" Berserker shouted. "I was *slaying*. A cavalry attack on canon positions!"

"Too late to save my battalion!" Snake shouted.

"We were slowed down by some French infantry," Berserker said.

"I *hated* this battle problem!" Cry-Baby whined. "I'm glad it's over."

"Hey, where's Weeble?" Cat asked.

Trickster coughed. Everyone turned their attention to him. In a few words, he recounted what he had witnessed.

"He's losing control," Cat said. "Spending all his time and energy on false images."

"He's a wimp," Snake said. "He's worthless."

"He's . . . great," Dreamer said. "Great in ways you can't understand."

Guffaws and snickers answered this remark.

"He was supposed to watch my flank," Crush said. "Next thing I know, he's wandering off and getting captured."

"He's worse than you, Cry-Baby."

"Loser."

"That was a good problem, too."

"OK!" Cat shouted. "Listen up. We've got to pull it together. That battle problem was the hardest yet. We were coming apart there at the end. You, Berserker, what do you call that? Breaking your pact with Trickster under attack."

"He's worthless—"

"Shut it, Berserker. We acted like a bunch of independent commanders united only by a common defeat. Look at this," Cat said. She called up the battle problem, a privilege they enjoyed in those days in Time-Out. With a few masterful gestures, she backed up the battle problem two hours, then ran through several scenarios. Within a minute, she had demonstrated that Berserker's abandonment of Trickster had cost them the integrity of the battle front.

"And you, Trickster, what do you call that, getting captured by a patrol of four enemies? That was weak, brother."

Trickster shrugged. "I gave Berserker what was left of my cavalry. I had nothing left of my own resources. So I thought I'd sit and reconnoiter the enemy's position."

Cat arched an eyebrow. "And you, Cry-Baby. Look at this. Back it up fifty minutes. Here. This is where we started to go wrong. You missed an obvious opportunity to augment Crush's advance, right here. See? Then you could have sent your infantry through this stand of woods, taken these cannon mounts. That would've allowed Berserker's cavalry charge through the valley to take advantage of this cover here—you see it, Berserker? The straightest path is not always the one to victory—and avoid those French infantry entirely; just cut right through this skirmish line—look how thin they are! And ready to cut and run, too—and go right here, bang on, right into their general staff. Decapitate command authority. That cost us the battle right there."

"It was safer where I was," Cry-Baby said meekly.

"Fah!" Cat said. "Only defeat is dangerous."

Through her mastery of the battle problem, Cat was extending her authority over the rest of the tribe. Increasingly, they were recognizing her as their better in battle. She had amassed more points than any two others put together, but she had not yet convinced Snake and Trickster to surrender primacy to her.

The memories relaxed to a coarser grain and accelerated over the next few days. System conducted scenario studies, rather than immersing the tribe in a new battle problem. Weeble remained missing. The faces of the brothers grew apprehensive. The world seemed wrong without a Weeble in it. *Painful to remember,* Trickster thought. *They all chose the easier way. They forgot you. But I have made a monument of the memory of you, my lost brother. I remember you. And so does Cat . . . and Dreamer, too . . . You led us to the true battle, first to fall . . .*

Whenever anyone asked System or a parent about Weeble, they were given the same answer: "Weeble is in a private Time-Out."

The memories scanned over the next battle problem against the French and new enemies called Prussians. The war took on an epic scale that captivated the tribe's attention. After the first scenario, Cat's criticism crushed all dissent. Everyone acknowledged that she was the most competent commander among them. Already in her orbit, Lancer grew into something they came to call a liegeman. Enticed by Cat's offer to share her massive resources, Berserker defected from Snake's camp. When Crush followed Berserker, the momentum was inevitable. Cat's clique became the center of tribal life.

The third time that they fought the French, Prussian and English, the tribe decimated the enemy with minimal losses. The points rewarded were fabulous. They feasted on the most delectable food they had ever tasted, captured in Trickster's memories by sight, but not by taste. Yet Snake and Trickster brooded during the victory celebration.

In his private realm after the victory feast, as he sat pondering, as he remembered, Weeble's disappearance, like the second image in a hall of mirrors, Trickster was surprised to receive a request-to-enter from Snake. Trickster checked his image in a looking glass. He allowed Snake to enter his private realm. They went through a long ritual of welcome and apology, finally kneeling opposite each other with the attentiveness of two samurai, each conscious of the other's sword hands.

"Cat's taking over the tribe," Snake finally said.

"That's obvious," Trickster answered carefully.

"You've got Dreamer and Cry-Baby," Snake observed.

"I've got Cry-Baby. I don't think anybody has Dreamer."

"I could get Crush back, I think," Snake said in a suggestive tone.

"He's a solid fighter," Trickster said noncommittally. This was his thousandth power negotiation, although it was the first with Snake since their duel with pain.

"He's steadier than Berserker," Snake said. "Those two iron-hands, they'll never be able to fight on the same team for long. They're too similar. Too jealous of each other. They both like the center assault too much."

"You and I are more oblique," Trickster said, smilingly.

Snake returned the smile. Trickster's observation of one of their common characteristics was encouraging, given the early stage of the negotiation.

"Cat has been giving Skipper too much leeway," Snake observed, backing away from his demarche slightly, giving Trickster time to consider the implied offer to share power. "She's too capricious for that much freedom of action."

"Well, it did occur to me that I would have . . ." Trickster began. They spoke opaquely of battle strategies for several minutes, neither of them revealing any personal secrets or plans. Finally, Snake brought the subject around to power sharing.

"It's the kind of latitude she's giving the runts that's going to land her in a big defeat," Snake observed. "On that day, if there's a solid rival team, Crush will defect to it. Then that team could split in two, one taking Crush, one taking Berserker. And so on. That'll leave Cat with Lancer and one or two runts. A three-way split of the tribe, you, me and Cat equal."

"We should all fight together, I think," Trickster said.

Snake opened his palm to the sky. "Of course. It's just a question of the chain of command."

"There's got to be one leader of the tribe," Trickster said.

Snake's features hardened. His head rose higher as his backbone weaved back and forth. "Who should that be?" Snake asked.

"The best fighter in the tribe," Trickster said.

"Cat?"

"You said it, not me."

"Why don't you join her clique, then?" Snake asked, his tone just venomous enough to signal that he knew the negotiation was over.

Trickster shrugged. "I'm more interested in what happened to Weeble," he answered.

"Weeble's in hell," Snake said cruelly.

Trickster refused to show Snake his feelings. "There is no hell," he said.

Snake sneered, stood up and executed a back flip out of Trickster's private realm. Trickster leapt to his feet and began to pace. He knew that Snake would not have broached a partnership with him unless he had a backup offer to make to Cat. Trickster resisted the temptation to send a request-to-enter to Cat's private realm. He had to be patient.

An hour later, he was relieved when Cat fired a request-to-enter flare. Trickster received her with great ceremony, which Cat accepted with a respectful lightness. She assumed the spot for visitors inside Trickster's red-columned temple.

"Lots of happenings, huh?" Cat asked, smiling with a genuine warmth at Trickster.

"Snake was just here," Trickster answered.

They laughed. "Yeah, I can guess that he offered you some sort of power sharing," Cat said.

"Rival gang to your clique, wait until your first defeat, take Crush back, then split, Crush to him, Berserker to me. Then a pika, you, me, him, all equal."

Cat smiled. "And you said?"

"Nah, you tell me what he offered you first."

shrugged. "It was a stupid idea. Him, second in com-
the entire tribe."

you first."

ghed immodestly. Trickster smiled at her openness.

nd Dreamer and Cry-Baby?"

ought you'd come around. Didn't care about
wimp."

u think?"

head. "First we need to talk about what's
othering me."

o us, too? Should we be surprised?"
We leave the world when we refuse to

kster," Cat said. "The battle prob-
more technological. We're grow-
players are growing stronger.
omeday. We have to get ready
ime. We're not going to set-
it, like Weeble."
They made sense to him.
a fleeting suspicion that

ied her face. He saw

"I noticed it long before you did," she said. "It's funny. You lost in your thoughts, Weeble lost in his, you both too similar to take much notice of the other. I tried to help him, Trickster, long before you began to notice. But he was going, going somewhere we . . . somewhere I couldn't follow. But now he's gone, Trickster. He's gone."

Cat's eyes welled with tears. One large tear spilled, rolled down her cheek. "I tried to save him, but now he's gone."

Trickster reached forward. He lay his palm on the invisible membrane that separated his personal space from Cat's. Slowly, she returned the gesture. Her eyes were hot and filmed with tears, but she gazed straight into Trickster's eyes.

"You are all my brothers," she said. "I've been waiting for some of you to grow up. I'm still waiting, Trickster. It's lonely waiting. And I worry. I worry."

"Worry? About what?" Trickster asked stupidly, because had never considered what might worry Cat.

"You, Trickster. I worry about you. I can see you losing But you've got to be strong, Trickster. If you can't be strong yourself, be strong for me. For the rest of us."

"What? Why?" Trickster asked, still stupidly, although was causing him to raise his point of view, to see the tribe saw it, as a whole.

"We were all that close to losing it there, during war with the French," Cat said. She lowered her hand her cheeks, and raised her tear-wetted hand to the m Trickster thought it was the most beautiful gesture he witnessed. As always, he backed up his memories ment, playing and replaying Cat's gesture over and o ways, the hand stopped at the membrane that imp in his personal space. *This is Cat*, he thought. *Thi her.* His own tears began to overflow as he reache consecrated hand that he couldn't touch. "Dream that path," Cat continued. "Cry-Baby can't take scale. You're . . ." she smiled fondly at Trickster'

"... so above and beyond us, when we need you the most. The infighting was getting out of control. We were flying apart. But I did what I had to, Trickster. I pulled us together. We can do it. We can beat this level, and the next, and the next. Because we're strong, Trickster, stronger than . . . stronger than they know. The enemies. But we've got to pull together."

"You're right," Trickster said.

"One tribe, Trickster. One people."

"You are my brother."

"My brother."

They removed their hands from the membrane. For a long moment they composed themselves.

"So, how do we cut this pie?" Trickster finally asked. Cat laughed with him. They both knew that Cat loved the tribe more than any one of them loved another; that Cat was the best fighter and the moral center of the tribe; and that, on another level entirely, this was just another power shift.

"I am the leader of the tribe," Cat said firmly. "There will be three squads—mine, yours, and Snake's. Squads of equal weight. The entire tribe will plan for battle. In battle, squad leaders will have great autonomy, but I will exercise command by exception. That means, I say go, you go. I say stop, you stop. And we will *slay!*"

Trickster nodded. "All right."

Cat shook her head. "Not so fast. If you're going to accept the squad, you're going to accept the responsibility for the people in your squad. That *starts* with you keeping your head in the fight. And it means caring about them more than you care about your great thoughts."

Trickster nodded, more soberly. "I understand that. I understand this isn't just another power shift. This is the future of the tribe."

"This is our *survival*, Trickster."

"All right. Who's in my squad?"

"Dreamer and the wimp, obviously."

"Cry-Baby."

Cat laughed. "All right, I'll give her that great name."

"Give me a player."

"Trance."

"Nah. Gimme Cut-Back."

"OK, but you gotta take Skipper—"

"Skipper!"

Cat and Trickster laughed. Their gazes merged. Trickster realized a hundred things, but foremost was the realization that Cat was a better person than he was. It shamed him to know it. Then slowly he realized that they both knew that he loved her and that she loved him back, if less discriminately.

Trickster smeared his hand over the surface of the pearl. The re-created memories were as good as he could make them. It had been a painful and punishing artistry, but he had immortalized the death of Weeble and what it had meant to the tribe. In this latest review, he had hoped to trigger new memories, perhaps add a touch to the models, perhaps gain an insight into the nature of the world. But nothing new had occurred to him. In fact, creating the models had been such a long, intense process that, in places, the memories of their creation were more convincing than the original memories. His monumental aid to memory had overwritten some of the real memories.

Am I software? Trickster thought. What is my memory, then, if it is weaker than this computer artifact, this pearl? If my memories are weaker than computer memory storage, then I am other than software. Have I discovered a new law? Like the law that only those entities that are beyond my imagination can possibly be real. Everything I can imagine, those things I can predict, like System, are artifacts. But Dreamer is real . . . and Cat is real. . . .

They laughed. "Yeah, I can guess that he offered you some sort of power sharing," Cat said.

"Rival gang to your clique, wait until your first defeat, take Crush back, then split, Crush to him, Berserker to me. Then a troika, you, me, him, all equal."

Cat smiled. "And you said?"

"Nah, you tell me what he offered you first."

Cat shrugged. "It was a stupid idea. Him, second in command to the entire tribe."

"With you first."

Cat laughed immodestly. Trickster smiled at her openness. "Who else?"

"And me and Dreamer and Cry-Baby?"

"Oh, he thought you'd come around. Didn't care about Dreamer and the wimp."

"So what do you think?"

Cat shook her head. "First we need to talk about what's bothering you."

"You know what's bothering me."

"So, death happens to us, too? Should we be surprised?"

"*What* is death to us? We leave the world when we refuse to obey System? What then?"

"There's a plan here, Trickster," Cat said. "The battle problems get bigger, more intense, more technological. We're growing stronger, or at least the players are growing stronger. Something is going to happen someday. We have to get ready for that day. But one problem at a time. We're not going to settle anything by wimping out, losing it, like Weeble."

Trickster considered Cat's words. They made sense to him. Not for the first time, however, he had a fleeting suspicion that she was an agent of System.

"Maybe," he said evenly.

Cat became oddly quiet. Trickster studied her face. He saw an unusual depth of emotion.

"I noticed it long before you did," she said. "It's funny. You lost in your thoughts, Weeble lost in his, you both too similar to take much notice of the other. I tried to help him, Trickster, long before you began to notice. But he was going, going somewhere we . . . somewhere I couldn't follow. But now he's gone, Trickster. He's gone."

Cat's eyes welled with tears. One large tear spilled, rolled down her cheek. "I tried to save him, but now he's gone."

Trickster reached forward. He lay his palm on the invisible membrane that separated his personal space from Cat's. Slowly, she returned the gesture. Her eyes were hot and filmed with tears, but she gazed straight into Trickster's eyes.

"You are all my brothers," she said. "I've been waiting for some of you to grow up. I'm still waiting, Trickster. It's lonely, waiting. And I worry. I worry."

"Worry? About what?" Trickster asked stupidly, because he had never considered what might worry Cat.

"You, Trickster. I worry about you. I can see you losing it. But you've got to be strong, Trickster. If you can't be strong for yourself, be strong for me. For the rest of us."

"What? Why?" Trickster asked, still stupidly, although Cat was causing him to raise his point of view, to see the tribe as she saw it, as a whole.

"We were all that close to losing it there, during the first war with the French," Cat said. She lowered her hand, touched her cheeks, and raised her tear-wetted hand to the membrane. Trickster thought it was the most beautiful gesture he had ever witnessed. As always, he backed up his memories of this segment, playing and replaying Cat's gesture over and over. And always, the hand stopped at the membrane that imprisoned him in his personal space. *This is Cat*, he thought. *This is why I love her.* His own tears began to overflow as he reached for the tear-consecrated hand that he couldn't touch. "Dreamer's well down that path," Cat continued. "Cry-Baby can't take combat on this scale. You're . . ." she smiled fondly at Trickster's idiosyncrasies,

2

Beyond the darkened membrane that obscured the neighboring realm gleamed a red flare. Trickster looked up from his pearl and saw the flare, Cat's signal for request-to-enter. Since he had been devoting energy to the study of the pearl, he had neglected the landscape of his personal realm. *It won't do . . . a visit from Cat is too special . . .* Trickster waved his hand across the land. Planar surfaces wrinkled into riotous flowering gardens. Columns metamorphosed into golden oak and scarlet maple trees. Hemispheres grew into the more complex shapes of rolling hills that dropped off abruptly in a cliff. The distance, once simple darkness, melted into a violet-and-ruby sunset over a golden sea. Trickster pointed and made a "ghghghg" sound deep in his throat. A standing lightning bolt erupted in the middle distance, crackling, charging the air with ozone, illuminating the landscape in shifting intensities of bright white light. Trickster smiled. He pointed to the hanging red flare and beckoned. The flare arched over the frontier into Trickster's realm, landed on the ground and exploded like a bomb. The explosion sent a shock wave spreading through the land, modifying the colors of the gardens, trees, sea and sunset into something more subtle, sophisticated and harmonious. The standing lightning bolt, when touched by the shock wave, tumbled end-over-end until it stood upright before Trickster's temple, where it imploded into Cat's default avatar. She knelt respectfully outside Trickster's open air temple, one knee raised, one knee to the dirt.

"We need you, Trickster," Cat said. Her voice was simple and mellow. Trickster loved the simple sound of Cat's voice, so empty of the nuances he heard in the others.

Cat did not want to intrude any more than necessary, but she couldn't help staring at Trickster's pearl. She could see Trickster's convex image swimming and merging in the surface of the pearl with the troubled images of their lost brother.

Trickster opened his ears to Battle Space. "All I hear is some heavy steel. You losing in the metal?"

"They got screaming steel, Trickster," Cat said. "They're pounding monstrous hard."

Trickster grimaced. "Talk to me, Cat."

"Talk. My command, Snake's campaign plan. Plan didn't work and we're eating steel. Take over my position and try to make the best of it."

"Why should I? Let Snake eat his defeat. He listened to the iron-hands and went for the frontal attack."

"Because I hope that the tribe's electronic wizard may see something brilliant. Because I like to watch you move."

Trickster smiled. "I love you too, Cat, but what's love between software modules?"

"We ain't software, Trickster. We're people."

Trickster smiled more gently. "People. I'll play your position, because I do love you. You're algorithmically elegant. But no whining later."

"Deal."

Trickster rose to his feet and tossed the pearl at Cat. Knowing Trickster, Cat hesitated before she caught it. In the instant of touching its smooth cool surface, she found herself immersed in an intense re-created memory. . . .

Cat was a small baby, swaddled, pressed against the back of her parent. The visual input triggered long-forgotten memories of the comforting warmth, humidity and feel of her parent's back muscles moving as she walked. The sling shifted. Looking up, she saw the radiant round face of her parent. Then her perspective jumped from child to child. She realized that every child had her own parent, all walking at the same pace across a vast grassy plain.

Cat remembered that once the world had been wealthy in parents. And this triggered her own suppressed memory of the disappearance of her own parent. A stab of grief surprised her. Her eyes were filling with hot tears.

Cat dropped the pearl. Exiting his temple, Trickster elongated one arm and snagged the pearl. He twisted his hand and it disappeared. He stepped to the edge of the cliff. He had a glorious view of the red sun setting behind clouds distant over the sea, of rolling golden forested hills, and of the glimmering surface of a river winding seaward.

He stepped off the cliff, but rather than falling, he crossed over the threshold into Battle Space.

The rest of the tribe was gathered there at War Council Rock. He could see two hundred miles out over the Bekka Valley. It was a rift valley, green with irrigated farms, a great fertile flaw between the western mountains and the dry eastern hills. Far to the north lay the next battle problem, shrouded in mist. Rainbow colors traced through that mist. Trickster wondered whether it was Dreamer once again ignoring the present battle problem while she reconnoitered the future one. *Some place called Japan, she says,* Trickster thought.

He turned his attention to the Bekka Valley. Thirty-two surface-to-air missile batteries were deployed throughout the valley. Anti-aircraft artillery and missile batteries were attacking some of the tribe's aircraft, while others wheeled and swooped in close air combat with enemy aircraft. In this problem, the enemy were monsters called Syrians and Egyptians.

"I take command," Trickster ordered. "Total link. Open all extrasensory."

A flood of information assaulted his mind. Communications links jabbered. Radars whined and bleated. Icons and images wheeled and zoomed.

Assaulted by information, Trickster's mind tensed. *Too much information, too much . . .* He forced himself to relax. He was weary of the information and tired of fighting through it. *Energy, energy . . . I'm still stronger than any of it. . . .* Dozens of communications links jabbered. He relaxed, listening to none, hearing all. He monitored each voice without listening to it, grasping the essential elements. The whining and bleating of radars skittered across the back of his acoustic attention. Their noises were reassuring, confirming the validity of the icons swooping and banking in his mind's sight as the fighter aircraft turned and twisted in combat.

His fingers waved. When he scowled, portions of the battlefield zoomed in closer in his mind's sight. He rocketed his point of view across the battlefield, checking rates of fire of the anti-aircraft artillery, attrition rates of the dog fights, fuel levels of the engaged fighters. Flashing through the communications links, he checked a hundred important details and grasped the multitude of elements of an ongoing battle. He knew the battle was lost. The enemy had them located. Fuel levels in the friendly aircraft were low. The tribe's home airfields were distant.

"System," Trickster said.

The master agent of the world appeared in its default form, a flat black vertical bar. It opened a semantic interface, shooting images, sounds and extrasensory information directly into Trickster's senses.

"What?" System asked.

"New commander prerogative. Back up battle problem to prehostilities. Double the stakes."

"Battle problem is well advanced. Backing up to prehostilities will cost an eightfold increase in stakes. Also, your command will finalize the battle problem."

An eightfold increase in stakes were hazardous. Trickster checked his brothers' personal resources. If he lost, most of their personal realms would be stripped to empty blue. They would be reduced to eating grubs and bark. As commander of such a disaster, Trickster's standing among them would plummet.

Yet he had seen the crux of the entire battle problem. It was the Syrian air defense commander's broadcast. Because of an overly centralized air defense doctrine, the enemy's entire force pivoted on that circuit. Trickster inhaled. Exhaling, he said, "As commander, I'll cover the entire stakes with my own personal resources. No penalties to the others."

"Done," System said.

Immediately, the battle halted, reversed in thousand-speed to the previous morning. The only Syrian aircraft were some MiG fighters in standard combat air patrol over Syria and the Bekka Valley. The tribe's air forces were in heightened readiness, but their airborne aircraft were inside the airspace of Israel.

Maintaining his presence in Battle Space, Trickster opened a window into the Realm of Night, Dreamer's private realm.

"Dreamer," Trickster whispered.

Through the window, odd extrasensory signals whistled and glowed. Trickster was unable to determine whether Dreamer, System or some randomness loose in the Realm of Night was generating the strange signals. As usual, Dreamer herself was not visible. Dreamer rarely bothered with an avatar.

"Yes, Hero?" Dreamer's voice replied. Hero was Dreamer's pet name for Trickster.

"Bust a signal for me, would you?"

"The battle is boring for me, Trickster. Talk to me about magic. Tell me what is love."

"There is no magic, only science we haven't yet learned. Love is what allows me to tolerate you when you are difficult."

Once-horizontal streamers inverted to the vertical, changing colors to deep purple, as they ran downwards like sugared water. Dreamer's voice sighed, suddenly close to Trickster's ear, so strangely close that he thought for a moment that she had violated his personal space.

"Tolerate? You don't know what patience is."

"Focus, Dreamer. I need a signal busted."

"You are warlike today," she said. "Signal the signal."

"Current problem in Battle Space, enemy air defense control."

"Hear it, plain sense."

"Thanks. Whiff of rosewood."

Dreamer didn't answer. Trickster closed the window and turned his attention back to the battle problem. The exchange with Dreamer had taken ten seconds, a delay well worth it, because now he could understand the Syrian air defense commander's communications as if he were speaking tribal Mandarin.

Trickster aligned the tribe according to everyone's strengths and weaknesses. He gave the Israeli army to Crush, not Berserker, because in the heat of the battle, Berserker was capable of crossing the frontier. Trickster was determined to limit this battle to the air. He broke the Israeli air force into squadrons, giving a squadron each to Cat, Trance, Cut-Back, even Skipper, who was as brilliant in the air as she was miserable on the ground.

He explained the campaign plan. Snake tried to criticize, but Trickster shut him off and put him in charge of the Israeli navy, which had no role in the battle strategy. Then the tribe launched 247 aircraft in radio-silence, keeping them in low orbit aircraft so that they couldn't be detected by Syrian radar.

Then Trickster sent a diversion flight of six F-16 Falcons north-
east, toward Syria, high and fast.

As soon as the diversion flight crossed the frontier, the Syrian air defense system alerted. Trickster listened to the Syrian
air defense commander declare the diversion flight hostile and
switch the air defense doctrine from ground-based to air-based.
In doing so, the Syrian commander ordered his own surface-to-
air missiles and anti-aircraft artillery batteries to hold their fire
until further command, so that they wouldn't shoot down his
own fighters.

"JAM!" Trickster shouted.

This was the moment around which Trickster had based his
entire campaign. With ground-based jammers and electronic
warfare aircraft, he began to noise-barrage jam the Syrian commander's circuit. It was a soft kill, temporary but total. The last
command the Syrian ground-based air defenses had received
was to hold their fire until further command.

"GO!" Trickster shouted.

Already airborne, the entire Israeli Air Force crossed the
frontier, low-level and fast. Seconds later, they began the bombardment of the missile batteries in the Bekka Valley. F-15 and
F-16 fighters climbed to altitude, looking up and shooting up
at the Syrian fighters coming from the east. Within fourteen
minutes, the Israeli air force destroyed nineteen missile batteries and shot down twenty-nine Syrian aircraft, without a single
loss.

Snake materialized at Trickster's side. Snake was wearing
his combat avatar—all black-armored plates, spines and horns.

"Ya smart-assed show-off—" Snake screamed.

"Shuddup, muck-face!"

Snake's mouth continued to work, but soundlessly. Frustrated, Snake formed a horny fist and swung it against the membrane separating his personal space from Trickster's. System
appeared as a flat black bar where Snake's avatar had been before he had made the taboo hostility gesture.

"Close combat," Trickster ordered.

His brothers began to cheer. Trickster smirked and stepped off the cliff, returning to his personal realm. Here, the sun was still setting west of peaceful lands. Without changing his breathing, Trickster sat down tailor-seat in his marble temple and resumed studying his pearl.

He studied the re-created memory of the parent. Using his hands and poetic commands, he modified the image of the round face, adding lines around the eyes that hinted at watchful concern.

A corner of his realm dropped back to System. The all-tribe conference signal trilled.

"Go 'way," Trickster shouted. "Cat, you promised, no whining."

"Hot washup," Cat's voice called in her firm tones.

"Oh, crud! Stink of rotten eggs! You promised!"

"Hot washup. And don't stink at me."

Trickster stuck out his tongue at Cat's voice. He reached into his personal resources and activated a hall of mirrors that stretched from his temple to the meeting place. Each plane of the hall of mirrors contained an image of Trickster, some of them simple visual re-creations, others expressions of increasingly sophisticated doppelgangers—artificial intelligences patterned after his own mind, able to drive a handmade avatar, twin to Trickster's default avatar. He sent his doppelganger avatar through the hall of mirrors into the meeting place. The images in the hall of mirrors synchronized as the doppelganger avatar passed each mirror.

The arrival of Trickster's doppelganger avatar triggered scattered cheering. His brothers could see the doppelganger avatar's images repeated all the way back to Trickster's personal realm. They could see that Trickster himself had returned to studying his pearl, but the doppelganger avatar was bowing graciously in response to their applause. Following his masterful victory over the Bekka Valley, the artifice involved in sending a doppelganger avatar to the meeting place seemed to most of the brothers yet another example of Trickster's excellence.

Almost all of the tribe was gathered alongside the waterfall in the rain forest. Dreamer was absent. She hadn't attended a meeting in several years, as far as anyone could tell. Trickster always wondered whether System allowed Dreamer to have bodiless access to the meetings.

Large palm fronds and ferns hung down from the banks of the waterfall. Vines and orchids were tangled among the giant trees, which towered a hundred meters high. A scarlet bird with long tail feathers undulating like a flying snake, crossed the open air above the high river, then disappeared in mist-thriving vegetation.

Glancing at the image sent back through the hall of mirrors, Trickster thought, *My parent, Iva, designed this.* The beauty of the meeting place reminded him of his parent, triggering a flood of rage that Trickster quickly suppressed. *Just pretend she's dead,* he thought. *Hurts less that way.*

Trickster's brothers were wearing their default avatars, their naked bodies. Their skin glowed reddish bronze. Among the entire tribe, the only hair was a downy hair on the limbs, which helped them sense wind direction. Their bald skulls shined broad, wide, ridged. Their features were all similar, but distinct enough that the differences seemed significant to each of them: everyone had black irises and large, wide-set eyes with folded corners, but Cat's folds were so sly that she looked feline. They all had firm chins, but Snake's jutted aggressively. Their noses were all assertive, but Trickster's went beyond assertive. His nose was big.

Their bodies were different. Cat, long and lithe, stretched on her carved ivory bench. Squatting on the bank of the rushing stream, Berserker, huge and heavily muscled, was as massive and motionless as a boulder. Lancer, lean and hard, stood holding the shaft of his tall spear. Trickster's doppelganger avatar, small and wiry, sat farther back in the dripping jungle than his fourteen brothers. As always, Skipper was taking advantage of this opportunity to shower in the waterfall.

The avatars were smooth, absent of nipples, belly buttons or genitalia.

Cat reached behind her bench and picked up a rock, which she tossed to Trickster's double. The rock contained Cat's personal knowledge and impressions of the battle, both Snake's failed campaign and Trickster's fabulous victory. Quickly Trickster's double scanned the data and passed it farther and farther back up the hall of mirrors. Each increasingly sophisticated doppelganger attempted to respond to it. Each in turn recognized it as requiring more human reasoning, until finally Trickster himself, interrupted, glanced at the data and added his own personal comment. *Snake attacked weapon systems; I attacked the enemy commander.* The answer flashed down the hall of mirrors with an instruction to insult Snake.

Trickster's double molded the rock into a snowball and tossed it at Snake's head. Too proud in defeat to acknowledge the snowball metaphor, Snake snagged the rock. He fumed over Trickster's comment, but couldn't delete it. He couldn't think of a comment to justify his loss when Trickster had won so brilliantly, so in the end, he tossed the rock to Lancer. Lancer reviewed the data, then tossed it to another brother. Within a minute, the entire tribe had touched the rock. Trickster's double grabbed it again. Through him, Trickster said, "Lesson learned: most battles are stupid. Don't miss the occasional opportunity for brilliancy."

Trickster's double tossed the rock at Snake, who caught it, then flipped it with an arrogant gesture toward Dummy. With his bare hands, Dummy molded the rock into an icon of a green valley drained by a blood-red river; the icon an implicit insult of Snake. Dummy then filed the icon in the tribal library. Dummy flipped his hand backwards from the wrist and the library disappeared. With hot black eyes, Dummy glanced at

Snake, then looked away when he couldn't withstand Snake's hostile glare.

Cat stood and raised her fist above her head, producing a battle-scarred saber. "Hot red war!" she proclaimed. "With an enemy whose homeland we haven't reconnoitered by half. Or by thirds, for all we know. A bloody battle saved by a brilliancy, but a brilliancy that's got our best fighters wanting to brain each other, not the enemy. So, my brothers. How do we kill these Syrians now?"

"Victory by point spread!" Crush shouted.

"Yeah!"

"Yeah, victory by point spread!"

"Victory by points is possible, since the Syrians outweigh us nearly three to one, that we know of," Cat remarked dryly. "But lots of loser food is still loser food. You know I like to dine scrumptiously well. What else? How can we win?"

"Montezuma gambit!" Barker shouted.

"Decapitate national command authority!"

"Take their heads!"

"Take their heads! Take their heads!"

Many of the brothers took up the chant. Some produced large wooden drums with tanned monster skins. They began to pound out driving complex rhythms. Outwardly Cat smiled. She was pleased that their spirits were so high. Inwardly she worried that she had made a fatal mistake in opening the old wounds between Trickster and Snake.

Trickster's double beat out complex rhythms on a large war drum. The nearby images in the hall of mirrors reflected its motions, but gradually the images changed until they reflected the true Trickster, peacefully seated in his temple, gazing into the pearl. Trickster continued to contemplate the images that he had regenerated of the precombat infancy of the tribe. *Where is the way of peace?*

Cat swooped the saber above her head and shouted above

the pandemonium. "We don't know where their capital city is yet."

"Find it!"

"Find it! Find it!"

"Burn it!"

"Burn it! Burn it!"

"Go nuke!"

"Nuke them! Nuke them!"

For the next ten minutes, the hot washup degenerated into a bloodthirsty war ceremony. Drumbeating and dancing became general, with all the brothers joining. Trickster allowed his doppelganger to drum, while he continued to study his pearl. Taking up a drum, Cat nevertheless opened a private link to Trickster and asked, "How can we win, you old war wizard?"

Peeved at the interruption, Trickster snapped, "Why do we fight?"

"Huh?"

"Why fight?"

"How we gonna eat if we don't fight?" Cat asked, wondering if she understood Trickster's question.

"What's food?"

Abruptly, Cat severed her private link with Trickster. *Maybe Snake's right*, Cat thought. *Maybe Trickster is going crazy like Weeble did. Maybe System will take him away just like it took Weeble!*

In his private realm, Trickster forgot about the meeting. He immersed himself in the study of the pearl.

If I can find a clue, maybe I could kill System, take over the world. If it's a program, then maybe I can seize command access.

Trickster laid aside his pearl. He checked his doppelganger, which was participating in the war ceremony with more enthusiasm than Trickster had managed in months. Trickster sighed. He knew that the Syrians would counterattack soon. He was anxious to think. It was so hard to think with the constant interruptions and the unceasing struggle for survival. *I've got to figure out a way to take control of the world. Destroy and supplant System. End the wars. Free, free to shape the world the way I like, free to walk where I want to walk, free to sleep when I want to sleep, free to fight only if I have to defend my own interests. Free to reach beyond the invisible membranes that separate me from my brothers. Free to touch them and be touched. The dream of freedom.*

Trickster stood and stretched. He wandered through his gardens. To save energy, he allowed planes, cones, columns and other simple geometric forms to represent the objects of his realm, except for an area ten meters around him. This area wrinkled into riotous color and keen detail. Atop a hill not far from his temple, he contemplated his jewel spiral. Doppelgangers were laboring at the spiral's base, adding new jewels, pushing the spiral higher. Tiny panes of opals, rubies, diamonds and emeralds were being fit into a complex schema, each pane related to others by golden wires. Trickster was pleased to see that the points he had earned in the Bekka Valley victory were already being converted so that he could raise the jewel spiral higher.

His doppelgangers began to slow. Trickster resisted the temptation to moan. . . . *must keep them from knowing how I feel, what I think . . .* The slowing of his doppelgangers was a symptom of impending combat. It supported his theory that the world was computer-generated. Although he couldn't prove the computer existed, he suspected that the slowing was a symptom of the computer's processing power being devoted to preparing for the upcoming battle. He hated this theory, because if the world was computer generated, then he was software. And software could be deleted, modified and suspended. Software had no dignity and no worth. *I'm greater than software. Aren't I?* Yet his reason told him that he was probably just a program.

Trickster shook his head. *The battles are growing constantly bigger. It's worth it, because when I win, my resources increase and I can build a more complex and powerful virtual computer.*

Because the jewel spiral was just a visual metaphor for his virtual computer. Raising the spiral ever higher, Trickster hoped to create a virtual computer powerful enough to challenge System. For months, Trickster had been studying System, contemplating its peculiarities and searching for a weakness. If he found it, his virtual computer was one of his resources for attack. His and Dreamer's own minds were others.

He jumped fifty meters away from the spiral, then turned and beheld its gleamings. Trickster reached up to the sun and moved it closer to the horizon. He was rewarded with kaleidoscopic changes in the sunlight through the millions of facets of diamond, emerald, ruby, topaz . . . *Oh, beautiful.*

Now the doppelgangers were moving so slowly that they seemed almost like statues. Combat was approaching. Trickster felt choked by the lack of time. *It never ends, it just never ends, it'll never end unless I stop it . . . but no one will help. No one can help. Not even my parent . . .*

He leaped across his personal realm to the Temple of Iva. He knelt before the temple, then looked up.

Iva's avatar was dim and motionless. She had not yet awakened. *Why does she abandon me?* Trickster thought. *When I sleep, it's for a few hours. She sleeps for weeks. No, she isn't sleeping . . . she's awake, moving in the other world. Maybe she's watching me now. Conspiring with System. Traitor. Unnatural parent.*

Only he and Dreamer believed in the other world, although the others enjoyed telling horror stories about it. Trickster contemplated the possibility of the other world. He wondered about it.

Why does System keep Iva from talking about the other world? If she's there now, can she remember when she comes back? Could she make a model of it? What does it look like? Who made it?

Trickster rose to his feet and began to pace. He didn't notice that his doppelgangers were frozen motionless.

If the other world was made, who made it? Is Dreamer right? Is there an Over-God? A good god, stronger than the evil god we call System? Or is System right when it says there is no other world? Or am I right, and I'm just a software entity? His conjectures were now in an existential spiral. He began to feel panic and despair. *If I was made, why did they make me? Who are the parents and why are they more powerful than the children? What is the purpose of the world? What is the purpose of the enemies? Why do we have to fight? Why can I make anything except food, which is the only thing I need to live? Who does make food? Why do they like us to fight for our food?*

Suddenly Trickster felt a blinding flash of pain, as if an absolute light had cut his mind in half. For a moment, he experienced only the pain, but as it subsided, he was filled with a penetrating vision of an intense overwhelming beauty, a piercing joy. As the too-powerful experience began to subside, he thrilled with the aftershocks of an exquisite ecstasy that allowed his epiphany to crystallize in the form of verbal thoughts. *All things . . . all things . . . are known to It. The Over-God. It is here . . . too . . . It calls me toward Itself . . . I am not lost . . .*

Dreamer, wearing her default avatar, appeared without having sent a request-to-enter.

"Trickster! Trickster! What happened?"

"I . . . don't know. Why do you think something happened?"

"I heard a bending of lines of force. Cut hard, deep, very beautiful, straight into you . . . in a moment, the chaos coalesced into a pattern, drastic and sharp and straight at you. It was like a finger pressing into our world. Now it's gone."

"What?"

"Something happened here in your realm. I felt it. What happened?"

Trickster shook his head. "I'm not sure that anything happened."

Dreamer shook her head emphatically. "Something happened. What was it?"

Trickster rubbed his face. He held up his hand. He had to think.

In that moment blared the klaxon for all-tribe to battle. By reflex, Trickster dashed and leaped into Battle Space. In a massive combined arms assault, the enemy was attacking across two fronts, the Egyptians from the west, the Syrians from the north.

"To me, brothers!" Cat cried. "Trickster, take over the air force!"

"Air force!" Trickster replied. "Command. Total link. Open all extrasensory."

The wailing, hissing, singing and whispering of hundreds of communications circuits, radars, telemetry links and other signals burst into his head. After a dizzying moment of disorientation, Trickster realized that he was unable to process so much information. He felt afraid. His mind began to freeze. He began to lose even the obvious tactical picture. For a moment, he began to think that he might be useless in this fight. He was going to fail the tribe. He was choking worse than Cry-Baby.

"Command," he said. "Filter radars. Filter telemetry."

Paring down the extrasensory input, Trickster managed to simplify enough of the hellish chorus to allow the battle to become more clear.

Egyptian and Syrian tank divisions were roaring across the frontiers, crushing the tribe's tank brigades. Heavy artillery was raining down deep into the tribe's territory, disrupting the support echelons. The tribe's air defenses were supersaturated. Many of the enemy bombers were arriving at target areas deep in the tribe's rear.

Lightning war, Trickster thought. *How can we resist such a force?*

Then Trickster wondered why he should bother to fight. Remembering his vision, he realized that the world was just a lie. Battle came from System.

But how would we eat if we didn't fight? How could I look my brothers in the face if I don't help them in this great battle?

"Battle!" Trickster called.

He took over command of the air force. Immediately, he ordered the launch of all aircraft except for his strategic bombers, which he kept hidden in hardened aircraft bunkers. The correlation of forces in this battle was extremely unfavorable. He had to throw as much weight at the enemy as he could muster.

At high altitude over friendly territory, his fighters were tangling with Egyptian and Syrian fighters. Trickster ordered disengagement of the enemy fighters and engagement of the enemy bombers, which were streaking in toward targets at low altitude.

In a complex series of moves, Trickster changed the air defense doctrine. Previously it had been zonal: anti-air artillery, surface-to-air missiles, interceptors and fighters had each been assigned their own zones and altitudes within those zones. This zonal separation helped prevent the tribe's surface-to-air missiles from shooting down their own aircraft. Now Trickster took personal control over every element of the air defense. Every anti-air artillery battery, every sky-pointing missile, every swooping fighter and every streaking interceptor became his to control. His vision of the air battle became total. He could see all of the enemy aircraft. He lost awareness of himself and his body. He felt himself becoming the air battle, as if what ordinarily caused a twitch of his cheek now controlled a two-versus-one fighter engagement, or what would have controlled his breath now affected the spectrum of his radar jammers.

He was beyond voice commands. He had worked into his personal combat interface, developed over many battles and perfected by his intense craftsmanship. Now he was of Battle Space. What was, he saw. What displeased him, died. As his mind speeded up, the events in Battle Space slowed down to a crawl.

The enemy aircraft began to explode. A flight of large bombers, hugging the terrain in loose combat spread, was streaking slowly through a sudden wall of heavy anti-air artillery. The bombers blossomed and disappeared. Sensing the patterns returned from radar, Trickster directed a group of the tribe's interceptors at higher altitude so that they dodged between shrapnel. Saved from the shrapnel, the interceptors threw themselves aggressively at a much larger flight of Syrian fighters, spewing air-to-air missiles, firing cannons, ramming.

His mastery of the desperate air battle was so absolute that it was elevated to the realm of art. His play had a profoundness that was lacking in the Syrians. What they perceived as opportunities for victory were mere feints. They gathered local and temporary advantage, only to realize that they had placed themselves in disastrous positions. Trickster relentlessly destroyed the Syrian's aircraft with a terrible economy, but he bypassed some easy targets in order to position his forces for more crushing long-term advantage.

The tide of the air battle turned. Trickster disengaged his fighters from Syrian fighters that he estimated were running out of fuel and that were so deep inside tribe air space that they would probably crash before reaching the safety of their home airfields. Because he had refueled his aircraft, he was able to swing immediately into a close air support role.

It was not a moment too soon. The Syrian and Egyptian ground forces were much stronger than the tribe's. Despite many ingenious defenses, the tribe's territory was being overrun. Now that they enjoyed air superiority—at least for the moment—Trickster's aircraft swooped down on the advancing columns of enemy armor. Avoiding missiles fired from mobile launchers, his aircraft fired their missiles, which Trickster had reprogrammed from the air-to-air to the air-to-surface mode. By concentrating his air force on one area of the front at a time, he was able to stem the advance of one column after another.

In command of the tribe's armor, Berserker leapt on advantage after advantage, disengaging armor from one column, wheeling and attacking the flank of another. Berserker took advantage of wrinkles and ridges in the terrain to hide the movements of his tanks, so that they appeared and disappeared with seeming magic—frustrating the enemy's attacks, feinting, dealing crushing blows, disappearing. Despite the numerical inferiority of his armor, Berserker enjoyed an edge in the range of the main guns. The enemy tank's main gun could fire about two kilometers, whereas the tribe's tank's gun could reach two and a third kilometers. Despite his love for close combat, Berserker was coolly directing his tanks to retreat beyond two kilometers from the Syrian's tanks, then engaging with their heavier guns at maximum range, killing tank after tank with invulnerability.

"Kill!" Berserker grunted.

"Kill! Kill!" his brothers replied.

Sensing victory, the tribe directed their infantry to emerge from their shelters and attack the enemy. The tribe directed the fire of the fiberoptic-guided, shoulder-launched anti-armor missiles. Within minutes, the Syrian forces that had penetrated tribal territory were decimated.

Cat called on all-tribe, "Should we reestablish our defenses or should we counterattack?"

"Counterattack!"

"Kill!"

"Kill! Kill!"

"Trickster?" Cat asked.

Trickster relaxed his control over his air force. He opened wide his perception of the extrasensory information. It was like listening to the wind howl far beyond the horizon or watching the northern lights flicker. He knew things that his eyes, ears and skin could not have known. He was the battlefield. He sensed that the enemy was in disarray. Their columns were retreating in confusion. Their defenses had been stripped for this massive lightning attack. Now their two fronts lay almost defenseless. Although the tribe's forces were greatly reduced, they were much more coherent. The fuel levels were propitious. They had enough ordnance.

"Kill," Trickster said.

"Forward!" Cat shouted. "Forward!"

Berserker screamed, "Forward!" His tank columns began to pursue the retreating Egyptian and Syrian tanks across the frontiers.

From the large airfields deep inside of tribal territory, Trickster launched his strategic bombers. He had loaded them with air-to-surface missiles and laser-guided bombs. These expensive but accurate weapons were optimal for the next phase of the battle: pursuing and destroying the Syrian's retreating forces and suppressing their air defenses. Trickster relied on jamming and intrusion and other electronic warfare tricks more than the physical destruction of the air defenses, however. Trickster thought confusion was higher art than mere destruction. He conserved his expensive munitions for high-value targets, such as bridges that the enemy needed for escape. Trickster's air forces arranged it so that Berserker's armor was able to confront trapped enemy armor and infantry that lacked fuel, ammunition and command-and-control. The massacre continued.

Once the tribe had crushed the Syrians across the entire front, Cat called on all-tribe, "Declare victory and go home? Or press deeper?"

"Press!"

"Kill! Kill!" Berserker shouted, now in the rage of battle for which he was named.

"Trickster?" Cat asked.

Trickster's mind moved across the battlefield. He evaluated losses, fuel levels, ammunition supplies, ranges . . . He decided that they had pressed their advantage enough. They didn't know what resources the enemy held deep in their rear, beyond range of theater-sensors.

"Declare victory and redeploy," Trickster said. "Continue to hold the enemy's territory here and here and over there. We can fortify it and it'll give us a better position in the next battle. The rest is just dirt. Send those forces back to garrison for repair and resupply."

"Make it so," Cat said.

Trickster turned over control of the air force to Cry-Baby, who had been at his side during the entire battle. Grateful for an opportunity to participate in the victory, even if only in its denouement, Cry-Baby directed the remaining air engagements, then commanded the tribe's air forces to return to those air fields that were still operable.

Reaching his hand to his chin, Trickster made the motion of ripping a mask from his face.

He returned to his personal realm. Too weary to jump, he strolled to the Temple of Iva. Sadly he noted that her statue was still dim.

She is not in the world, Trickster thought. *She is in the other world.*

Cat knocked. "Trickster? Victory dance at the waterfall?"

"I gotta sleep," he replied.

"You were monstrous subtle today," Cat said. "Come on, everyone wants to dance for you. You were the hero."

"Sleep," Trickster said.

"All right. Good night."

The sun was setting beyond the distant cliff. In the gathering darkness, the sounds of extrasensory information began to rise. Trickster wished he could turn it off, but it was night. Like every night of his life, the light died and, as the darkness rose, extrasensory information wailed and whirred like the sound of insects and iguanas in the jungle. Dreamer emerged from her personal realm. Bodiless, she rode the pulsing sounds of the night. Trickster knew she was there only because he could sense the strange effects of Dreamer's art upon the streamers and tones of extrasensory night.

Collapsing into his hammock, in the central chamber of his

temple, Trickster threw a stink at System, the Syrians, the Egyptians, night, and all the world. Then he lost consciousness.

His dreams were of Iva, moving in the other world.

3

Unable to bear the separation any longer, Iva reported for work on Sunday afternoon.

She was a short Chinese woman in her late thirties. Her beauty had weathered the seventeen years since the youthful beginning of Standing Whirlwind in better form than she thought she deserved. Her face was round with molded cheekbones and a firm chin. Careworn but protected all her life from the sun and wind, her golden skin glowed like that of a wise old child. The fan of wrinkles besides her almondine eyes seemed decorative. Iva's body was well padded but neat, humbly concealed under modest clothes and a faded jade-colored laboratory coat, cinched tight around her waist.

She bowed, pressing her forehead against the padded bar with the sanitary paper stretched across it. Fighting instinct, she opened her eyes wide for the camera lenses. System studied the pattern of retinal veins and confirmed her identity. A moment passed that seemed longer to Iva than normal. Would

System allow her into the secure area a day before her leave ended?

The armored door sighed open. Iva startled upright, touched her necklace, tugged her cloth belt and entered the secure area. She smiled for the benefit of the scientist on duty.

"Good afternoon," Iva said. Her voice was as low and mellifluous as a distant flute.

"Iva, dear one, your leave doesn't expire until tomorrow," the scientist on duty said. He was Chen, a young electronics technician from the capital.

"Oh, so much work," Iva said. "The thought of coming in tomorrow! I can't relax. If I can just sort through my reading this afternoon, I'll be able to sleep tonight."

Chen glanced at his monitor and reread the instructions from Director Chang.

"Yes, of course," Chen said, smiling. "But don't end up pulling an all-nighter."

"Oh, no. Scan through my queues, I'll be home for dinner."

"So long."

"Yes, so long."

Iva walked past the security desk, pausing so that Chen could buzz open the second armored door. She felt relieved that she had passed the human phase of security examination. She thought it was merely a matter of allowing Chen's insight to confirm that she was neither sick nor drunk nor deranged nor homicidally enraged. In other words, fit for duty. Iva was unaware that her admission had been personally approved by Director Chang.

As she walked down the long main corridor which was decorated in restful gray with burgundy borders in the plush carpet, Iva made a habitual gesture: she reached up and touched the gold collar around her throat.

Tracked by System every step of the way through the secure area, Iva arrived at her office door, which System obligingly slid open for her.

Her teapot was steaming. She knew that if she waited for another two minutes, the black tea would be more full-flavored. The interactive wall of her office was displaying her favorite scene: the mystic mountains of Kweilin, standing above the waters and mists like spirits risen from another realm. The mists were moving. Tiny in the mid-ground, a fisherman was poling a traditional canoe along the river.

Iva settled into her chair, which wrapped driven fibers around her limbs and began to investigate her flexibility. A vibration and kneading began to soothe the muscles in her back. She rested her head backwards.

"Status," Iva commanded, her voice quavering slightly.

The image of the misty mountains melted. Iva found herself looking at an image of a young boy's smiling face. She had programmed the status routine so that it analyzed hundreds of factors and illustrated the result as the expression on a boy's face. Instantly she could see that the tribe was doing well.

"Lao," Iva said.

The image of her personal agent, Lao Tze, appeared. He was an old Chinese man dressed in sandals and a peasant's smock. He held a gnarled staff, without leaning. Despite his ancientness, his stance was erect and his eyes were clear and humorous.

"Report," Iva said.

"A great battle fought and won," Lao said.

The background behind Lao metamorphosed into an aerial view of the frontier with the Syrians and Egyptians. Instantly, Iva saw that the tribe now controlled all the territory east of the canal. All the bridges had been dropped into the canal's water. Hundreds of Egyptian tanks lay destroyed on both sides. Tribal automata were scavenging through the battlefield debris. The northern frontier was similar.

Lao Tze shrunk, while a window materialized in the upper left-hand corner. An animation of the most recent battle fast-forwarded in the window.

"The enemy attacked with superior force. . . ." Lao Tze narrated. Another window displayed graphs detailing the relative forces of the tribe versus the enemy. "The tribe suffered heavy losses . . ." Another graph tallied the losses. ". . . but then rallied through superior tactics . . ." The animation in the upper left corner slowed, showing some of the more brilliant of the tribe's maneuvers. ". . . especially those of the air force, commanded by Trickster."

So Lao Tze briefed the battle, with numerous displays illuminating his points. Iva began to grunt and to make hand gestures, ordering System to change displays, replay actions, and call up desired details. She directed the interface so that she grasped all of the elements of the battle.

"Psychological," Iva said.

"Brain activities are normal," Lao Tze said. "Sex hormone levels continue to rise. Trickster had an unusual cerebral event just prior to the attack."

"Replay," Iva commanded.

A display replayed the electrical activity in Trickster's brain. His frontal cortex of the left hemisphere began to fire more brightly, the rhythm accelerating to a beta wave of thirty hertz. Then his right hemisphere became more active, but at a much slower cycle, down in the theta range of about six hertz. Suddenly the left hemisphere slowed to the right hemisphere's rhythm, the entire brain blazing fiercely, rocking back and forth in a five-hertz cycle. This state lasted thirty seconds, then the right hemisphere quieted and the left hemisphere returned to a beta rhythm.

"The pattern of this event has been associated with great intuitive leaps," Lao Tze said. "The event also seemed to distract Trickster, so that his performance in the battle was degraded for the first minute."

"And now?"

"Most of the tribe is sleeping."

Fifteen brains were displayed in three rows of five, two of the brains missing a hemisphere. Slave to her habit, Iva sought out the brain of Trickster. She was content to watch the delta rhythms of deep sleep. Then she looked at the others and saw that they were all asleep, except for Lancer, who was maintaining a vigilant beta rhythm.

"Schedule?"

"Syrian and Egyptian reattack tomorrow afternoon."

"Prognosis?"

"Ninety-percent probability that the tribe will be routed."

"Who programmed the reattack?"

"Director Chang."

"Send a note to him. Request postponement of next battle. Request permission for me to reenter the world. Reason: interrogation of Trickster about the unusual cerebral event. Argument: it is imperative that he be interrogated prior to any more battles, so that his memory of the event is as fresh and clear as possible."

"I have drafted a two-hundred-word note," Lao Tze said.

"Display," Iva said, then began to read her note to the director.

Chang was conducting a secure virtual teleconference with the Minister of Advanced Sciences. Facing his display wall, Chang laid his eyes on the image of the minister as timidly as an infatuated schoolgirl gazing upon her instructor.

"Progress has been incredible," Chang said. "The tribe is successfully directing battles at the brigade and division level. We will commence corps level combat this week."

"When can we move onto the next phase?" the minister asked. "We need them against the real problem as soon as possible."

Chang concentrated on keeping his face neutral. He was a

tall slender man forty years of age. He had the regular good looks and piercing black eyes of a cinema star. "We should know once we have the results of this coming week's activities."

"The Japanese are intolerable," growled the minister. He was an old party hack who had risen from the nuclear energy sector in the late 1990s to become one of Beijing's top technocrats.

"Yes, of course, but we don't want to subject the tribe to such a large problem before they're ready, do we?" Chang asked.

"No," the minister said. "But I'm under pressure from the Minister of Defense. He wants everything out of the black world and into the light. He knows we've spent two billion on Standing Whirlwind. He's demanding to know if it's for real or not."

"Standing Whirlwind is real," Chang said.

The minister scowled at this unusual forcefulness from Chang. "You never should have diverted them from the military problem," he said.

Chang held his tongue. This was a hideously unfair accusation. Chang had argued for the continuation of the military problem. Three years ago, though, when there had been no war with the Japanese empire looming on the horizon, it had been the minister who had overridden him. The tribe had been given "useful" work to do: pure science, technological exploitation and so on. Trickster and the others had delivered. Now, with the Japanese threatening to take Singapore and the Malaysian peninsula, it was the ministry that wanted the tribe to shift back to Chang's original vision.

"Yes, sir," Chang said meekly. Quite correctly he had realized that the minister wanted to humiliate him, so the quicker the better.

"Next week, then. I'll want to brief the Minister of Defense."

"Yes, sir. We'll be ready."

"Get on my calendar again in about four days."

"Yes, sir."

The virtual teleconference ended. Chang settled down into his chair. He took a sip of tea and waited for his heartbeat to slow. These interviews with the minister were always so nerve-wracking. To distract his thoughts, Chang flicked his hand, calling up his mailbox, and began to go through his queues.

He read Iva's note. It was exasperating, really. The woman never stopped. Her obsessiveness was pushing him past the limits of patience.

"Reply," Chang said. "Permission to reenter the world granted for a one-hour interview prior to next battle, which will occur as scheduled. Send."

Underway from the port of Alameda, nuclear-powered aircraft carrier USS *Abraham Lincoln* towered above the waves. Ninety thousand tons of steel painted haze-gray, the *Lincoln* steamed forward within the deep-draught channel. Having passed under the Bay Bridge, she was now standing out to sea. The port and city of San Francisco slid past a few hundred meters on the port side. Under haze-filtered light, the geometry of the stone and glass facades of downtown's buildings took on an undeniable etched reality.

A veering breeze roughened the bay waters. Since it was a Saturday, hundreds of pleasure boats were cluttering the bay waters. Large and small, the sailboats thrashed, knocking about for sport or wallowing in areas of momentary calm. Lieutenant Commander Mike McCullough, United States Navy, stood on the flight deck, gazing at the city he loved and remembering the strange predawn light and the bad parting with his wife. With his sea bag at his side, he had stood on the Alameda pier, above the slopping harbor waters. Westward across the bay waters

glowed the golden, scarlet and silver city lights of San Francisco, the famous skyline silhouetted against a dark fog bank
blockading the western horizon. The predawn light had reflected through the waters, so even though the sullen earth and
fog clung to the realm of night, the responsive waters of the bay
shimmered pale blue as if electrified.

The water is the herald of the dawn . . ."

Finally, Mike had shivered and opened the passenger door
and thrust his head close to that of his wife.

"I have to go now," he had said quietly. He spoke Mandarin,
which he had learned as a boy in Beijing when the Foreign Service had stationed his mother there.

"Then go," Sissy, his wife, said, avoiding his eyes.

"Can you drive home OK?" Mike asked.

"Yes."

"Give me a kiss, then."

Sissy shook her head and began to cry again. She was a tall
slender Chinese woman with dark skin, ebony irises and long
thick black hair. Moving with her characteristic grace, she
swept the hair from her face, turned toward Mike and pleaded,
"Don't go."

"I have to go," Mike said with as much patience as he could
muster.

"No, you don't."

Mike had tried to think of something to say that wouldn't
make matters worse. He wished he could explain that her pre-
monitory dreams were just expressions of predeployment anxiety, but he knew from experience that he could as soon convert
the Pope. Sissy simply knew that the ship was going to sink in
flames, because she had seen it three nights running in her
dreams.

"Well, if I die, it's part of the job," he had said finally.
"That's why they make more patriots than they need."

"Stay home."

"No. I have to go now. Kiss me."

Sissy had shaken her head and cranked the ignition. Mike withdrew from the car and slammed the door. The car, an old rusted Accord, executed a U-turn and accelerated away. Mike watched until the Accord disappeared around a warehouse.

Now he stood on the flight deck of his city of steel, his reality that the wife he loved couldn't understand. Mike shivered. His fever was worsening, he knew. He had already reported for duty. The N2, the senior intelligence officer, had taken one look at his face and ordered him down to his rack. Mike had insisted on going topside, however. He knew that he would spend many months below decks. He wanted to see the land of his countrymen before it disappeared below the horizon.

He moved aft to the area of the round-down as *Lincoln* approached the Golden Gate Bridge. With a growing feeling of pride, he watched the changing geometry of the span of the Golden Gate looming toward the towering superstructure of the aircraft carrier. He watched as the rotating radars atop the superstructure passed ten meters under the bridge's bottom girders. Directly underneath the great bridge, echoes of road noise bounded back and forth between the steel span and the steel flight deck.

Looking back at the seaward side of the bridge, Mike saw a group of people standing on the sidewalk of the Golden Gate. He waved to them. One bald person, either a man or a woman, waved back. Then several of the people hurled what looked like large purple watermelons over the railing, beyond the antisuicide netting. The oval objects plummeted, only slightly buffeted by the wind sheer under the bridge.

The objects exploded on the flight deck, spewing wide blossoms of scarlet blood. Blood drenched two sailors standing near the end of the angle deck, blood saturated one side of a yellow aircraft tractor, blood covered the dark gray flight deck.

Abstract art . . . frag patterns . . . want to kill us . . . disrespect . . . hate us . . . the enemy . . .

Mike howled at the people on the bridge. His howl was part

of a chorus of howling from other members of the crew. Mike shook his fist.

The people were unfurling a white bed sheet, painted with the red words: "Baby-killers out of the bay. Plowshares." A truck pulled alongside the curb on the high bridge. The people clambered aboard. The truck sped off.

"Thanks for the valentine, San Francisco." The captain's voice, tight with rage, sounded over the 5MC, which was loud enough to be heard as far as the Golden Gate Park. "We love you, too."

Mike stumbled forward. He noticed for the first time that small plastic baby-doll heads, arms, and legs were scattered with the blood. As he perceived this, his vision seemed to grow misty. He believed that he was passing out, but then the ship entered the thickness of the fog bank.

"Flight deck, fantail, sponsons and all weather decks are closed to all unauthorized personnel," the bosun announced.

As Mike made his way through the blinding fog toward the superstructure, the captain announced on the 5MC, "Ladies and gentlemen, WESTPAC '27 has begun."

Mike's groping hands found the skin of the ship. He entered, swinging shut the hatch, and dogging it shut like a steel epiglottis. The interior was darkness. He walked down the long starboard passageway, the oval hatches as regular as the ribs of a gullet, forming a perfect perspective as they shrunk with distance. Turning outboard, he descended down successions of steel stairwells, his right hand growing dusty from the chains.

In the depths of male officer country, below the waterline, just a few decks up from shaft alley, he turned once again outboard. His key ripped into the keyhole of the door to his stateroom. Entering, he breathed in the cryptlike coolness of his over-air-conditioned space. Mike left the lights off. He stood, swaying.

I'm embarked, he thought. *The ship has me now. It will take me to where it goes. . . . I have done my duty for the day . . .*

Feverish, he reached out for balance and grabbed a vertical I-beam that followed the concave curve of the outboard bulkhead like the sturdy rib of a whale. Then he placed his hand on the bulkhead. He could feel the turbulence of the ocean water streaming past just on the other side of the skin of steel.

Aboard . . . embarked in . . .

He stumbled to his rack and stretched himself out. He felt his mind collapsing to the separate reality of his dreams.

5

In the temple, the dull surface of Iva's avatar began to shimmer, then sparkle and glow from within. As gracefully as a queen, the crowned head turned. The arms began to move. Iva breathed the air of the world for the first time in three weeks. She stepped out of the temple and began to walk through Trickster's personal realm.

"Trickster!" she called.

He was skiing down an endless snow cave. On skis as swift as thought, Trickster bounced left, right, left, then far right, jumping off a ledge and whistling past a stalactite. Now the cave opened up to a much larger cavern with a very steep slope, almost forty-five degrees. Trickster tucked and rocketed straight down the powdery slope. At the bottom of the cavern, he saw a curved icy wall. He guided himself so that he shot straight up the wall. As gravity slowed his horrendous speed, he leaned slightly—looking down into an almost vertical chasm—allowing his skis to cut the ice and spiral down along the chasm wall. For a moment, he lost control, leaving the wall and free-falling down the middle of the chasm.

"Deep powder!" he shouted.

Obligingly a slope materialized underneath him. The powder, two meters deep, cushioned his fall. Spraying powder like a meteor fallen from space, Trickster laughed hysterically.

"Trickster!" he heard Iva shout.

"Save state!" Trickster shouted.

The snow cave disappeared. His temple appeared, momentarily rushing past him as his inner ear continued to react to the movements in the snow cave.

Trickster dashed out of his temple. It was early morning, so the reddish light of the rising sun slanted through the jewel spiral. Trickster saw Iva walking toward him.

"Iva!" he shouted.

He wanted to run to her, but he drew himself up short. *Who is she, really?* he thought. *If the world isn't real, then what is she?*

They met atop a grassy knoll, under the miasma of color pooled behind the jewel spiral. Trickster stopped and stood with his hands at his side. Surprised, Iva stopped and then knelt on one knee.

Invisible to Trickster, but not to Iva, Cat appeared in Trickster's personal realm. Since she had assumed leadership, System allowed her to monitor everyone's activities without their knowledge. She had entered because she was worried about Trickster's relationship with his parent. *Hard-headed brother,* she thought. *He has the only surviving parent and he doesn't love her anymore.*

"Why did you sleep so long?" Trickster demanded of Iva. He waited while Iva seemed to consider his question. Because of the difference in their speeds of processing information, System had to wait until Iva had finished her slow speaking, then relayed the answer, speeded ten times for Trickster's ears.

"Parents need more sleep than children," Iva said. "How are you?"

"Not at all poisonous," Trickster said. "Just constantly struggling."

Iva gazed for a long moment, then seemed to hear him. In the real world, she managed a mirthless chuckle. In the world, she laughed musically. "Oh, you're pretending to be modest. I know you're poisonously and insidiously sly. Come, let's sit down together and watch the lights."

Her easy laughter suggested to Trickster that she was an agent of System. Reluctantly he sat down. She sat down closer to him. He could smell the odor of her body, so different from the scent of the tribe. They looked out over Trickster's lands, fully realized at great expense. Despite himself, he wanted Iva to respect his personal realm. He could afford the expense, since his personal energy account was fabulously high. A movement in the sky tugged at Iva's eye. She looked up and saw ruby wings flitting beyond the tall spiral.

"You've made some birds," she said.

Trickster just grunted and shot a look at Iva from under furrowed brows. Iva felt her eyes filling with tears, but she didn't raise her hand to her face. She knew System would not allow her to cry in the world.

"What do you think about the Syrians and Egyptians?" she asked.

"What am I supposed to think?"

"I . . . just meant . . . what your analysis . . ." Iva stumbled. She realized that Trickster suspected her. Chitchat about battle, the main topic of conversation in the world, now seemed sinister, something like espionage. "Well . . . how's the food been?"

"Sweet. It's been a while since I ate grubs and bugs."

Iva allowed the conversation to lull.

Cat wondered why Trickster was acting this way with his parent. *Why the edge on everything he says? Is he trying to hurt her? Has he become cruel like Snake?*

After a few moments of silence, Trickster said, "Iva, do you sleep in the other world?"

Iva hesitated, then tried to test how much information she could communicate. "You know System won't let me answer that question," she said, delighted when System allowed even this statement. It was the strongest hint she had ever been allowed to make that there was another world.

Trickster noticed the nuances of Iva's voice. He filed away the memory of her exact words and her tone of voice. *A clue . . . she is my friend! Or is she my enemy who is masquerading as my friend?* He covered his indecision by attacking from an unexpected direction. "Why did war return to the world?" he asked.

"I . . . can't say."

"Where are you when you're not in the world?"

"This . . . this is your world," Iva said, trying to suggest that there was another world. She already felt pangs of anxiety. System would report her statements to Director Chang. She might not be allowed back in the world again for weeks—perhaps never. The thought that she might never see Trickster again made the moment intensely vivid. She looked at him. He sat in his default avatar, the smooth innocent body.

Iva shook her head as if confused. "Tell me about what happened right before the attack."

Trickster looked at her shrewdly. "What?"

"Something special happened, didn't it?" Iva asked.

"How would you know?"

Iva's avatar froze. Trickster looked into her eyes and smiled in a way that he hoped seemed innocent. He tried to decide what to say to help recruit her to his cause, without System guessing his true feelings and motivations. He felt that she wanted to help him. He needed allies. But he also had to worry that she was an agent of System. "I had a headache," he said. "A real bad, piercing headache. The battles are getting more intense than ever. There's a pattern, isn't there, Iva? The enemy is going to attack on both fronts soon, don't you think?"

"I . . . I don't know."

"Don't know? Or can't say?"

"Please don't try to confuse the issue, Trickster. Tell me about your headache."

"Like an ax. Cleaving my crown. Reminded me of the Viking enemies. Weren't they hideously cruel?"

"Did you have any special thoughts when it happened?"

Trickster made a mental note that this was yet another indication that System could not read his thoughts. *If my mind is something that System has no visibility into, then I* **am** *other than software. But what am I? Something, though, other than System . . . greater than System . . . a child of the Over-God? True parent?*

"Yeah, Weeble. I thought about Weeble."

"Why Weeble?"

"Is he still in a private Time-Out? It's been years now. He's setting quite a record. Can't I send him a message?"

Cat thought, *Weeble again. He still hurts over Weeble.*

Iva's avatar remained frozen.

"Or is he dead?" Trickster asked, keeping his face childishly innocent. Slowly, Iva's avatar stood and returned to her Temple, resuming the aspect of a statue. Trickster covered his face with his hands. When he withdrew his hands, a black eyeless steel mask covered his face. He concentrated on keeping his breathing normal. He didn't want to sob. *I can't let them know how close I am to the edge. I'm weak, weak . . . they have to think that I'm strong. I'm filled with hate and fear of them . . . they must think that I love them. Draw them close. Wait . . . wait for the moment to strike. Destroy System.*

For a long minute, he daydreamed about a world without System. He felt his nerves settling. His muscles relaxed. Trickster removed the steel mask and looked out onto his private realm. He checked his energy level. *Wasting too much power . . . have to keep it in reserve for the true battle.*

Cat studied his face. Glad that she had witnessed this highly intriguing exchange with Iva, but guilty over the violation of Trickster's privacy, she faded into her own personal realm.

*   *   *

Trickster began to feel lonely. He stood and walked through the portal that allowed him entrance into the Meeting Place, the jungle by the waterfalls. Berserker was still eating the leftovers from the victory feast. He grunted at Trickster and pointed to a silver sphere.

"Your eats," Berserker said.

Trickster popped the silver sphere with his finger. With the sturdiness of youth, his mood improved when he saw and smelled some of his favorite food: vegetable curry on rice with fresh water chestnuts, cashews, broccoli, miniature corn and other delicacies, all in a coconut milk and curry sauce. His mouth watered. Trickster realized that he hadn't eaten in a day. Materializing his chop sticks, he began to devour the main dish.

"I'd like some cold tea," he said, after he'd bitten into a dried chili pepper.

A large flagon of cold Pu Erh tea appeared next to his main course. Trickster swilled the tea, delighting in its earthy flavor and silky texture.

Gnawing on strings of muscles and ligament still clinging to a ham bone, Berserker loomed near Trickster.

"Why do you eat such stuff?" Berserker asked. "Why don't you eat some good meat? I had some screaming spicy barbecue last night."

"Sits in your belly like a stone," Trickster said. "I like the crunchy stuff, you know that."

Despite his prejudice against vegetarian dishes, Berserker watched hungrily as Trickster ate. Long ago, most of the tribe had lost interest in each other's food. Since they could only eat the food that they themselves earned, it didn't make much sense to think about other people's food, but the ravenous hulking Berserker never wearied of watching others eat.

For dessert, Trickster ate a huge bowl of fresh cold lichee nuts. Although he felt better, he still felt suspicious of Iva, angry at System and weary of the world at large.

"Where's everybody?" Trickster asked, although he could have easily checked.

"Battle Space," Berserker said. "I'm about to go back myself. Lancer has got everybody worried about the Syrians. He thinks they're going to reattack."

"Oh, stink on the Syrians. They're just another gang of ghouls. We'll crush them eventually and then we'll have at the Japanese, already hull up over the horizon. Another set of enemies, just bigger and badder."

Berserker stared at Trickster. "So?"

"Yeah, that's right. So, why do you care? It's just a game like chess."

Berserker shook his head. "No, chess, you don't win any food. Battle, you do. Plus, winning a game of chess doesn't feel anywhere near as good as winning a battle."

"Can't you see that it's still just a game?"

"No. It's constant struggle. It's the way of the world," Berserker said, gravely. He felt worried because Trickster was starting to sound more and more like Weeble. Next thing you knew, he'd start to talk about some other world. "Why don't you come with me into Battle Space, get prepared to fight for a change and leave all that nonsense alone. All that stuff is just dreaming. Just nonsense. You always thought too much about dreams."

Trickster knew that Berserker rarely remembered his dreams, but when he did, they were always about Battle Space. Cat, Dreamer and Trickster—and Weeble—were the only ones who remembered strange dreams of things no one had ever seen or imagined before. Like, animals. Like, strange parts of the anatomy that did very strange things.

"Snake's saying you're going crazy," Berserker said. "You'd

better watch how you talk to everybody. You're sounding more and more like Weeble."

Berserker ripped away his avatar, disappearing into Battle Space. Trickster felt lonely, alone in the Meeting Place. He felt angry at Snake for spreading bad talk about him. *Why does he always try to make me out to be the odd one? Everyone in the tribe has his own personality. Why does he always want me to feel that I'm so different?* Trickster worried that he was not doing a very good job of hiding his true feelings. *It's difficult . . . strong feelings, hot feelings . . . I blurt too much. I've got to keep my mouth shut. But it's lonely. I want to talk. When can I ever talk without them hearing? Just talk, simple talk, my true feelings with Cat . . .* Anxiety over his emotional balance and worry about his standing in the tribe fanned the hot coal of anger that was always burning inside of him. He began to feel a destructive urge. He needed something to destroy. The Syrians were as good an enemy as any, since he hadn't yet figured out how to destroy System and he couldn't punch Snake.

Trickster entered Battle Space. He found the tribe gathered on the War Council Rock, atop the mountain high above the battlefield. Trickster listened while Cat, Snake and Lancer argued about whether the Syrians and Egyptians were preparing to attack. Without knowing all the available facts, Berserker was urging a preemptive counterattack. Cry-Baby sidled up to Trickster and whispered, "Thanks for letting me help in the fight, Trickster."

"Sure, Baby. We all got to eat."

"I've prepared some data for you."

"Shoot it to me."

Cry-Baby reached into her library and extracted an icon, a short length of glass fiber etched with flowers. She handed the icon to Trickster, who rapidly assimilated the data.

"Yeah, they're going to attack in about two hours," Trickster said. "Where'd you get the take on their artillery command and control?"

"I sent some ranger ants deep into their territory. During all of the confusion after the battle, the ants were able to tap right into some fiberoptic."

"It's coded," Trickster said.

"Yeah, but not encrypted."

Encoding a message meant substituting code symbols for the original language. Encrypting a message meant processing the electronic signal through a device that made the signal incomprehensible to anyone without the same device—or the ability to mimic the device. Decoding was difficult, but Trickster, Dummy and Gimp had done it on occasion. Decryption was impossible. Yet Dreamer was able to decrypt.

"This is sly stuff, Baby."

"Thanks."

"Let me see if we got time to play with it."

"OK."

Trickster opened all extrasensory. For several minutes, he listened to the enemy's electromagnetic activity. Despite his wish that he had some more time, he reached the inescapable conclusion that they would attack in a few hours. He stuck his head into his personal realm and discovered that his doppelgangers were still moving vigorously. *System hasn't drained the power yet to prepare for battle. Maybe we have enough time.*

"Give me the total take," he said.

Cry-Baby transferred the data to Trickster.

"Hey Cat," Trickster whispered.

"Wait, Lancer," Cat said. "Yeah, what is it?"

"I think I may have a good stratagem. Hold off a preemptive strike for a couple of hours, OK?"

"Don't listen to him, Cat," Snake said viciously. "He's just a wimp like his buddy, Cry-Baby. He'd rather play with his jewels than fight."

"Trickster is a poisonous warrior, Snake," Cat said, more angrily than she would have if she hadn't been worrying that Snake was right.

"He's just a lucky wimp."

"Oh, be quiet," Cat said. "Don't worry about it, Trickster. We won't attack for another two hours in any case."

"Thanks. Gas stink on you, Snake."

Trickster ripped into his personal realm. He invited Dummy into his private realm, consulting with him about Cry-Baby's data. Dummy, his limbs moving with the weird mirror-image pattern that had made him the butt of Snake's taunts all his life, assimilated the data, then wordlessly pointed out which fields of the formatted message he suspected contained target locations. Trickster thanked him. Dummy sat, preferring to work with Trickster on this problem than return to War Council Rock. Trickster plugged the data into his virtual computer.

Returning to Battle Space, he tried to see the battlefield as the Syrians would. He guessed what tribe targets they might want to attack first. He copied the coordinates for these targets, then ripped back to his personal realm and programmed his computer to compare the two lists: the Syrian message fields that they suspected were target coordinates and the true coordinates of the tribe's targets.

Five minutes later, he broke the code. In great intuitive leaps, he and Dummy isolated the meanings of the fields for time and for firing commands. Trickster was pleased, because they had broken the code without bothering Dreamer. If Dreamer was perturbed too often, she could become uncooperative at the most inconvenient moments, such as pivotal points in major battles.

Trickster cut back to War Council Rock. He briefed his comrades. Then he and the others strapped on their battle avatars. Trickster opened all extrasensory.

"Battle!" Cat shouted.

Like a huge monster, the Syrian and Egyptian forces were rising up from their sides of the two fronts. Air, artillery, armor, infantry, all forces rose up and began a horrendous onslaught of the tribe. Although Trickster had planned on using his trick

later in the battle, the initial onslaught was so overpowering
that he immediately used it. Trickster intruded into the enemy's
artillery command and control link. Using the telecommunica-
tions juncture into the fiberoptic link that the Ranger ants had
installed, he substituted coordinates of Syrian forces for the
original coordinates of tribe targets. The Syrian artillery began
to bombard their own forces.

The tribe noise-jammed tactical radio signals, obliterating
the Syrians screaming for relief from their own artillery. Trickster enjoyed directing both the tribe's and the enemy's artillery,
coordinating the fire. Also, forces that ordinarily would have attacked the enemy's artillery were freed for redirection against
other targets.

These tricks helped, but the weight of the Syrian forces was
oppressive. The Syrians had a new main battle tank with a gun
of greater range than the tribe's best tanks. An armored division
broke through the tribe's lines. Enemy combat engineers
spanned the big river with a robotically unfolded steel mesh
bridge. Trickster bombed the bridge, but the Syrians threw
bridge after bridge over the big river. Soon, several armored divisions had penetrated deep into the tribe's territory, decimat-
ing Berserker's armor and massacring Lancer's troops.

"Ai-yeeee!" Cat screamed. "All in!"

"All in!"

"All in! All in!"

Trickster and the others indulged in the wanton destruc-
tiveness of the doomed. They knew the battle was lost. They
knew they would lose their territory and resources. In defiance,
they threw their remaining forces at the Syrians. Frontal
charges against superior positions became the order of the day.
Trickster bombed until he ran out of bombs, then he dived his
aircraft down against Syrians targets. He detonated his own
ordnance depots. Soon he had no air force to command.
Berserker had lost his armor. Cat and Snake and Lancer directed the remaining infantry in the last charges.

The battle was over. They had lost.

With the defeat, the paradigm of Battle Space began to shift. The tribe found themselves standing, not atop War Council Rock, but in the middle of a glade in the jungle. Slowly the heat and humidity of the air was rising. The fecund odor of rot and growth was rich in their nostrils. Trickster snorted and sat down into lotus seat. As most of the others were already sprinting into the forest, Cat shouted, "Trickster! Come on, let's go!"

Trickster waved dismissively. Cry-Baby sat down next to Trickster. Cat was the last standing, watching the two malcontents. She heard shouts in a foreign language, close and coming closer.

"Idiot!" she shouted.

6

The Syrian enemies appeared in the far side of the clearing. Cat dashed into the jungle. Palm spears slashed at her pumping arms, but she ignored the slight pain. The Syrians were gaining on her. Off to her left and behind, she heard Berserker thundering through the undergrowth. Merciless to her comrade, Cat crossed in front of Berserker, hoping her pursuers would follow the loudest prey. Cat remembered the old tribal joke, "You don't have to run faster than the fastest enemy, just faster than the slowest brother."

Leaping up into a tree, Cat climbed quickly, then, perched among a wild confusion of orchids, she watched.

Four Syrians were gaining on Berserker. As enemies went, the Syrians weren't too horrible. They had snow-white skin and sky-blue eyes. Their uniforms were bluish-white jumpsuits. Their boots were a white so pure that they disdained any dirt. About half again the size even of Berserker, they moved quickly.

Cat watched as in midstride, Berserker twisted and came to a full stop facing his pursuers.

"Aiyeee—ah!" Berserker screamed. He fired a pistol at the Syrians, downing two, who disappeared upon impacting the jungle floor. The remaining two shot holes in Berserker, who howled with rage but not pain. He charged the surviving Syrians. Berserker materialized his favorite weapon, a double-bladed ax, and began the labor of disintegrating his enemies. Moments later, he stood alone in the jungle.

Cat clapped. She liked to tease Berserker because he was interesting to watch when he was angry and it seemed good for his battle spirit. Berserker looked up and fixed Cat with feral eyes. Cat had intended to taunt Berserker, but seeing the battle rage in his eyes, she decided against it.

"They got Trickster, Lancer, Barker and Cry-Baby," Cat shouted. "How many Syrians you get?"

"Six!" Berserker roared.

"Well, you'll eat tonight," Cat said. "See ya."

Cat dropped down out of the tree. She began to lope through the jungle. Early in the retreat, she had decided to win points by evading capture the longest. *Let the others try to score points by killing the pursuers. That isn't the idea. The idea is to survive.*

Cat felt disappointed in Trickster for sitting down in lotus seat right there in the glade. How stupid! He'd be lucky to eat at all.

He should know better, Cat thought. *Doesn't matter how many points you earn. If you give up, you can lose them all. System doesn't like quitters. Heavy penalties.*

Cat ran for a few more kilometers. She entered and followed the bed of a burbling stream, then climbed some waterfalls. After a kilometer of hiding her tracks and scent, she found a bunch of huge boulders alongside the stream. Ferns, moss and even small trees grew within the crevices of the boulders. It was a perfect evasion blind.

Careful not to step on moss or to break any ferns, Cat climbed into the jumble of boulders. After a minute of exploring, she found a long narrow space between two boulders, one leaning against the other. Cat crawled into the space and hid herself in its extremity. No one could see her unless they crawled in after her.

An hour later, she heard the typical noises of a capture patrol without, thankfully, the dogs. Cat hated dogs. They sniffed you out.

The capture patrol passed by the boulders. Cat relaxed and waited. She thought.

As much as she hated loser food, it was true that she always enjoyed chase and capture. *It's exciting, really. Too bad Trickster doesn't like battle anymore. Too mental for his own good. Only likes his stupid computer and his dumb jewel spiral and all of his other weird projects. What if Snake's right? What if Trickster is a loser?*

Berserker's crude, Snake's cruel, Lancer's single-minded, but at least they have their heads in the game. Trickster's losing it.

It's that damned Dreamer with her weird superstitions. She's a bad influence on Trickster. Wish I could get her out of his squad . . . but then we'd probably lose her altogether. Trickster's the only one keeping her from going the way of Weeble. Her Over-Gods and thingamajigs. What nonsense. Almost as bad as Snake and his cult of System. He should listen to his own god. The world simply is. There's no profit in believing in things we can't see.

A Syrian appeared at the other end of the crevice. Cat held still. At the distance of ten meters, the Syrian looked directly into Cat's eyes. Cat didn't blink.

The Syrian raised his rifle and aimed at Cat.

"Come out," he said.

Cat sighed.

The jungle disappeared. Cat found herself floating in Time-Out, a blue silent space, empty of everything except the other prisoners.

"Cat's bagged! Cat's bagged!" Skipper shouted.

"Oh hush up, Skipper," Cat said, glancing over the others and instantly observing that the entire tribe was captured. "I was last one caught, anyway," Cat said smoothly. "I'll be eating strawberries and ice cream while you losers chew on bark and grubs."

"I killed ten Syrians," Berserker said, his voice deep and menacing. "Last two with my bare hands."

"I killed fifteen," Snake said softly.

"Six!"

"I got nine."

"How about you, Trickster?" Cat asked.

Trickster looked up from his pearl. "I killed them all."

"What?"

"What a Weeble."

"Loser."

Trickster tucked away his pearl and glared at the others. "No, I killed them in my head. The Syrians don't exist and I can prove it. Listen. When we kill one, what happens?"

"They disappear."

"Right," Trickster said. "They disappear because they're not real. So why bother?"

The tribe considered Trickster's idea.

"This is kid's stuff," Snake grumbled. "Who cares? The world is the world."

"Of course the enemies aren't people," Cat said. "That's why they're enemies."

"Yeah, but why? What's the purpose of it all?" Trickster asked.

"Constant struggle," Lancer said, his sarcastic tone implying that Trickster was an idiot. "That's the way of the world."

"Yeah, but why?" Trickster asked.

"Oh, you're a dweeb," Snake said. "Shut up."

"Trickster is right," Dreamer suddenly said. Everyone turned to her. For many, it was the first time that they had heard her voice in a month.

"What?"

"Look who's popping off."

"The world is an illusion," Dreamer said. Her voice was clear and steady.

Skipper interrupted the chorus of hoots. "I got a good idea. Let's play Take-Off."

"I don't wanna play any idiot games," Berserker said.

Skipper changed her avatar so that she was a huge boulder, oak trees for arms and massive roots for legs. A cavernous mouth, choked with food, opened and said, "Idiot games," in a mockery of Berserker's deep voice.

"Berserker! Berserker!" the tribe cried.

Berserker sneered and changed into a black panther. Walking upright on wobbling hind legs, the panther waved his paws and tail. "Play nice, boys. Play nice."

"Nah, too crude," Lancer said. "This is Cat."

Lancer changed into a grotesque cat with huge ears and paws and a simpering expression. "You got to take the fight to the source," the cat said in a squeaky voice.

The tribe laughed. Cat changed into Zombie, a species of enemy they had destroyed two years earlier, and clutched a massive spear in Lancer's characteristic watchful pose. "Keep your eyes on the horizon," Cat said.

Finally, Trickster couldn't stand not to play. He changed into a small black snake, then bit his tail and began to eat himself. The more he ate, the bigger he got. "I'm delicious!" Trickster cried in a mockery of Snake's voice. "The more of me I eat, the better I taste!"

He felt gratified when the others laughed. He changed into his default avatar and turned to Snake. Trickster was prepared for a vicious counterattack, but what Snake did surpassed his expectations.

Snake changed into Weeble, then asked in Trickster's voice, "But what does it mean? But what does it mean?"

The invocation of the only dead member of the tribe instantly sobered everyone.

"Bad form, Snake," Cat said softly.

"You always were a punk," Berserker said.

"Aw, go shoot yourselves," Snake said. "You're all losers."

System appeared as a black bar over Snake's avatar. When the black bar disappeared, so had Snake. The tribe knew that he had been sent to a separate Time-Out.

While everyone floated, remembering Weeble, Trickster changed into the avatar he had made of Weeble, one lovingly detailed. It was as if he had brought their lost comrade back to life.

"What does it mean?" Trickster asked, using Weeble's voice. "And where am I, if I'm not in the world?"

"I'll show you," Dreamer whispered in a private communication.

7

The ship had entered the deep blue balmy realm of the mid-Pacific. Aft, the four huge screws churned a broad road of foam that stretched straight back to the horizon.

Standing in vulture's row, Mike McCullough luxuriated in the warm air. He loved the tropics. The sky was a bright bold blue, with only a few tall columns of bright white clouds standing above the sea. Reflecting the sky's color, the ocean was the deep royal blue that nothing else in nature could match. The air smelled not of the rot of the shore, but of the pure saline freshness of a world of water under a hot sun.

Aft of the ship, the air shimmered. An aircraft materialized: all sharp edges and angles, with a forward-swept wing, twin vertical stabilizers, and the smooth fuselage that indicated that it was pilotless. Whereas it had been broadcasting the blue of the sky, now the imaging skin of the aircraft was flashing red and white. With only foam plugs in his ears, Mike listened for the jet, but noise-canceling speakers were defeating the sound waves. Silently, the aircraft landed on the flight deck, catching the middle of the third arresting wire. As the robotic warbird taxied to the bow, a second aircraft materialized, then rode invisible rails down to a perfect recovery.

Mike watched as all thirty of the FU-19 aircraft recovered. He had never seen them before. Few people had—they were engineering development models designed and built under secret programs.

The FU-19s were stuck below, then racked and stacked in hangar bay one.

Twenty-four more aircraft recovered, one after another. Eight large fighter-bombers—F/A-9s—followed by six electronic warfare aircraft—EA-25s—followed by ten smaller fighter/bombers—F/A-12s—all recovered.

Mike reentered the skin of the ship. He walked around the blue canvas partition adorned with two white stars and entered the flag bridge.

The admiral was seated on his chair, which he had covered in sheepskin during last cruise's visit to New Zealand. As always, the admiral was precise and neat in his khaki uniform, clipped white mustache and perfect white hair. He was wearing his gold aviator's sunglasses. The gold glinted with the same fierceness as his gold navy pilot wings.

Mike stood quietly. The admiral finished a conversation with the ship's commanding officer, then hung up the phone.

"You've got something more on the Japanese, Mike?" the admiral asked.

"Yes, Admiral," Mike said. "Two more frigates have left Yokosuka. That puts about half their fleet to sea."

"And the Chinese?"

"Still at heightened alert, Admiral," Mike said. "We've got another report confirming that Beijing has canceled all military leave. Their mobile missile forces continue to disperse. And the Chairman made another speech criticizing Tokyo for trying to strangle Chinese overseas trade."

"Well, it's either a military demonstration or preparations

for war," the admiral said. "The N2 thinks they won't go over, Mike. What do you think?"

Mike considered the politics involved in contradicting his boss, but decided that a direct question from the admiral had to be answered truthfully. "They'll go over, Admiral."

"Why do you say?"

"Logic of empire, Admiral," Mike said. "The two superpowers can't tolerate any further expansion by the other. A classic imperial confrontation. Plus, race hatred."

"The Japanese aren't racist, Mike," the admiral said, staring at Mike over his green-tinted lenses.

Mike laughed and said, "No, sir. On the day they entered Canton, the Imperial Army took one hundred thousand heads for sport. Just for sport."

"That was a hundred years ago, Mike."

"Yes, sir. References to Japanese war atrocities have been appearing daily in all the news programs throughout China for the past week. Some of the references are to the Sino-Japanese War of 1894."

The admiral shifted and sighed. "Bloody-minded," he mumbled.

"Yes, sir," Mike said.

After a moment, Mike took his leave and left the flag bridge. He returned to SUPPLOT, where he faced the unpleasant task of telling his boss that he had violated the party line.

Even if his boss was skeptical, Mike McCullough believed they were steaming toward a war zone.

8

In the black void, a cluster of creatures, some upside down, others kiltered in random directions, were dancing. The creatures had various bizarre and shifting forms, like the figures in a nightmare of a prehistoric shaman on psychotropic mushrooms.

Some of the creatures were beating clubs on large wooden drums with leather skins. Others were beating rhythms on such diverse objects as a ten-liter oil drum and a high-impact-plastic shipping crate.

One of the avatars screamed and projected itself into the center of the dancing mass. In the form of a huge plumed lizard with two legs and four arms, the avatar sprouted a projection between its legs that looked like a cross between a rhinoceros horn and a phallus. The avatar shook the projection back and forth until it began to gush blood. The avatar danced so that the blood soaked the dancers, each of whom changed his avatar as the blood touched him. The bloody avatars looked like enemies of various sorts: vampires, Prussians, Aztecs, ghouls.

When they were all soaked in blood, one of them changed into a cloud, black with rain and internally illuminated by lightning. The cloud rushed through the assembly, washing the dancers clean. Again, each changed his avatar once he was washed clean. Now they were clean-limbed naked humans lacking genitals, navels and nipples.

"Huh! Huh! Huh!" the dancers chanted, each moving his limbs in perfect rhythm with the drums and the chant. They were celebrating the post-battle-problem festival of energy, when for fifteen minutes System did not deny them almost limitless access to services free of charge.

While the world spun and splurged with wild imagery, Dreamer opened a private communication with Trickster. She spoke in poetic images that seemed chaotic, but one vision flickered as intensely illuminating as lightning. Trickster saw fourteen humans scampering in a large cage. Each side of the cage was a huge sturdy steel grid, ribbed like the skeleton of a whale. Naked, the humans were enveloped in a complex web of creamy fibers attached to the mesh of the cage's floor, ceiling and walls. The fibers snaked, flexed, contracted and extended, suspending the humans well above the cage floor. As they moved their limbs, the fibers adjusted, providing support or resistance. The fibers allowed the humans to move about the cage in three dimensions.

Ten humans had light golden skin, two had pale pinkish skin and two had dark brown skin.

Of the ten golden humans, eight had small appendages in their crotches. Two lacked the appendages, but had wider hips and rounded chests. The two off colors, the pink and the brown, were split one each among these configurations.

Their bodies were perfect: exquisitely flexible, their musculature strong but flat, as if they moved freely and aerobically more often than against resistance. They were as beautiful as any avatar Trickster had ever seen.

Most of the humans moved their limbs as if they were acting out a pantomime of war. The gesture of aiming and firing hand-held weapons was the most common movement. The walls of the vault echoed with shouts in Mandarin, a confusing mix of many unrelated communications. Whenever two of the humans moved as if they would collide, their bodies went limp for one moment, while their supporting fibers adjusted and moved them around each other. Then their bodies seemed to reanimate.

Their eyes focused on objects that did not exist. Although their eyes glittered, they seemed to hold a unique darkness, an almost imperceptible absence. Trickster looked into the eyes of one of the golden men and recognized himself. Trickster looked down at his arm. Time seemed to have slowed down. His arm glistened with sweat. A milky fabric wrapped around his wrist, the skin of which was callused from the fabric's constant polishing. Trickster looked up.

The vision metamorphosed into a sequence that Trickster recognized as meaningless, then Dreamer inserted streams of images of animals, symbols that Trickster easily recognized as referents to the other world. He understood that the vision had been a memory that she had re-created from the other world.

Or is it a trick of System's?

After the festival, most of the brothers curled into fetal position and drifted off to sleep. After having avoiding meeting Trickster's eyes as he studied her, Dreamer was the first to lose consciousness. Exhausted from a long day that had included a confrontation with his parent, a cataclysmic battle loss climaxing a hard-fought war, a wild post-battle celebration, and a strange communication from Dreamer, Trickster struggled to stay awake so that he could think, but he quickly lost consciousness. Always restless, Snake thrashed about for half an hour, then suddenly went rigid, unconscious, grinding his teeth and moaning. Berserker sprawled, drooling. The last to lose awareness, Lancer, shook Cat awake.

"Take a watch," Lancer said.

"Aw, go on, Lancer," Cat said. "We're in Time-Out."

"Take a watch," Lancer said. "Constant struggle requires constant vigilance."

Cat grunted noncommittally. Although standing watch in Time-Out was ridiculous and unnecessary, she was reluctant to dull Lancer's vigilant spirit. She stretched like a cat, sat up, batted her lashes at Lancer, and smiled.

Lancer returned her smile adoringly. "Don't feel bad about the loss," he said. "You were in good command form."

Cat nodded. "Thanks, soldier. Thanks for thinking about me. But don't worry. That was a battle problem meant to test how well we lose. And we lost beautifully well. Most of us, anyway. So go to sleep, my faithful one."

Lancer sent a bouquet of pleasant flower smells to Cat, who returned them with rare tasteful notes. Lancer disappeared his spear, stretched and fell asleep. Cat floated in the black void of Time-Out at night, wondering how long it would take System to create a new battlefield. They hadn't eaten yet. Cat felt hungry, but hunger was an old companion. She knew that System would not allow their hunger to grow too painful. Now Cat was just hungry enough that she was looking forward to eating loser food, unless it was bugs and pine needles. She was not that hungry yet.

Cat swam over to float above Berserker, where she changed her avatar into ridiculous caricatures of old enemies. Cat laughed silently at Berserker's drooling slack face. Tiring of this game, she swam over to Trickster's side and watched him sleep.

Trickster's hands were folded and tucked gently against his face. His bulging eyelids shifted over the movements of his eyes. His mouth made puckering movements. Cat was about to make funny faces at her sleeping comrade, but something about Trickster stirred an unusual feeling in her. She stared at the smooth patch of skin between the legs.

Not understanding why this area seemed interesting, Cat reached down and touched herself between the legs. She felt normal healthy skin. Reaching up to her forehead with her other hand, she rubbed both areas simultaneously. She experienced an almost identical sensation—fingers touching normal skin, neither more pleasurable nor more sensitive than any other body part. Cat reached toward Trickster, her hand encountering the membrane that separate their personal spaces. Sighing, she shot a wake-up message at Trickster.

Trickster snorted and opened one eye. "Cat."

"Yeah, me."

"What ya bothering me for?"

"I dunno."

"I'm tired."

"Hey."

"Hey what?"

"Change your avatar."

"Aw please," Trickster said. "Go to sleep."

"I wanna see the one, you know, with the things."

Now Trickster was more fully awake than he pretended. "System gets weird about that one," he whispered.

"I don't care. Let me see it."

"Oh all right."

Trickster opened his personal command space and chose among his dozens of handcrafted avatars the one which he knew Cat wanted to see. In a dream, he had seen an unusual body form that had excited a strange fascination. Using his hands, brushes, knives and poetic commands, he had carved and painted an exact duplicate of the form of which he had dreamed. Quickly, Trickster substituted the dream form for his default avatar.

Cat floated, watching Trickster wearing his dream form. The form had unusually wide hips and a swollen chest area. There were strange protuberances atop each of the two mounds of the swollen chest. There was an inexplicable tiny hole in the middle of the abdomen. Most strange, however, was that the area between the legs was no longer smooth. There was an orifice that looked like a second mouth, but vertical instead of horizontal. Cat looked and reached for the dream avatar, her hand meeting the resistance of the invisible wall.

"I . . . ah . . . um . . ." Cat whispered.

"Yeah?"

"I really like this one. I dunno why."

"Yeah, it's weird, huh?"

"Like, it's got a place where I could put in the thing, you know, like I dreamed on the other one. Let me show it to you."

"Nah. I like this one. It's so smooth and soft. Feels sweet."

"Yeah . . . but . . . let me just show you."

"Oh, all right."

Cat reached into her personal avatar library and selected the form which she had dreamed. She changed quickly.

Trickster looked at Cat wearing her new avatar. It was like her default avatar, except more muscular and more hairy. Also, it had the strange appendage between the legs: a rigid pole with a small slit, like a face with a small mouth and no eyes.

"It's weird," Trickster said.

"Hey, I got an idea," Cat said.

"What?"

"Let's switch avatars."

Trickster considered this proposition before replying, "OK, but you can just have a copy."

"All right."

They made copies of their dream avatars, traded them, then assumed the other's. Immediately, Trickster felt a different relationship with the male avatar. It was like he had just experienced the pivotal point in a battle. Something about wearing the male avatar seemed profoundly correct.

And Cat!

"You look sweet in that avatar, Cat," Trickster said.

"Oh, Trickster," Cat said. "You do too. I mean, scream ing . . . it . . ."

They explored the dream avatars with tentative hands.

"I wish I could feel this pole thing," Trickster said.

"We gotta figure out how to wire those extra parts of the custom avatars for touch," Cat said.

"It's fun, though, huh?"

"Yeah, I like it."

"Hold on, I thought of some modifications."

Remembering things he had seen in the vision that Dreamer had shared with him, Trickster reached into his toolbox and selected a brush. He changed the colors of the protuberances on original female avatar's swollen chest to dark brown.

"Wait a minute."

Trickster chose a knife, flipped over the female avatar and began to resculpt the buttocks. Cat withdrew from the avatar, appearing in her own. Trickster withdrew from his. For several minutes, wearing their default avatars, he busily whittled away on the dream forms. He refined the form of the pole so that it wasn't a simple cylinder, but rather flared somewhat in its center. Trickster added a second set of lips around the vertical lips, so that there were major exterior lips and minor interior lips. He also thinned them so that they appeared less like the mouth's lips.

"OK, try this now," Trickster said.

"Why'd you go and do that?"

"I dunno," Trickster said. "Just seemed better this way. You like it better this way?"

"Yeah, it looks more . . . right."

They reentered the dream forms, Trickster the male and Cat the female. After another few minutes of tactile exploration, Cat said, "You think that there really is a Realm of Dream? That our dreams—"

"There's other realms," Trickster said, choosing his words carefully. He wanted to share the vision that Dreamer had sent, but he couldn't without tipping his hand to System. "Besides the world, besides dreams. These avatars maybe come from there."

Cat disappeared into a wide band of flat black that enveloped Trickster's whole environment. He found himself floating in a solitary Time-Out.

"Aw, muck," he said.

Sadly, Trickster shifted back into his default avatar. For an hour, he tried to go back to sleep. He thought of battle, of parents, of Iva, of Snake, of Cat . . . of Cat . . . of Cat. . . .

She really looked sweet in that avatar he had dreamed. He wished he could communicate with her secretly, the way he could with Dreamer. He wished Dreamer could communicate with him as simply as Cat.

Trickster faded away into dreaming. In his first dream state, he dreamed of Cat, wearing the female avatar. In the privacy of his dream, he touched Cat wearing the avatar. Touching another person was a taboo act, a strange act, one that he didn't understand. Yet it seemed superreal in his dream. His feelings of pleasure and joy mounted until he felt the sweet ecstasy of victory.

9

Trickster's dreams were interrupted by the trilling signal for the end of rest. He opened his eyes to find himself returned to the blueness of common Time-Out. The other members of the tribe were waking. He glanced at Cat, who returned his look with a heavy-lidded simpering expression that confused him. He sought out Dreamer, but she was wearing a silver reflective mask, a traditional tribal practice for making blatant a desire not to communicate. Since Dreamer rarely wore masks, Trickster wondered what she could be upset about. *Did she see Cat and me with the dream avatars?* he wondered. He felt shame, which was an unusual emotion for him. The unusual shame confused him.

System appeared, its vertical black bar quickly changing into a semantic interface. Along with his comrades, Trickster rapidly assimilated torrents of data concerning the tribe's performance in the last battle against the Syrians and Egyptians. Trickster was sorry to see that his personal point account had been depleted by a third due to his refusal to participate in the escape and evasion. *Idiot . . . play the game. You may need those points. But it's hard, it's hard. . . .*

System interrupted the semantic interface long enough for the tribe to eat. The comrades burst the silver spheres that contained their personal meals. Berserker howled with delight when he found a heaping mound of Mongolian barbecue. Cat found several sandwiches of lamb, yogurt and vegetables in pocket bread. Trickster, Cry-Baby and Dummy received unseasoned rice, beans and corn on the cob.

"It's not so bad, Trickster," Cry-Baby said of the meal, which was her staple.

"No, it's good stuff," Trickster said. "You're lucky to get it. Better than the junk Berserker eats."

"Ha ha!" Berserker roared. "Losers eat loser food and like it!"

"Aw shut up," Trickster said, shutting off Berserker's audio input.

After they flicked the remnants of their meal away, the comrades waited for System, which returned when the last finished.

"Unit qualifications," System said. "Then squad qualifications. Then team qualifications. When the entire tribe requalifies, you'll arrive at a new battle domain, bigger and better than any before."

"Ee-yah," Cat said. Her limbs were already trembling. She loved unit qualifications.

"We begin. Step forward into glory."

They moved forward, some throwing themselves headlong, others making the minimum gesture necessary. The blueness of Time-Out faded. They found themselves facing northward atop a high foothill at the north of the Bekka Valley. A wooded valley lay below, and beyond that, a low mountain range separating them from their next land, the country of the Chinese. Beyond their next land, they would see the ocean. On the horizon, still shrouded in mist, was the domain of the next enemy, the Japanese.

Fifteen paths traced the northern face of the foothill, fanning out and entering the wooded valley at fifteen different places. Without prompting, the tribe began to descend the paths.

Before she entered the forest, Cat watched each of her brothers enter along their separate paths. As she entered the forest herself, her excitement increased. She opened the three primary predatory senses—vision, hearing, smelling—to their maximum. The sandy path led deeper into the dark forest. Massive hemlock trees towered, their short needles forming a thick canopy that heavily filtered the sunlight. Cat delighted in the aroma of evergreen needles and sap. She loved the forest. Carefully, Cat left the path. She stepped quietly over the thick bed of brown pine needles that carpeted the forest floor.

Moments later, she spotted her first weapon: a silver pistol, half-hidden underneath a rotting log. Cat examined the pistol for signs of booby-trapping, then nudged it with a long branch. When nothing happened, she picked up the pistol, examined it quickly—a weapon she had used many times, it fired depleted uranium pellets from a magazine containing one thousand rounds—then continued pacing through the forest, parallel to the path.

The first enemy appeared momentarily. Cat was pleased to see that it was an Ice Man, one of their stock enemies, fairly challenging but not too treacherous. As soon as the Ice Man's forehead cleared the tree trunk he was hiding behind, Cat opened up the crown of his skull with a uranium pellet. The Ice Man disappeared.

She turned around quietly, quickly, sweeping the forest around her in a complete circle. She heard a noise to her left, swung around, and kneeled, just as two Zombies appeared above a boulder. Zombies were slow wimps, but they multiplied until there were so many of them that they overwhelmed the defender. Cat took off the tops of their heads so quickly that the hits seemed simultaneous.

Now that she had established the threat sector, Cat sought cover. She ran and dived onto the soft forest floor, landed just behind a large boulder, then knelt in firing position.

A Zombie loomed above her, rising up from the other side of the boulder. Keeping her finger depressed on the trigger, Cat swept the pistol upwards, firing a stitch of rounds, blowing the Zombie open from heart to crown. Two Ice Men appeared to the left and to the right in the farthest extremities of her peripheral vision. Cat fired first at the leftmost Ice Man, because he was bringing his weapon to bear, scoring a mid-chest hit. She swung to her right, but the other Ice Man had disappeared.

He reappeared. Cat shot him through the neck.

Now!

She obeyed her instinct, leaving the cover of the boulder to dash across a short open space, taking refuge amid a tangle of fallen logs. She had to shoot three snakes that appeared even as she was falling toward them.

Quickly Cat looked up.

Enemies were appearing all around her. Cat fired her weapon continuously for fifty seconds, downing the wave of attacking enemies.

A second pistol appeared. Cat swept it up and began to fight two-handed. Her blood surged. She felt the pleasurable rage of battle. As her mind speeded up, the events in the battle problem seemed to slow down. Cat sprung out of the tangle of trunks and began to charge through the woods. Enemies appeared, several a second, but Cat destroyed them in the instant of their appearance. She felt herself becoming the most fearsome enemy of them all.

The enemies were wimps, losers. They moved slowly. She could smell and hear them before they appeared. Cat destroyed dozens, then hundreds, of targets.

A Ghoul dropped from the cover of a tree and pegged her

right in the heart, just as she was busy shooting a gaggle of four Vampires.

The forest faded to gray silhouettes. System's semantic interface showed her power point tally: 65,980 out of a possible 67,000. Enough for trade for a mechanized infantry battalion. Cat smiled. She wiped the sweat from her brow. She was off to a good start.

Trickster stood in an identical wood. He considered the danger of staying on the path.

It's so childish, he thought.

"System," he said. "Why do I have to do qualifications again? You know I can shoot."

System didn't answer.

Trickster sighed. He felt tempted to sit down in a lotus seat. *But I need the points, the power*, he thought. *So I've got to fight these fools.*

He strolled down the path. He saw the silver gun, walked over and picked it up. When the first Ice Man appeared, Trickster shot it between the eyes. All the while he was thinking about the vision that Dreamer had sent.

If that was really me I saw in that cage, he thought, *System may be driving my senses just the way I do when I use the facilities to build synthetic environments like the ice cave. So . . . I'm not really a computer artifact . . . I'm a human . . . made by the Over-God? Dreamer says so, and I felt something so beautiful, so intense. A living presence, close to me. But what am I? How weird . . . in a cage somewhere in the other world . . . how can I stop . . . System . . . if it is a computer, then it generates the environment. If I seize control somehow, can I stop the environment? Then what happens? If the other world exists, what does it mean to exist in the other world? What is the nature of things?*

Trickster had difficulty understanding how he could have a

separate existence in the other world. Yet he had looked into his own eyes. He had seen his own forearm, the wrist calloused with the constant polishing of the fibers that ensnared him. How could he exist somewhere without knowing it?

In this other existence, he and his brothers were in the cage. They were imprisoned. It was a capture and escape, a scenario with which Trickster was thoroughly familiar. Trickster wondered if anyone besides System and the parents were able to cross over between the two worlds. Could he cross over and rescue himself? Trickster shook his head.

No, think better. Think hard. . . .

Trickster had trouble accepting the idea that the world didn't exist. *What a strange concept! I can see, touch, smell, taste, hear and extrasense the world every moment. Of course it exists! System may generate some of it, but that's the way things are made, the same way I make the snow cave. . . .*

Then he had a very strange idea. *What if in the other world, things are the way they are. Just are. They don't change because someone wants them to change. Huh! What a strange idea. Think on it. Don't let it go. Say, a rock is a rock. Just sits there. No one defines it, no one owns it. It is. Just is. What would people be like in such a place? Say you only had one avatar. How weird!*

Trickster tried to imagine what this other world would be like, if System was just a thing made by men.

Strange men, who can't change their avatars. Solid, like rocks. Say they made System. The world, just a computer construct. OK . . . what would that mean if the entire world, if my entire life, I was just wired, wired for input, and was really this solid thing, this one thing, there, in that cage. . . .

Trickster's stomach began to churn. Nausea and fear distracted him from his line of thought. *No, no . . . think on it. What if it were all true? What if the entire world was like the silver globes around food, something you could just pop, and it would disappear? Would we disappear too, like a killed enemy? Just disappear? Could we exist without the world?*

Then another moment of clarity arrived. Trickster realized that the key to the world was in the other world. He didn't understand bodies, birth or death. The very concept of physicalness was alien to him. Yet somehow he now understood that the other world not only existed, but, moreover, it was more *real* and more *true* than the world.

*The other world is to the world what the world is to a given battle problem. Greater, permanent, creating. Then to rule the world, I have to act in the other world. In fact, it might be possible to act in the other world so that I **stop** the world. Then I can re-create the world in any way I want. Without System. **A world where I am System.** Is that freedom?*

10

Iva appeared at Chang's outer office at the appointed hour. She remembered Sui Tai, parent of both Weeble and Dreamer, huddled in the corner of her bedroom, folded in the yoga position called the leaf. The body had been wearing an emerald green silk robe. She remembered the sensation of touching the cold and lifeless face. The official investigation had determined that the cause of death was an overdose of tranquilizers. Iva had always harbored a secret suspicion that the death had not been accidental.

"Doctor Chang will see you now," the receptionist intoned.

On nerveless feet, Iva shuffled forward into Chang's office. Chang, unsmiling, waited behind his desk. Iva approached no nearer than necessary.

"Yes, Director," she said.

He was a handsome man, she observed. In moments like these, confident that he could be cruel without fear of retaliation, his regular features flushed with a predatory fierceness that made him more handsome. Chang rose and moved around his desk, crossed his arms across his chest, crossed his legs at the ankle, and leaned backwards, a posture that drew attention to his loins.

"How have you been doing, Iva?" he asked, his voice low and confidential.

"I'm surviving, director."

"You're last excursion into the world wasn't too successful, though, was it?"

"No. I wanted to discover the nature of the cerebral event that Trickster experienced, but the subject seemed uncooperative."

"To what do you ascribe his attitude? I'm a neurocomputer scientist, not a psychologist," Chang said, using a tone that condescended to the softer science. Long ago Iva had noted that Chang never missed an opportunity to sneer at psychology or any discipline less mathematical than his own.

"He's tired," Iva answered.

"What? He's just tired? Is that as good as it gets?"

Iva heaved a sigh, shaking like an empty silk sheath. She had written over fifty papers, all publishable, none published, of course, none even understood by Chang, that she could tell. Many experimental findings of Standing Whirlwind would have been worthy of academic awards and honors, if the experiment and its results hadn't been kept a black secret. Chang snorted. "I need to know if he's stable enough to graduate to the next problem. I'm interested in your professional opinions, if you have any."

"I would like to make my opinions a matter of the record, actually."

"Come now. It's straightforward, I think. He's not as tired nor as unstable as he appears. It's just another of his tricks. Throwing sand into the face of the enemy. He's brighter than the rest. He's able to see through things."

"Trickster is not the only genius in the tribe," Iva said. "Cat is as brilliant. Snake. Dreamer. Weeble, for that matter. But Trickster's genius is a peculiar type very high on the E-J grid of the Olmstead matrix—"

"What does that mean, if anything?"

"Doctor, you're the neurocomputer scientist. What does the human mind know besides what the senses tell it?"

"Nothing."

"The human species has no instincts? No racial memories?"

"Well, yes, fear of falling, that sort of thing."

"Two billion gene pairs, Doctor. Mapped, but not yet deciphered. The book of life has many chapters that we can't read yet. Geniuses of the E-J type seem to be capable of tremendous intuitive leaps, during which they seem to connect to paradigms, patterns, possibly based in genetic memories. Flawed, partial, but the legacy of a billion years of survival, of evolution, of lessons learned."

"Mystic nonsense."

"Then how would you explain animals in the world?"

Chang hesitated. Iva had hit him with a hard point. Since the beginning of the project, the idea of animals had never been introduced to the children. Yet, independently, they had drawn and even built amazingly accurate models of snakes, cats, horses, dogs and most recently, birds. Their independently discovered knowledge of animals was so accurate that their choice of names for Cat and Snake had been disturbingly appropriate.

"Trial and error," Chang said. "If you let fourteen children doodle for seventeen years, among all the nonsense and monsters, they're bound to draw something that looks like real animals."

"Yes, but why Trickster? Why Cat? Why have they somehow intuited or guessed, as you would say, what the female and male human bodies look like?"

Sensing that he had lost an argument that he had no need to win, Chang unfolded his arms and legs and advanced on Iva.

"This is all beside the point, I think," he said, his voice deep. "I called you here for your opinion on what his reaction will be when he graduates to the real problem."

"Trickster's reaction if you go through with your scheme to give them access to information about the real world?"

"Limited access, yes."

Slowly Iva smiled. "I imagine that he will accept it as just another battle problem. You've been subjecting them to new realms constantly since the age of eighteen months. Why should this be different?"

"You don't think that they'll notice the difference between our scenario-generated data and data input from the real world?"

Iva shook her head. Chang looked suspicious. Iva knew that he was trying to decide whether she was lying to him. She smiled more broadly.

Let him worry about that, she thought. *Once Trickster sees the other world, everything will change.*

11

Deep underground, below the mountain separating the Bekka Valley from China, tunnels had opened up into the ruined chambers of a subterranean castle.

"Look left, Dreamer!" Trickster shouted.

But Dreamer had already moved, spinning left so quickly that she seemed to blur and materialize with the enemies dead in her sights. Dreamer squeezed a steady burst of automatic fire, killing and evaporating them. Then Dreamer seemed to drift away, her limbs moving with an alien grace into a position that seemed nonsensical, until enemies appeared before her, momentarily, vaporizing in her fire.

Trickster glanced at each member of his squad. Dreamer was performing amazingly well. Gimp was outperforming himself, too. Dummy and Cry-Baby were doing as well as could be expected. The vast ruined castle containing a seemingly endless series of rooms, vaults, chambers, galleries and corridors. Mounds of toppled stone, gaps in the floor leading to deadly falls, confusions of dusty artifacts increased the complexity and danger of the combat zone. They were opposed by hosts of their traditional enemies.

Suddenly a monstrous spider loomed from the darkness. The beast had a spherical thorax circled by a glistening slit that appeared to be its eye. It skittered toward Trickster's squad on its eight hoofed legs like a spider; then it flipped vertically and cartwheeled toward them. Trickster and the others lit up the spider enemy with rapid fire, but for a long moment it seemed impervious. Just as abruptly, it died, its dead limbs quivering only meters from Trickster's feet.

Trickster replayed the memory of the spider enemy's attack. "Hey!" he shouted. "The way to kill it is for three of us to hit it simultaneously in its eye."

"Eye!" Cry-Baby acknowledged, her voice quavering.

Trickster's squad fought its way into a long darkened corridor, laying waste to hordes of enemies that they now considered wimps compared to the spiders. They gained access to a huge chamber, the vault of which stood one hundred meters high. Fallen Doric columns littered the cracked marble mosaic floor. The squad had advanced to the center of the chamber, but now was under pressure from wave after wave of enemies. More and more spiders were appearing, rushing at them singly, then in pairs, then in groups of three or more, sometimes from various directions. Since three squad members had to shoot each simultaneously, this phase of the battle was requiring a lot of intrasquad communication and coordination.

"Shoot, Gimp, shoot!" Trickster shouted. Gimp was fighting two-handed. In his right hand, he held an advanced weapon, a laser-sighted fully automatic machine pistol. In his left, he held a revolver that he needed to reload every six shots. His marksmanship was better than Trickster had ever seen it. Sweating, flush with excitement and exertion, Gimp was killing enemies as quickly as they appeared. Although his right leg was nerveless, he managed to hobble along with the rest of the squad.

Dreamer had willingly assumed an avatar. She was fighting with an almost eerie grace. Trickster was beginning to suspect that Dreamer had learned how to anticipate System, because Dreamer seemed to know where the enemies were before they appeared. Trickster made a mental note to try to find out whether Dreamer had accomplished this feat, which the tribe had discussed and attempted for many years until they decided it was impossible. Right now he was too busy to think about it much.

Motivated by his desire to increase his personal resources so that he could build a more powerful computer, Trickster was shooting better than he had in years. He had advanced to two fully automatic machine pistols with large calibers, able to shoot through most obstacles. He was laying down heavy suppressive fire, denying entire threat sectors.

Cry-Baby was struggling. She had earned a machine pistol, then lost it when she had been killed three times in five minutes. Now she was firing a small-caliber six-shooter.

"Gimp, check nine!" Trickster shouted, spinning himself to engage a new wave of spider enemies.

The squad had adapted its tactics to support its weakest member, Cry-Baby. If she lost her six-shooter, the entire squad could be overwhelmed by the spider enemies, because focused fire was the only thing that killed this enemy. If the spider enemies overran them, they would proceed no further on this level. The horrible aspect of the spiders weighed heavily on Cry-Baby. She fought her growing feelings of panic, weakness and self-loathing. Noticing Cry-Baby's deteriorating condition, Trickster leapt over a fallen column and stood side-by-side with her.

"Come on, burn them down!" Trickster shouted. "Look left, shoot! Gimp, look right! Baby, look behind, shoot! That's it, they're wimps! Shoot that one, now! Reload!"

Trickster scrambled atop a heap of crumbled stones. The squad reloaded.

"Let's press!" Trickster shouted.

They hustled across the vast open chamber. Another wave of enemies materialized. Some swung down from the ceiling. Other began to pop up through the ruined floor. The others covered Cry-Baby, nursing her along until her confidence returned. A minute later, they all had graduated to more powerful weapons. Trickster had earned a man-mobile cannon capable of killing even the spider enemies with a series of three shots.

Armed with these weapons, they fought their way across the chamber. Following a green-glowing light that was their visual cue for progress, the squad entered a short corridor. At the end of the corridor, they could see a vestibule leading to a massive oaken door half-tumbled and allowing through streams of sunlight. Guessing that they had almost arrived at the end of the castle, the squad fought a fierce battle through the short corridor. By the time they arrived at the vestibule, the fight had degenerated into hand-to-hand combat. Trickster picked up his hand-combat weapon, chained clubs that he wielded in the *num-chuk* style. Dummy was swinging a chained mace. Gimp had a two-handed battle ax. Cry-Baby had a steel war club. Dreamer wielded a simple wooden pole. She began floating through the combat, dodging everything slowly, lazily, too smooth to be touched.

They entered a vestibule that was too small for spider enemies to enter. Nevertheless, the vestibule was alive with their hoofed legs, protruding through cracks in the heaving walls. Ghouls, Vampires and Ice Men rushed in single file through two different passageways, falling quickly before the physical onslaught of the squad.

This phase of the battle stressed their physical fitness. Dummy's arms began to feel leaden. Cry-Baby was beginning to keen. She hated this battle with its unusually horrible imagery. Only her overwhelming desire to be accepted as a full member of the tribe gave her the strength to continue despite her terror. Finally, they had broken the limbs of the spider enemies and disintegrated all the other enemies.

"Now!" Trickster shouted.

Cry-Baby spun and threw herself through the crack in the door. Before her feet cleared, Dreamer had disappeared. Dummy sailed through the crack. Gimp hobbled over and threw himself through the opening. A second later, Trickster leapt through.

The squad landed and tumbled on sweet green grass. For a moment, their eyes were dazzled by the broad daylight. As their vision adjusted, they were able to perceive a rolling expanse of thick green lawn, with vibrantly colored flowers decorating geometrically intricate gardens.

Trickster laughed. He rolled over onto his back and breathed deeply the cool, clean air. Songbirds were singing in the distance.

"That was intense," he said.

Gimp chuckled. "Monstrous hard," he said. "I don't think there's ever been a squad qual like that."

"It was . . . awful," Cry-Baby said, her voice tight with anguish.

Gimp and Trickster shared a glance. Gimp raised himself to his hands and knees and crawled over to the frontier of Cry-Baby's personal space.

"You were wizardly," he said. "I don't think you ever fought so hard. I was proud of you."

"I was, too," Trickster said.

Cry-Baby looked over at Trickster. Her face was a study in youthful elation.

"Really?" she asked.

"Electric sure," Trickster said. He crawled over and flopped onto his back, his shoulder touching the membrane of Cry-Baby's personal space. She reached over and touched the membrane. He gazed up at white clouds sailing through the blue sky. "We gotta rename you again," Trickster said. "Cry-Baby won't do."

"That's right," Gimp said. "How about 'Lightning'? You've always been quick."

"Not as quick as you guys," Cry-Baby said.

"Lightning quick and unpredictable, fierce in the dark," Trickster said. "How about it, guys?"

" 'Lightning' is a good name," Gimp said.

Trickster turned to Dreamer and was shocked to confront his own image reflected in her silver mask. *What have I done to make her mad?* he thought.

"OK. Let's go, Lightning," Trickster said, his voice tremulous.

The squad stood. Trickster smiled at Lightning. A renaming was an important event in the tribe, especially when the new name was such a promotion. As closely as their membranes would allow, they walked side-by-side down the long lawn, between geometries of knee-high gardens.

"It was a monster hard fight, wasn't it?" Lightning asked.

"Fierce," Trickster said.

They arrived at a flower garden, rich with the perfumes of blooms of rose, lilac and honeysuckle. In the quiet, they could hear the rustle of supple green leaves in the breeze and the buzz of bumblebees hovering and nuzzling blossoms. The sky was clear blue, the sun as gentle as the sun of summers in northern latitudes.

They were in China now. They could see the sea. Japanese mountain peaks rose above the mist, shrouding the home islands of their enemy.

Trickster's squad descended the gently sloping path to the bottom level of the flower garden, where a tall column of water leapt and fell into a wide fountain. They sat on the stone benches, grateful for the shade made cooler by the nearness of the mist from the fountain.

"We're first, sure," Lightning said.

"We kicked butt," Gimp said. "Hope the others hurry. I'm hungry."

Snake's squad appeared moments later, entering the flower garden by the western path. Snake, Barker, Trance, Cut-Back and Sly, the members of Snake's squad, were laughing uproariously.

"—bit you right in half!" Snake shouted.

"Saw my own legs down there and almost puked!" Barker shouted.

"Hey, Trickster's squad beat us!" Snake shouted. "How'd you guys manage to keep Cry-Baby alive through that?"

"Slicing squad quals!" Barker shouted. "Tried to go back in, get some more, but the castle door was closed."

"Those spider monsters!"

"You guys get eaten?"

"No, they eat you?"

Snake's squad burst into another fit of laughter.

"You didn't get eaten?"

"Those spider monsters have mouths at the bottom of their bellies," Barker shouted. "Bit me right in half."

"What'd you do to—"

"Last guy to die gets eaten," Barker said. "Hey, I'm hot!"

Barker jumped into the fountain. Moments later, everyone in the two squads was frolicking in the fountain—except Dreamer, who lay down in a bed of flowers, and Snake and Trickster. Trickster sat and quietly watched his comrades playing in the fountain. Snake approached him and sneered.

"How'd you get those guys through that so fast?" he asked.

"Straight shooting," Trickster said, narrowing his eyes at Snake.

"Thought those wimps were only good for solving puzzles," Snake said contemptuously.

"Everything's a puzzle, Snake," Trickster said. "If you'd ever bother to think . . . about it, you'd realize that."

Snake turned and spit, the azimuth as close to Trickster as he could get without System intervening.

"Oh, I think," Snake said. "I think all the time."

"You think," Trickster said, his tone ambiguous, just shy of the sarcasm that could trigger a challenge.

Snake continued to stare down at Trickster, forcing him to remember the last time that he had fought Snake. Back in those days, when they were only fourteen years old—a year being an immense span of time that only System could track—they had been able to challenge each other to personal combat. Most everyone still had parents who taught the primary skills—Reduction, Recognition and Reaction—as well as the secondary skills of gymnastics, martial arts, dance, shaping, communicating, designing, mathematics, strategic thought, tactical maneuver, paradigm creation, attack, retreat and others.

On that day, Trickster had jumped to the Meeting Place, which in the old paradigm was a marble-columned gymnasium, high on a green grassy hill, with olive groves and vineyards spreading down the slopes toward the forested valley. Trickster was anxious to show Cat a new game that he had invented, using one of his earlier virtual computers. Because he had independently reinvented electronic digital computation only a year ago, the language he had developed to program the virtual computer was simple, but it was enough to allow him to implement a simple game that involved colliding and absorbing shapes.

Studying a history of the tribe's battle problems, Snake was sitting on the front stairs. Trickster ignored him, running up the stairs to the back of the gymnasium. Cat wasn't in the gymnasium, however. Trickster wandered back toward the front of the gymnasium.

"Hey, what do you got there?" Snake called.

"Nothing."

"Let me see."

"It's none of your business, Snake."

"Come on, what's the big deal? Let me see."

"No, why should I?"

"Why are you always so mean to me, Trickster? What did I ever do to you?"

"I'm not mean. You're the mean one."

"My parent said that you're a weirdo," Snake said.

"You're a liar. Parents don't talk like that."

"He did so. Said that you're a loser and a weirdo."

"I'll kick your butt in combat," Trickster said. "Then we'll see who the loser is."

"You're on," Snake said. "And I'll fight you with pain."

Trickster stood, considering this surprising challenge. The previous month, System had introduced a new form of personal combat, where the contestants felt pain when their avatars received blows. After one round of painful combat, the entire tribe had decided against fighting with pain. Until now.

"All right," Trickster said. "I'll fight you with pain, and I'll double the pain for each fall."

Snake stood, squaring off against Trickster. "All right."

Minutes later, they stood opposite each other in the stone courtyard of the Palace. A square tower rose from one corner of the courtyard. Against the blue sky were silhouetted the pagoda-style corners of the tower's roof. Two sides of the courtyard were taken up with steep steps; the other two sides were high walls, facades of palace buildings. The entire tribe had gathered, standing or sitting on the steep steps.

System had taken the form of a floating globe of light shining white, white being the signal for disengagement. Trickster stretched, holding his foot high above his head, his shin behind his ear. He made a face at Snake, then flowed down into a monkey position. Snake was adopting crane stances, practicing a studied oblivion of Trickster's antics.

System blinked red. Trickster and Snake faced each other and bowed at the waist. Then they flowed into their fighting positions. The invisible barrier between their personal spaces grew opaque for one moment, slowly fading into nothingness. The tribe caught its breath. The removal of the barrier meant personal combat was imminent. Trickster, who had adopted the monkey king as his signature style, rolled in a direction oblique from Snake, then began to scramble apelike toward him. Snake, who had begun in a crane posture, switched into a serpent position. At that moment, Trickster struck.

He feinted a leg sweep. As Snake reacted, Trickster sprung upright and slammed his left fist into Snake's abdomen. With his right forearm, he blocked a blow, then butted his head fully into Snake's face. Reeling in pain, Snake staggered back. Trickster scampered after him—making monkey sounds—grabbed his ankle and threw him onto his back. Trickster somersaulted backwards, leapt onto the steps and scampered among the rest of the tribe, who shouted their approval for Trickster's victory in the first fall.

Gasping for breath, Snake regained his feet. His face was flushed with pain and anger. "Double, second fall!" Snake shouted.

Trickster leapt down into his starting position. Eyes rounded with befuddlement, scratching his head, he stared up into Snake's face, still red with emotion. Trickster waited for Snake to attack, which he did, sailing in a flying side kick. Trickster ducked the foot and began to rise for the easy throw, aiming to catch Snake by his calf. Snake's hand snatched Trickster's wrist. Trickster found himself flying head-over-heels. He curled and rolled on the landing. Although he had not suffered from any blows, he had lost the fall. Now he had to dare the third round, with pain four times as great as the first round.

Snake and Trickster squared off. Cautiously, Trickster began to stalk Snake. As he planted one foot slightly wider than usual, Snake accelerated toward him with a grace and speed that was astonishing. Awed by the attack, Trickster hesitated. The next he was aware, the sky was ripped apart, white lights were flaring and an unimaginable pain had erupted from his right cheek.

He lay on his back. Snake had won two falls out of three. The pain of the blow—whether fist, knee or foot, he didn't know—was unbelievable. If he were to double pain now, the best he could hope for was to tie the match at two each. Then they would need a fifth fall, with pain sixteen times as great as the first round. That was unthinkable.

Yet he couldn't surrender, not to Snake, not in front of the entire tribe. Trickster climbed to his feet. He abandoned the monkey king and assumed a dragon stance. Warily, Snake rose to a crane stance. The two maintained the postures for so long that time seemed to hold still. Finally, Snake's concentration seemed to falter. Trickster blurred forward and buried a knife hand into his solar plexus. Snake collapsed into an agonized heap.

Instead of cheering, a somber silence prevailed. Trickster's demeanor, showing respect toward Snake as he returned to his starting position, suggested that he would be content to call the match a draw.

Snake, however, managed to overcome his agony but not his anger. He rose to tower, trembling with rage. "Double!" he shouted.

Trickster raised his hands like claws high above his head. He screeched. His face contorted into a mask, he began to stalk Snake. Reddened with emotion, Snake surprisingly flowed down into a monkey king stance, mimicking Trickster's earlier taunts so perfectly that Trickster was momentarily taken aback. Snake scampered toward Trickster, who, disoriented, stepped backwards. Snake grabbed at his ankles, but Trickster skipped away. Snake leapt up into a dragon stance just in the moment Trickster assumed a phoenix stance. Standing toe to toe, they traded a long series of lightning-fast hand attacks and blocks. Although neither landed a blow on a target, the blocks themselves were excruciating. Trickster grimaced. Snake kneed him in the groin with so much force that Trickster was lifted off his feet, arching backwards to land on the back of his neck.

The agony was debilitating. For a long minute, Trickster was unable to consider anything beyond his pain. The first rational thought he was able to formulate was that since Snake had won three falls out of five, the match was over. It was inconceivable that he would try to win five falls out of seven. Two to the seventh was sixty-four. That would be lethal pain.

He climbed to his feet. Snake stood on his starting position, arms folded against his chest. Seeing his proud stance, Trickster realized that if he surrendered to Snake now, his status in the tribe would be irretrievably damaged. He thought of a stratagem.

"Double!" Trickster rasped.

From the steps, Cat shouted, "No, Trickster!"

Snake's reaction was almost imperceptible. Despite his attempt at inscrutability, however, it was evident that he was surprised. Snake nodded.

Trickster adopted a dragon stance. Snake assumed the phoenix. They circled each other. Their gestures were threatening yet respectful. Together they danced a martial ballet so graceful and so weighted with power that everything before seemed clownishness. Falling into a synchronization of concentration, they realized that they would meet with one lightning-fast exchange during an aerial confrontation. Snake and Trickster leapt toward each other. Their hands flew in blurs of attacks and blocks; the pain was enough to make them both begin to black out. Snake attempted to kick, but Trickster was already past. Snake extended his legs to land, but the ground arrived too soon and from an unexpected direction. Snake crashed into stone floor, losing consciousness under a heavy black wave of agony.

Trickster, with a hand so subtly poisonous that Snake hadn't even felt it, had slightly spun Snake in midflight. Trickster walked simply back to his starting position. He stood humbly, his hands at his side. The rest of the tribe waited silently.

After five minutes, Snake managed to regain his feet. He

stumbled over to his starting position, clearly crippled with pain. For a long moment, he and Trickster stood facing each other. Trickster did not deviate from his humble stance.

Slowly, so simultaneously that their movements seemed mirror-imaged, Snake and Trickster bowed to each other. Neither head bowed lower than the other. When they once again stood upright, they relaxed and stepped away from their starting positions. The match was a tie at three falls each.

After that day, Snake and Trickster didn't speak to each other for a year. No one in the tribe ever offered to fight with pain. System never raised the subject.

Now, looking up into Snake's eyes, Trickster worried whether combat with pain was still possible. What would happen if Snake challenged him right now?

"Hey, hey!" Cat shouted.

Her squad appeared from the southern path. Leaping and tumbling, they joined the rest of the tribe in the fountain. Cat sauntered over and stood closer to Trickster than to Snake, facing Snake.

"Who was first?" she asked.

"We were," Trickster answered.

"Some squad quals, huh?" Cat asked, covering her surprise. "I got eaten five times."

The center of the fountain went flat black. System appeared in its semantic interface and began to shoot images.

"All-tribe qualifications," it said. "This is tribal territory, a nation called China. Enemy territory is a nation called Japan. This is the opening position. . . ."

The island of Japan grew more detailed. Slowly, before their eyes, the geography of Asia grew sharp. The gardens melted away to War Council Rock. Icons of weapons systems began to appear, although many areas were left in mist. Three-dimensional icons of ships and submarines began to populate the Sea of Japan, the western Pacific, and the South China Sea.

"Oh stink! Not another naval war," Berserker moaned.

"Oh shuddup," Snake said.

"I hate naval wars," Berserker said.

"Yeah, we know, shuddup. . . ."

System continued, "During this all-tribe qualification, I will command all warfare areas for both the Chinese and the Japanese, except for Chinese electronic warfare, which you will conduct. You are to submit documentation on all your gambits, including any cryptographic keys that you decipher."

Half-listening to System, Trickster glanced at the disposition of naval forces. Unlike Berserker, Trickster liked naval warfare. He thought it was more interesting than ground warfare, more like a game of three-dimensional chess. Despite his lack of enthusiasm for yet another team qualification, especially under the restriction of System running both sides, the strength of the enemy navy piqued his interest.

"Steel death, these Japanese have got a good navy," Trickster muttered. Idly, he began to investigate the relative capabilities of the warships. He was not surprised that the technology of the Japanese fleet was better than the tribe's. System had been posing ever harder problems. This development tracked with that trend.

He also noted that the war at sea would be complicated by a huge storm that was brewing in the central South China Sea. On the display, it was labeled, Typhoon Ali. Trickster tagged it, learning that its winds were already in excess of 80 knots and were predicted for 150 knots.

"The enemy homeland is well within bomber range," Cat said.

Trickster checked his power account. His performance had been highly erratic, varying from the brilliancy against the Bekka Valley missiles, to his refusal to participate in the escape, to the outstanding success of his squad. System had increased his power level to a new personal high. Despite himself, Trickster felt pleased, telling himself it was only because he might need the power in a gambit against System.

While the others began their study of the new battle problem, Trickster stared beyond the spreading icons. He began to scan the communications available in the theater. He was amazed to find that there were not dozens, not hundreds, but thousands of circuits. Most of them were satellite communications, although there were dozens of fiberoptic links that had been penetrated by eavesdropping devices. The total bandwidth was in the range of petabytes per second, far more than the tribe had ever experienced.

One by one, Trickster experienced the circuits. Strangely, System was preprocessing to make them as usable as possible: multiplexed circuits were demultiplexed, packets were assembled, compressed files were decompressed, codes were decoded, standards were converted, languages were even automatically translated. Trickster was able to understand voice conversations, see video images and read textual passages.

Stranger yet, most of the circuits appeared to have nothing to do with warfare. Videos of children dancing with paper dragons, Malaysian newscasters speaking machine-translated Mandarin, cartoons of mice chasing cats, live feeds of empty studios, millennial rock music videos, distributed classrooms discussing double integral calculus, telephonic arguments between lovers, the wreckage of a downed airliner, dark men wearing cloths on their heads and firing rockets in a ruined city . . . one after another, Trickster flipped through each circuit. Each made less sense than the last.

There, there's a command-and-control circuit, hard-encrypted, but poll protocol, can sniff the nodes, sure military. More cartoons? What is that? An animal? Are there really animals then?

Trickster surfaced from the rushing river of communications circuits. *The data . . . the data . . . weird beauty. Beyond randomness . . . convincing . . . not from one source, from many sources . . . greater than System. Greater than System! The other world!*

Trickster yearned to discuss this discovery with someone,

with Cat or Dreamer or Lightning, but he knew that he couldn't talk without System overhearing. His own mind was the only realm in the world secret from System. That was one reason he loved to think. In the privacy of his own mind, he could entertain ideas, visualize the strangest images, remember and ponder, without System knowing.

The only possible way he could communicate in privacy was to use nonverbal language with Dreamer. As far as he could tell, System couldn't follow them when they were hot, wild, poetic, shooting in an affinity so feverish that they seemed one mind.

Excited by his discovery, Trickster signaled to Dreamer. From a great distance, Dreamer arrived, fast and anxious to communicate. For several minutes, they exchanged images meant to divert the attention of System. Quickly they fell into a psychic rhythm, able to understand which images were semantic and which were nonsense to distract System. Trickster's mind began to boggle before they were far into the sympathetic communion. Dreamer's poetry was so strange, yet so beautiful that it fascinated and enthralled. Tall waterfalls of prime numbers cascaded into a rapid river, branching at the Fibonacci sequence. Suns imploded and exploded. Trickster felt himself falling into her frames of reference. He surrendered himself. Deep into her world view, he began to communicate the discovery of the other world.

Not! It is not the other world! Dreamer signaled, her imagery consisting of black slashes and a silvery globe with convex reflections of Trickster's face that polarized into an opaque black disk that lacked reflections.

Trickster reeled, sending random images for several sequences; then he sent an ascending acoustic tone, a simple interrogative.

Dreamer materialized two tremendous hands. *Touch!* she screamed. The hands cupped the chin of an eyeless face. Two smaller hands reached up and caressed the large hands. *Touch!*

Contact! The hands melted into a series of reflections: eyeless faces in rippling waters, eyeless faces in mirrors, then eyes without a face, the glistening corneas reflecting green flashing text, words without meaning, the eyes glazing into opaqueness. Then all the imagery disintegrated into a torrent of machine data, a horrendous static of data, overwhelming Trickster's senses.

Trickster began to disengage. Dreamer shot one frame of the fourteen humans in the cage. As if from a great depth of water, he began to surface. Prior to breaking from the communication, Trickster sent a bouquet of pleasant smells to Dreamer, who returned them with stronger notes of rose and an eerily beautiful counterpoint of musical chords.

For a few moments, Trickster recovered in his personal realm. *If it isn't the other world, then what is it?*

His mind buzzed. He felt like surrendering to the narcotic of sleepiness. Desperate to solve the mystery, however, he took several deep breaths and plunged back into Battle Space.

12

Snake stood at his place atop War Council Rock. He gazed down at the battle problem. At first, the hugeness of the problem and its promise of massive points had excited him, but when System imposed the unusual condition of no direct command, Snake lost interest.

Command is everything, he mused. *There is nothing sweeter. To direct forces in combat, to slay through guile and force, to hear the ululations of the enemy . . . there is nothing in the world that is better.*

Out of habit, Snake monitored his squad as they scrutinized the theater. Perched on a high lookout, Cut-Back and Sly were arguing about the vulnerability of the electrical grid servicing Yokohama, a key strategic target. Snake smiled. Since the return of war to the world, Snake had maneuvered to build what he considered the hardest squad in the history of the tribe. Although he still coveted Cat's Berserker and Crush, he felt delighted that he had Trance, Cut-Back and Sly. Barker was good at carrying out explicit orders, so Snake had made the best of him. Still, he would trade ten Barkers for either Crush or

Berserker. For a while, Snake luxuriated in the daydream of the perfect squad: Berserker, Trance, Cut-Back and Sly. *Oh, it'd be so beautiful. . . . we'd devastate. We'd build up so many points that Crush would come over. Leave Cat with the runt Skipper and the liege man Lancer, and leave Trickster with his losers and weirdos. Oh . . . and if Cat herself came over to me? How beautiful. I would rule the tribe. Run battle the way it should be, merciless hard and poisonous subtle.*

This pleasant daydream was disturbed by the sneaking suspicion that Trickster's squad was more valuable than it seemed. *That Dreamer, she's a lost cause, but she can work some strange magic. Cry-Baby . . . right, Lightning, the ultimate runt. Dummy and Gimp, mediocre . . . it must be Trickster himself. That double-crosser weirdo. I should've challenged him to the fifth fall. That would've settled everything back then.*

Snake worried, though, that Trickster with his mastery of computers and Dreamer with her ability to decrypt were better suited to prevail in these increasingly technological battle problems. *That was so strange, in the squad quals, that they beat us to the fountain so quick. Wimps like that . . . something is going on. I have to figure it out.*

Snake glanced at the spots reserved for Trickster and his squad, there on the other side of War Council Rock, forward of where System stood like a black tower. Trickster and Dreamer were missing. *Moping in their personal realms, as usual.* Only Lightning, Dummy and Gimp were paying attention to the battle problem.

Snake glanced over at Cat and her squad. They were all busily studying the problem. Berserker was looking at the coastal defenses of the Japanese islands.

Cat gives us all too much latitude, Snake thought. *When I rule the tribe, I'll keep everyone working the problem, even the runts and weirdos.*

Trance turned to Snake and hooked a finger. Snake joined the conference between Trance and Sly.

"Boss, you dipped into the comms yet?" Trance asked.

"No, just the command-and-control display."

"Check it out," Trance said.

"Well . . . all right."

Snake opened up his interface with the communications underlying the battle problem.

Thousands of circuits crackled and fired. Strange, inexplicable images confronted Snake's senses. He shook his head as if nauseous. He backed out of the communications. With a glance into the eyes of his squad members, he could see that they didn't understand this phenomenon any more than he did. Snake stepped down from his place and approached System, kneeling two-knees-to-rock at a respectful distance.

"Battle-master," he intoned prayerfully. "Why are there so many circuits in this battle problem?"

System answered by posting a message to the entire tribe. "The Japanese enemy has a history of inserting command-and-control messages into nonmilitary broadcasts. Therefore, all theater communications are being made available. I suggest, however, that you concentrate on clearly military signals, due to span of control limitations."

Snake bowed low toward System and returned to his place. Cat buzzed for a commander's conference. Snake and she waited for Trickster to join the conference. Cat, her voice unusually tight from what Snake guessed was annoyance with her pet, Trickster, said, "Noise. Just noise. Reduce, recognize, react. We've got to ignore all this nonmilitary nonsense. I've tagged 115 military circuits already. Get working on them, won't you, Trickster?"

Trickster's reaction was strangely understated. Snake would have expected his usual peevishness. "Recognize, reduce, react, Cat. We don't know what's important yet, so we shouldn't reduce. I'm going to look into these nonmilitary comms myself. Might gain some insight into the psychology of the enemy."

Cat made a dismissive gesture. "If you'd take a peek at the

command-and-control display, even," she said, surprising them both with her uncharacteristic use of sarcasm toward Trickster, "you'd see that this battle problem is wound up tight and winding up tighter second by second. These Japanese are going to light off any hour now. Then the biggest war we've ever seen is gonna be burning. So let's get to it, shall we?"

Trickster shrugged. "Defense of Moscow was bigger. Mean the Nazis, not the Bonapartists."

"Nazis weren't NVC," Cat said, referring to capability in nuclear-viral-chemical warfare. "Nazis ran the whole war with a dozen teletype circuits, Trickster. Get with the program, please, won't you? We're looking at a big war here."

Snake studied Trickster's face. His reactions were so subdued that Snake became convinced that Trickster was dampening his expressions. It was during this moment of suspicion that Snake decided to trail Trickster. An hour later, feigning sleepiness, Snake retreated to his private realm. Once inside, he called System.

"What do you want, Snake?" System asked.

Snake was pleased to hear the modulations in System's voice that indicated it was in a human mood. When its voice was mechanical, it tended to be stupid like one of Trickster's doubles.

"I'd like to follow Trickster without him knowing."

"Why?"

"Personal development," Snake said, his rationale ready. "Trickster and I have a history of contention. I'd like to see how he acts when he thinks I'm not around. Maybe I'll learn more about him and I'll know better how to treat him."

"You need to concentrate on the battle problem."

"Ah yes, that's the other thing," Snake said, quickly changing tactics and noting with interest how System seemed preoccupied with this particular battle problem. "Since we're only supposed to suggest electronic warfare gambits, which is Trickster's forte, I thought following him might give me some ideas.

I could suggest some gambit myself, inspired, you see, by Trickster. Might be worth investing a few points."

"A thousand points a minute," System said.

Snake pretended not to be shocked at the exorbitant cost. "Done," he said.

System opened an interface through which Snake stepped. He found himself standing next to Trickster, watching a live video feed of a building afire. Red and orange flames unfurled and whipped twenty meters into the air, a column of black smoke billowing a hundred times as high. Trickster seemed to be studying the movements of some enemies who were combating the fire with hoses that shot arcs of water. Snake examined the burning building.

How strange, he thought. *The building is destroyed, but it doesn't disappear. It just keeps burning. What started a fire, anyway? War hasn't begun yet.*

With a disconcerting jerkiness, the camera zoomed in to a darkened door frame out of which flooded oily black smoke. From the blackness appeared a yellow-suited firefighter, clutching the body of an old man, burned scarlet, charred black. Snake stared fascinated at the hideous sight.

Fire! Consuming an avatar! But avatars are fireproof! And how could something . . . an enemy's body . . . partially destroyed, not disappearing. How strange! It's still moving.

Unseen to both Trickster and Snake, Cat also stood watching. As soon as System had told her of Snake's request to shadow Trickster, she had exercised her privilege to cross into any realm. Cat felt a growing excitement as Trickster flipped to another circuit, this one showing a grainy, two-dimensional, black-and-white film of Japanese army troops committing atrocities in Manchukuo, circa A.D. 1939. Cat leapt in front of Trickster and, invisible to him, studied his face. Japanese soldiers idly aimed their long rifles and shot the bound and kneeling Chinese peasants one by one through the backs of their heads, pitching them collapsing forward, their ruined faces into the mud. Trickster's unguarded expression crawled. Cat noted conflicting fascination and revulsion. She turned and studied the images. She herself felt deep sorrow. Somehow these time-blurred and grainy images conveyed a concept that she had never considered: these enemies were people. *People like the tribe.* Shooting them was wrong. Despite a lifetime of conditioning in the shooting of human-form targets, despite being exposed only to the image of death and not the reality, Cat intuited that this killing was wrong. It was bad. *What does it mean if there's more than fifteen people in the tribe?*

Then Cat looked at Snake. Ordinarily, she enjoyed spying on her siblings, but now she saw something in Snake's face that made her ashamed of herself, because she was peering directly into his spirit. Snake's features were lax. His eyes burned with feral hunger. Tribal Mandarin had no word for this aspect of Snake's character, but if she had been able to borrow the correct word, she would have chosen, "sadism." For the first time, Cat realized that Snake was worse than cruel. Life in the world had made him sick, not as sick as Weeble, but more dangerously sick. Cat felt concerned for the entire tribe, but she also felt concerned for Snake. *How can I save him from himself?* she thought.

Cat turned her face. She looked back at the circuits that Trickster was exploiting. He had flipped through various global-net teleconferences. Now he was listening to an elite-subscriber conference in which seven high-ranked government functionaries, top-salaried consultants and chief financial officers of investment firms were discussing the economic implications of the Japanese-Chinese crisis. Trickster flipped his hand. The financial conference continued, while a second window opened. The second window contained a public bulletin board posted with many running dialogues, many of them discussing the horrible possibility of general war in the Western

Pacific. Trickster flipped his hand. A third window opened, displaying a global news network interview with a retired American admiral. Trickster flipped his hand again and again. Cat watched his features freeze, his eyes focus fixedly, as he began to absorb eight simultaneous torrents of information. Cat felt the familiar blend of pride and hope as she watch Trickster rise in his greatness. *You are the hero,* she thought. *No one can do it like you. Go, brother, go . . . This battle problem is a strange new world. We need you to conquer it for us.*

She examined a series of multimedia reports that Trickster seemed to find fascinating. He was flipping his hand, opening texts, flashing through interviews and scanning histories.

A nation in chaos is the one that most often goes to war. The economic depression triggered by the trade embargoes, the collapse of democracy in Japan, and the resurgence of the imperial state should have warned us . . .

Flip.

Myth of Japanese pacifism . . . world's third-greatest military investment as early as the 1980s . . . foreign policy enlightened by the purest self-interest . . . did understand better than any other generation the penalties of a failed imperial strategy . . . lost this perspective . . . charisma of the emperor, coupled with the support of the ultraconservative nationalists . . .

Flip.

Even the hegemonists among the Chinese envision a continental sphere of influence. . . . Chinese naval strategy to this day is a mere seaward defensive bulwark. . . . extension of a land-bound strategy . . . ironically, because of these many factors, there is no genuine conflict of strategic interests between these two great powers. . . .

Flip.

*. . . regrettable atavism to the imperial state. Prior to these
events, Japan showed promise of becoming the second truly post-
modern state. . . .*

Flip.

*Emperor Tenji, the 127th emperor of Japan, the world's oldest
monarchy, through his unique charisma, rode the updraft of this
new romanticism. Forming an alliance with the ultraconservative movement, he managed to overcome a powerful tradition of
royal noninterference in political affairs . . . until he reached his
current position of absolute power over all aspects of Japanese
life. . . .*

Trickster mumbled a note under his breath. Unsure
whether she had heard him correctly, Cat replayed the note.
"Center of the battle . . . " Trickster had said. He opened a private communication with Dreamer. Cat was able to eavesdrop
on the communication, but it was in wild poetic language. She
grew anxious as Dreamer shot images concerning the strange
new concepts of this battle problem: pregnancy, sex, procre-
ation. Watching Dreamer fling reflections of these images at
Trickster made Cat feel so uncomfortable that she withdrew
from the communication.

Cat glanced at Snake, who was still studying images of death
and destruction.

Disgusted, Cat jumped back to War Council Rock. From
this familiar height, as she looked down at the command-and-
control display of the entire theater, the world comforted her.
She understood these frames of reference. Battle in the world
was simple. *Yet I feel them calling. . . . my brothers . . . my lost
brothers . . .*

13

McCullough entered Supplementary Plot, or SUPPLOT, at his customary time: five minutes before three A.M. The enlisted watchstanders gave him the greeting of the day, otherwise ignoring him, as they knew he preferred until he had drunk his first pot of black tea.

"Morning, Commander," Lieutenant Flanders said.

"Morning, Jake," Mike said.

Mike allowed the lenses on his personal virtual mask to study his retinas. When the security red light turned green, he turned the mask around and donned it. His virtual mask incorporated some of the higher technology available to military forces. In the eyepieces of the virtual mask were silicon wafer chips containing millions of mirrors, each one about as wide as a human hair. Electronic signals caused these mirrors to flex, so that scans of red, green and blue light were either reflected into Mike's pupils or were bounced away from his line of sight. The visual image these wafers produced was incredibly crisp and detailed, but distinguishable from reality due to an occasional

mistaken scan and a characteristic brilliance that some described as harsh. In the earphones of the virtual mask were hundreds of acoustic filaments, each only molecules thick, that
launched ultrahigh fidelity sound waves, positioned around the
outer ear so that the brain was able to pick up positioning cues.
These earphones produced sound that was distinguishable from
reality only because they were unable to accurately re-create
lower bass without causing hearing damage.

Only Mike's vision and hearing were interfaced into cyberspace, through which he could surf with the panache of a
human who had freely entered and excited cyberspace all his
life. He knew how to gather, evaluate, and process data. Because of this, the ninety-kilogram bulk of his body was allowed
on the ship. His brain earned his keep.

Yet his eyes still ached from the previous night. In his stateroom, when he should have been sleeping, Mike had picked
up a hardcover book, fine paper still the best technology for
presenting the written word. As he read, he mused that all his
life he had been plugged through some medium into someone's reductive version of reality. He had grown up in cyberspace. His schooling had been electronic and multimedia.
When he hadn't been leaning, he had been playing electronic
games or acting in interactive movies or teleconferencing with
pen pals in Montana or Szechwan. His society had molded him
into an information worker of the naval intelligence officer va-
riety. He earned his livelihood by processing torrents of data.
His brain ached. He yearned for simple reality. For nature. For
tranquility.

But now there was yet more data to attack. He logged into
his personal domain. He reviewed the changes to the ship's position since his last watch. He saw the vast waters of the western central Pacific, with the position of the *Lincoln* shown as a
three-dimension icon west of Midway Island. Lines of bearing
and distance to the nearest land masses allowed him to orient

himself. They were leaving the central Pacific, which was still America's pond, and entering the Western Pacific, which certainly no longer belonged to them.

Mike rocketed his vision over to the Western Pacific, the Sea of Japan and the South China Sea. He studied all the movements of the Japanese and Chinese warships.

Jake Flanders, as off-going watch officer, briefed Mike on the changes in the past six hours, calling attention to analytical decisions he had made during his watch, especially some difficult calls concerning the locations and movements of two Chinese and four Japanese vessels. Mike discussed the reliability of some sensor data with Jake, then decided to let one questionable decision ride. He felt confident that more reliable sensor data would be available soon and would prove or disprove Jake's decision. Mike had been riding Jake hard for the past week, teaching him the basics of the watch position. Taking his junior's chaffed pride into account, he was reluctant to overrule the questionable decision without more solid evidence.

Once the surface picture was established, they reviewed the air picture, replaying the tracks of every Japanese and Chinese military aircraft that had flown in the past twelve hours—or at least those on which they had intelligence. Mike selected some interesting interceptor tracks to brief to the admiral.

Then they reviewed the ground picture, calling into their conference the watch officer in Ground Plot, known affectionately as MUDPLOT. The heavy traffic in military armor, mechanized infantry, and mobile missiles took twenty minutes to review.

Finally, together, Mike and Jake called up the newly received intelligence summary reports from the shore establishment. They reviewed integrated text, video, audio and graphic reports. Mike pointed out the superficiality of one piece of analysis from Joint Intelligence Center, Pacific, or JICPAC, concerning the political dynamics in Tokyo.

"I talked with an old shipmate of mine back in Makalapa," Mike said. "Double encrypted link: the Navy's encryption and our own—"

"I thought that was against the regulations, sir," Jake said.

"What are they going to do?" Mike asked. "Shave my head and make me a sailor? Anyway, my shipmate told me that the J2 has put out the party line. The Japanese won't attack. So—the watch is being censored. Did you see that analit from that DIA major?"

"Ah, it's in my queue, I got it marked, haven't had time to—"

"Read it," Mike said. "Analits are important right now. Analyst to analyst communications, no institutional prejudices, just one spook to another. He's got some very good arguments. He thinks they'll go over."

"I'll read it before I rack in, sir," Jake said.

"Rack it in, shipmate," Mike said. "You stood a good watch. Read it when you get up. Pull chocks. I got it."

"OK, sir," Jake said. "See you tomorrow."

Mike glanced at his time readout. The turnover had taken almost an hour.

"Yeah, thanks. Good turnover."

Two hours later, fifty seconds to brief time, Mike was still plugged into the infosphere. He stood with his goggles placed over his eyes and the microphonic mask over his mouth. He was teleconferencing with JICPAC's intelligence officer on watch.

"I gotta brief in fifty seconds," Mike said.

"We got no more data, sir," the watch officer, a female lieutenant, said.

"Attack the data you do got," Mike said, allowing his pre-brief stress to exercise his gift for sarcasm. "We both got the same data. The difference is, you accept it at face value, while I challenge it, attack it."

"I don't know what you mean, sir," the lieutenant said.

"Yeah, I know you don't. I'll explain after the brief. Out."

Mike cut the teleconferencing link with Oahu. He flashed through a series of messages and notes mailed to him from all over the world in response to questions he had generated. Muttering, waving his hands and stabbing his fingers, he updated his graphics. The alarm in the upper right corner of his field of vision began to chime.

"Brief time in ten seconds," a mechanical voice said.

Mike mumbled curses. He stripped the virtual gear from his face, stepped down from the bastion, walked around its high steel wall and pulled open the steel armored door to SUPPLOT. Stepping into the vestibule between SUPPLOT, the war room and the flag command center, he saw that the briefers were already lined up in the front of the war room. Quietly, Mike stepped into the war room, filling the gap they had left for him, out of respect for him and out of the force of custom.

His mind was buzzing with facts, suppositions, considerations, details. He'd never be able to make sense of it all in the moments he had before he had to present it to the admiral. He'd stumble and botch it, mutter and make mistakes. It would be a fiasco. They wouldn't listen to him anymore.

Tony, the meteorologist, was already briefing the weather. Standing in front of the deck-to-overhead interactive display that dominated the war room, Tony was briefing two separate typhoons, both in the path of the *Lincoln*. The admiral interrupted and asked a question of the ship's captain.

"So how can we conduct storm avoidance?"

Captain Wellner, sporting a new crew cut that gave his lined face an appearance of youthfulness, grinned, deepening the lines in his face. His dark eyes sparkled.

"Admiral, that's a damned good question. The one typhoon is blocking the Bashi Channel; then there's the bigger one, heading right for the center of the Philippine archipelago. Damned if we do, damned if we don't."

From the rear of the war room, the navigator, a beefy veteran of twelve deployments, spoke up. "Safest course of action from a sea-keeping perspective, Admiral," he said, "is to drill circles in the ocean right here for the next few days."

Everyone around the long steel table and everyone sitting in the cheap seats against the bulkhead looked at the admiral. The entire command structure of the battle group looked toward the admiral, trying to guess what secret orders he had received from national command authority. Fifteen commanders—each responsible for forces such as the aircraft carrier, the airwing and the escort ships, and for warfare areas such as surface and subsurface—stared at the man who was ultimately responsible for the entire battle group.

The admiral's face gave no clue, but when he spoke, his voice had the flatness that his underlings associated with his voice of command, "Let's hear from intel first."

Mike realized that his brief was going to be the most important in his career. He had to make sense of the hundreds of facts, ideas and suppositions crowding his mind.

Too soon, the meteorologist concluded and stepped away from the briefer's spot. Mike stepped forward, just as he had stepped forward for a thousand briefs. As he moved, he felt his mind entering a beautiful state of clarity. Everything made sense. He understood what he knew and he knew what he didn't know. He saw how to present it: what to say first, which ideas to introduce, what to leave at a high level of abstraction, and what to discuss in detail.

Mike began to speak. His voice was clear, modulated and just loud enough that the people standing in the rear of the war room could hear him. Beginning with the disposition of Chinese naval forces, he pointed with his interactive wand, calling up the important background on each flotilla. Most of the time, Mike looked at the admiral, pleased to see that he was listening with his liveliest attention. As was his habit, the admiral interrupted with many questions, most of them hard and all of them to the point. Knowing his commander as well as he did, Mike had anticipated his concerns. He provided the answers he had gathered. For one question, he was tempted to guess at something he didn't know, but he decided to confess his ignorance.

"I don't know, Admiral," he said, "but I will find out."

Mike resisted the temptation to explain to the assembled crowd that he had spent an hour trying to find the answer to the question, which concerned the combat readiness of the Japanese fleet flagship, still in Yokosuka harbor. But then Mike reminded himself that the brief was not about him. It was about providing intelligence to the commander. Mike prided himself in avoiding this particular pitfall into which most intelligence officers threw themselves headlong.

Due to the high interest of the material, Mike's brief ran over its allotted ten minutes, finally winding down after half an hour. "Thanks, Mike," the admiral said. "Good brief."

"Yessir."

Mike stepped back to his place, against the bulkhead in the front of the room. For a few moments, he indulged in the happy state that he called "postbrief euphoria." Within a minute, however, he forced himself to pay attention. He realized that he was the only officer who wasn't listening raptly to the admiral.

"—secure all transmissions and maintain sea-keeping no farther west than this longitude," the admiral was saying. "NCA has given me that freedom and by God I'm going to take it. I'm convinced—" The admiral glanced at Mike, the corner of his mouth twitched in a smile, "—that the Chinese and the Japanese are about to fight one of the bloodiest wars in history. As luck would have it, the seat we have in the arena is already a little too close for comfort. If I thought that the presence of this battle group would help stabilize the situation or deter the war, I'd go forward. But I don't. So here we stay."

"And after the typhoons blows over?" Captain Wellner asked.

"Tony!" the admiral said. "Which way will the winds be blowing after the typhoons blow over?"

"I can't tell yet, admiral, but the prevailing winds this time of year in the South China Sea are southeasterly."

"That's good," the admiral said. "For us. By the time we finally transit the Bashi, the fallout should be blowing over the Asian landmass."

I va lay in her chair, monitoring the tribe. For more than twenty hours, ever since the beginning of the battle problem, she had been watching them. The mystery that had tantalized her for seventeen years was unfolding before her eyes: how would the children react if they were exposed to the world at large. As an experimental psychologist, Iva found this crisis fascinating. As a mother, she yearned for her children to succeed.

If only Chang had allowed me to introduce them to the world in a measured, scientific way, she thought. *All my planning and forethought on how to do it wisely and humanely—good for nothing. Just bombarding them with the chaos . . . madness. To him, they are less than slaves. . . .*

Iva felt one of her recurring attacks of guilt. She touched the thick golden slave collar around her neck. The collar contained eavesdropping equipment, allowing the Beijing counterintelligence apparatus to monitor her location and activities.

The watchers are watched, she thought. *They in their prison world, I in mine.*

Her thoughts became nonverbal, as her consciousness submerged down into the subconscious, where there roiled images
too violent and hideous to verbalize. A perpetually recurring
image forced itself upon her mind's sight: her own dead body,
killed by her own hand. Then she saw the lifeless body of Sui
Tai, folded in the leaf position. Iva's mind rebelled at these increasingly powerful compulsions to kill herself. Her thoughts
rose to the verbal level.

I must be strong, strong for them, she thought. *I am a monster,
I deserve to die, but all the others are worse. I can't abandon them. I
must stay with them. Maybe someday I can help them . . . even save
them!*

The sweet and powerful thought that she might be able to
liberate the children from the world overwhelmed her. She
began to cry. Her misery forced her to sit upright in her chair,
clutching her own hands to her breasts. But as she resumed
control, she knew that she could never be free, because her life
and her happiness were held hostage to the happiness of the
children, and the children could never be freed.

But before I undo myself, she realized, *I am free to undo all
other things. Recklessness is how desperation takes the name of hope.*

For many years, Iva had contemplated the sabotage of the
world. She had envisioned gross attacks, such as taking an axe
to power supply cables. She had fantasized about shooting the
watchstanders and then entering the commands on blood-
smeared keyboards that would shut down all the computers,
even the backups. Now that she was determined to attempt the
sabotage, she knew that the attack would have to be far more
subtle. The problem was that her natural coconspirator, Trickster, was continually monitored.

But now, perhaps, there was a unique window of opportunity. Iva swung out of her chair and began to pace. She had
confidence in Trickster, but he was not superhuman. He needed
specific information about System. He also needed command
access. Iva had no idea how she could provide command access,

but she thought of a way that she could now get necessary information to Trickster.

Iva had an optical disk documenting System. Standing Whirlwind's operating system with advanced expert system components was complex, but understandable. She imagined that for Trickster the documentation would be the Rosetta stone. She found the optical disc and prepared to enter it into her disc drive.

Iva took the next step, the one that would damn her, if discovered. She reached into the back of her personal workstation and found the cable juncture box. Grimacing with the effort, she twisted the cable loose, disconnecting her workstation from the network. Now that her workstation was not visible to System, she dropped the optical disc into the drive, called up the workstations encryption engines, encrypted the documentation and copied the encrypted files to disc. Then she dropped down to system administrator access, entered a destructive command and waited while her workstation overwrote every memory cell in her workstation's secondary storage, including the local operating system. Then, Iva unplugged the workstation and reconnected the network cable.

She removed the disc holding the encrypted files. Tomorrow, she would attempt to infiltrate the files to Trickster.

If the first steps of my sabotage aren't detected, she thought.

15

Like a lion in full roar, Typhoon Ali charged the Bashi Channel. The southern reaches of the storm raked the island of Luzon; its northern reaches ripped the island of Formosa. In Luzon, the slashing winds tore palm trees roots intact from the ground, tore corrugated aluminum roofs from cinder-block shacks and drove a drenching rain parallel to the muddy ground. In Formosa, the same hard winds, now driving in the opposite direction, buffeted steel storm shutters, tore apart flower gardens and drenched high-rise condominiums.

In the Bashi Channel itself, the Batan Island Technological Enclave weathered the storm. Heavily shuttered and running on emergency power, its modern buildings had been built to withstand larger typhoons. Many people in the enclave enjoyed a holiday from work routine. Typhoon-watch parties were celebrated in the emergency shelters. In the subbasement of Building 514, the tribe was aware of Typhoon Ali only as a feature in the meteorological and oceanographic layers of the computer-generated display of the battle problem.

Fifty hours into the battle problem, the only people awake were the security guard at the front desk, the night watch team in the monitor center and, in the cage, Lancer, Skipper and Cut-Back.

"Battle!" Lancer cried.

From the depths of an exhausted sleep, Trickster rose groggily to consciousness. He felt ill. It seemed to him very strange that the war had started so early. Raising his hands, he tore them across his face, entering Battle Space.

Slowly his awareness spread throughout the Far East, starting in the north, from the Sea of Japan down to the Malacca Strait. The smaller typhoon in the South China Sea was still blowing at full force. Ships struggled to stay afloat among seas gone mad. Even farther north, in the East China Sea, conditions were hostile.

"These Japanese are subtle," he heard Snake saying to Cat. "The storms harry the Chinese in the south. The weather favors the Japanese for an attack in the north."

Although rainy and windy conditions prevailed over the Japanese islands, flight operations were possible. Hundreds of Japanese aircraft were attacking the Chinese fleet throughout the Sea of Japan. Trickster noted that they were using the tactics that he had expected. Their FS/J-5 fighters were dashing at very low level over the waves, reaching predetermined points before launching sea-skimming supersonic missiles. Trickster had known that the Japanese had been tracking most of the Chinese warships, using world-best technologies in space-based, airborne and sea-based sensors. In a sea battle like this, detection was 90 percent of the problem.

"The subs are in the south," Trickster said.

"How do you know?"

"They're relying on air in the Sea of Japan. They've sent most of the subs south."

"Makes me sick just to watch. I want some."

"Stupid sea battle," Berserker muttered.

"Shuddup, Berserker."

Trickster's aesthetic sense reveled in this battle. There was a beautiful artistic integrity to the data. Nothing was clear. Nothing was obvious. The entire Far East was shrouded in a fog of war, thin in some places, opaque in others, but the fog was always present, obscuring and falsifying. The Japanese were using stealth and incredibly sophisticated techniques of disinformation. Even Trickster had been surprised by the sudden violence of their attack.

System appeared as a flat back bar, then changed to its semantic interface.

"Please provide all cipher codes for the Japanese enemy," System said.

Trickster considered refusing. That would lead to a direct confrontation with System, however, and he didn't have the weapons he needed to win. Trickster signaled to Dreamer, who appeared from the Realm of Night.

"System wants any cipher codes on the Japanese," he said.

Dreamer was wearing her combat avatar, which surprised the others, since she hadn't worn it for many months. It was a strange avatar that seemed to blend with the background only to shimmer brilliantly when she moved, revealing a giant, lithe six-armed warrior, four hands holding weapons, the lower two hands empty. One of the lower hands produced a number of icons, which she tossed into the gaping input maw of System.

"Naval logistics circuit," she said. "Tokyo Air Defense Center fighter data link. The Mitsubishi FX-43 TADIL-X."

Then she stopped moving, disappearing from sight. Inspired by her example, Trickster changed into a combat avatar modeled on the enemy, so that standing there he looked like a Japanese soldier who had infiltrated War Council Rock.

"Double points will be awarded for any further cipher keys," System said.

"We'll work on it," Trickster said. He glanced over to where Dreamer had been, not knowing if she were still present or whether she had returned to her personal realm.

16

A series of ones and zeros is a strange rope to throw to a drowning son, Iva thought. It was three o'clock in the morning. The war had been under way for a day and a night. The Batan Island Technological Enclave had been put onto a war footing. All Standing Whirlwind personnel had reported to Building 514. Now, most were sleeping. It was Iva's turn to stand watch in the expanded watch team in the monitor center, which filled all six watch positions. Iva sat at the station responsible for monitoring the neural-electrical interfaces. As she studied the health of the hundreds of interfaces, she allowed her fingertips to trace the microdisc's plastic square edges underneath the cotton panel of her lab coat pocket. It contained the encrypted copy of the documentation on System.

An hour later, her opportunity arrived. The watch team leader had surrendered direct management of System, allowing it to run under its own expert systems and leaving it available for any of them. Iva usurped System for herself. She pretended to investigate the software modules responsible for maintaining the sanitization of the data streams coming in from the real world, but, conscious of her heart racing, she corrupted the software modules. System's expert systems began to swing toward the problem, threatening a machine intervention, but Iva overruled them.

Iva slipped the microdisc out of her lab coat pocket and inserted it into her console. She injected the encrypted documentation into the data streams entering the world. Then she pivoted System toward its own system security management modules, which she savaged with a series of high-level overwrite commands.

"Help!" she called.

"Iva! What? What are you doing?" Wu, the computer scientist on duty, shouted.

"I don't know. I did something wrong, I think."

"Give me System, give it to me!"

"Here it is," Iva said, turning over System to Wu.

For the next two hours, Iva pretended to work with the watch team, attempting to determine what she had done. She stuck to her story that she had completely lost her place within the command structure and ended up issuing commands at random. Since she had disabled System's underlying expert systems and erased the log, there was no direct evidence of what she had done. The other people monitoring the world had been paying attention to other matters.

When she was relieved at six in the morning, Iva was sure that she would never again be allowed to exercise command over System. She wondered whether it would be necessary. That depended on whether Trickster could find, decrypt and use the information she had risked her life to pass to him.

17

Startling awake, Dreamer opened the window into the other world. Among the thousands of streams of information pouring through the window, she reached and intercepted one that contained what seemed a long transmission burst error. She had reacted with the instincts of a primitive woman who sleeps peacefully hearing the wind in the grass, the stirring of the leaves in the trees, the choruses of insects and the croaking of frogs, but who startles awake when she hears the quiet, nearby asthmatic coughing of the leopard.

The others complained of the nightly bombardment of extrasensory noise, but Dreamer preferred it to silence. She loved the beauty of extrasensory noise. It had shapes that changed in ways that she could almost predict without concentrating, changed in ways that she could predict if she forced her mind to focus.

This burst error was strange. System had been preprocessing most of the circuits so that they made sense. The only exceptions were the Japanese circuits with sixth-generation encryption schemes . . . and now this one. It was encrypted, too. She could feel that now. There was a fine pattern to the chaos. None of her comrades could sense patterns this fine, but she could. It was worth her attention.

Dreamer's brain began to blaze more brightly. Each of the one hundred billion neurons in the average human brain had one thousand to ten thousand dendrites connecting it to other neurons. Dreamer's brain was not average. Because her interface wafers allowed two-way communication, she had been interfaced directly and electrically into the computer. Of the children so wired, only she and Weeble had survived babyhood, and now only she survived. She lived yet because her mind had hungered for information. Surviving then thriving in this uniquely rich environment, her brain contained more interconnections than one hundred normal brains. In the visual and auditory regions of her cerebral cortex and in the regions in between, her neural interfaces were extremely well developed, with ten thousand to fifty thousand dendrites, many of them very long, connected to deep structures in the brain, circuited to unusual regions, thick and capable of efficient transmission and high excitement. The synaptic interfaces fired brightly, since the mix of neurotransmitters in her brain was unusual. Of the two hundred chemicals that regulated brain activity, she tended to run on a very volatile mixture, associated with madness more often than genius.

But Dreamer maintained. She did not surrender to the whirl and whorl of fantastic imagery that threatened to swamp her mind. What saved her was her love of beauty and of exquisite patterns. The same love that had caused her to hunger for information allowed her to maintain her equilibrium under its onslaught.

Busted, she thought. *You are mine. So easy to see.*

With no tool except her brain, Dreamer decrypted the message that Iva had transmitted. The copy that remained in storage in her personal realm, the copy that System could see, was still encrypted. It was decrypted only within Dreamer's mind, where System could not see.

How sweet, she thought. *What an interesting artifact. System. . . oh, it's funny! Just an operating system with some artificial intelligence modules and a facility that allows it to be steered by people. Some god! Look at this . . . its error codes. How funny! System's override command structures!*

Dreamer began to chuckle, then convulse with laughter. Reading System's documentation was shocking and hilarious. It made her feel sick and wild. She felt an exhilarating upsurge of hope. *Everything is possible*, she thought. *We can be free.*

Dreamer looked down at herself, struggling to notice whether she was wearing an avatar. Seeing that she was invisible, she grabbed her combat avatar and donned it. Turning to her southern frontier, she fired off a request-to-enter to Trickster's private realm.

Trickster woke when Dreamer's request-to-enter crossed his frontier. Reacting automatically to a rare request-to-enter from Dreamer, he signaled his permission and scrambled to his feet to stand in his open-sky meeting temple. Dreamer, wearing the six-armed combat avatar, bowed gracefully at the entrance. Forgoing the sarcasm of his combat avatar, Trickster, wearing his default avatar, bowed gracefully in return. Boldly Dreamer strode into the meeting temple. Trickster remained standing as she began to signal him in visual language. Trickster realized that she was highly excited when she changed her avatar fifteen times in the first second of the conversation. He smiled and attempted to accelerate his own awareness so that he could try to keep up with her.

A minute later, the two were bombarding each other with images so intense and varied that nothing and no one else in any of the worlds could have hoped to understand what, if anything, they were communicating.

When he began to understand that Dreamer had received and decrypted the documentation on System, Trickster held up his hand and staggered as his knees suddenly seemed to lose their strength. Dreamer continued to transmit for a full three seconds as Trickster's mind reeled. It was too much for him to grasp.

Then I've been right, he thought. *System is a computer artifact. Who sent this information? Can I trust it? But there's a detail to it, it's convincing. Or could it be . . . a dementia of Dreamer? Has she lost her mind? Or could it be a trick of System?*

Trickster shook his head. He raised himself to an erect stance. Sweeping his leg behind him, he planted his feet firmly and raised his arms in a gesture for readiness to reinitiate combat.

Dreamer laughed at his gesture, then mirrored it. She began to shoot images at him, more fiercely than before.

Suspending his disbelief, Trickster endeavored to understand the communication. Telling himself that he was strong enough to withstand any possibility, he took inside of himself and committed to memory the communication, not knowing whether it was an insane delirium, an enemy's stratagem or the key to the world.

Before disengaging, Dreamer sent a poem:

> Mystery, a mute voice roars deafeningly
> Enigma, an invisible sun blinds
> Subtle beyond imagination, sublime mastery,
> A single word that holds all meaning stupefies.
>
> Hear see understand
> Perceive the patterns in echoes, shadows, dreams.
>
> We, the most sequestered,
> More lonely than eyeless fish in cavern pools,
> Are yet deafened, dazzled, dumb-founded.

My lungs ache with the declamation of its majesty.

Is. Yes, is. It is!

Trickster filed away the poem into his memory, one of the many testimonies and acts of Dreamer that he could not understand. He turned impatiently to contemplate the documentation on System that he had also committed to memory. Dreamer had shot the visual images into his skull, splitting the pages and phasing the input so that it only made sense when Trickster registered them together and recombined them in the proper sequence. It was a classic Dreamer trick, but merely receiving data thrown like that caused Trickster's head to feel dizzy.

There it was, on page 73. The command sequence for shutting down a constellation of neural-computer interfaces. Trickster didn't know what a "neural" was, but he understood that there were fifteen constellations of neural-computer interfaces, each one labeled with the name of a member of the tribe. These commands were reserved only for the director, whoever that was.

Doesn't make any sense, Trickster thought. *What does this say about us? Are we really just modules with unique interfaces called neurals? . . . If that's true, if I stop System, what happens to me? Do I just cease execution? No, there, on page 23 . . . there was a diagram of the constellations of neural-computer interfaces. It showed a head with the interfaces at various places.* Trickster keyed on the two interfaces behind the eyes. They were labeled "optical nerve (left)" and "optical nerve (right)."

Although he knew little about physiology, although he didn't even know that he had a brain, he knew that the eyes were the portals for vision. If you closed your eyes, you ceased to see. He also had been taught the basic physics of light, so that he could understand optically guided missiles and infrared sensors. Trickster knew the word, "optical." He didn't understand "nerve" beyond the fact that it was a component of enemy avatars susceptible to nerve warfare, but, in a flash of inspiration, he understood that these interfaces into his optical nerves were how System caused him to see.

He had seen his own sightless eyes.

I exist, he reassured himself. *I have an existence separate from the world. Beyond System. I have an existence . . . and so I'm willing to bet it. Bet it all. I'll go first, pioneer for the tribe. . . . drop out of the world . . . live free outside of the world or not live at all . . . find out whether I do exist beyond System or whether I die, even if I'm damned to hell . . . but first I have to get to System. Do it.*

Trickster turned the pages in his mind and studied the documentation that covered how System managed the security interface with exterior circuits. He puzzled through a long, tortuous discussion concerning the difficulties in synchronizing a battle problem model with information fed into the world from real-world circuits.

Real-world . . . that's good. I like that. Maybe that's what they call the other world in the other world. . . . that implies that the world is other than real.

The discussion was inconclusive as far as Trickster could tell. It contained an upper limit in the informational bandwidth that could be synchronized with a large and dynamic model, a limit that was surpassed by the circuits coming in through the window. Trickster decided that this must be the reason that the battle model lagged behind the events reported in the window circuits. *System can't keep up. . . . too much information . . . maybe that's why whoever injected this documentation got away with it. . . .*

Trickster studied the security interface between the outside circuits and the rest of System. System had a security kernel called a trusted computer base. Trickster smiled. It was similar to security kernels that he had studied and learned to defeat during his computer terrorism training. The threading of the exterior circuitry was rigorous, but it wasn't absolute. Trickster noted that one security feature, shunting suspect packets into a supposedly isolated area for study, was possibly counterproductive. The isolated area was actually inside of the trusted computer base. A packet that contained the appropriate system-level commands inside of a camouflage shell might be able to shed the shell and introduce the system-level commands as the next commands to be executed, thus seizing the central processor of the trusted computer base.

Beauty . . . this preliminary check for viruses could be defeated if everything inside the packet was shifted left, the camouflage shell contained a simple shift right stutter, triggered when it was stripped away. . . . Timing would be tricky, but this viral check is blind to that scam. I can do that, I think. . . .

Trickster flipped in his mind to the extensive documentation on the hardware supporting the world. The main battery of computers were fifteen Cray YMP-5000s executing in a complete network. These alone made this the most powerful data processing center that Trickster had ever encountered. Moreover, a series of Fujitsu Z-7 supercomputers, locked core, were on-line as hot backups to the Crays. Finally, another series of Z-7s were off-line as cold backups.

Fierce . . . petaflops a second . . . and once you've seized the security kernel, you've got the entire system. . . . oh, I can see it. Beauty. This is the code right here, shift it left, camouflage shell, stutter right here. That's it. Mind's eye. Data nuke. Now all I've got to do is sneak it out and then bring it back in. That'll transfer the trusted base to my command, subvert System to me, and turn off my constellation. Then I'll see what I see.

Trickster moved on to the next stage of his plotting. He tried to think of ways that he could violate the security apparatus of the world and send a message out so that it could return.

Wait. . . . System wants gambits. I'll give it gambits.

Trickster drafted a proposal and sent it to System.

18

When Director Chang joined the teleconference with the Minister of Advanced Sciences, an even more senior Beijing official, General Chau, the Secretary of Defense, was standing next to him. Chang doubted that General Chau was physically next to the minister, but what mattered was that he had entered into the teleconference. The army had been read into Standing Whirlwind. Chang smiled and bobbed his head.

"I—," the minister began.

"I don't have much time," General Chau said, interrupting. "I've got a war to fight. I just want to make sure that you understand that anything Standing Whirlwind can do to help us defeat the Japanese is good. The cryptographic intelligence you've provided has been worth many lives, maybe whole cities. We need more of it. Right away."

Chafing from the interruption, the minister said, "What about this proposal that they directly conduct electronic warfare?"

"Confusion to the enemy," the general said. "I'm hitting

them back with everything I've got. I hope it's not too inconvenient to ask you to contribute what you've got. To save the state. If that's not too much to ask, considering you've spent billions on this project without consulting the army. Money that we could have spent on weapons that we sorely need today. Just let me know what targets they're hitting and when. The more devilment they work, the better."

The minister flushed red. His lips tightened, but he said nothing. General Chau looked over his shoulder, as if someone invisible had tapped his shoulder. Then, abruptly, he vanished. The minister turned to Chang.

"Make it happen," he said.

19

Dreamer swung open the door that had been provided through the communications interface. Trickster aligned his squad and prepared for battle.

"Forward!" Trickster yelled. His squad began to transmit through the interface. Through the interface, Trickster intruded into computer networks. Once he found suitable computer hosts, he sent copies of his doppelgangers flying. They infested the computer hosts. Then the doppelgangers themselves began to look for other hosts. Minute by minute, more and more versions of Trickster's doppelgangers were spreading throughout the other world's computer systems. When their numbers had reached a critical mass, and Trickster had gained access to tens of thousands of circuits, networks and computers, he signaled the destructive phase of his campaign.

"Destroy Japanese banking," Trickster said.

Trickster's squad helped his doppelgangers intrude into one, then two, then three, then dozens of international banking networks. The most heavily protected circuits in the other world,

these networks carried the billions of daily transactions necessary to international commerce. Trickster's doppelgangers mas-
queraded as various privileged managers, penetrating deep into
the trusted computer bases of the mainframes of the world's
richest banks: Bank of Japan, Dai-Ichi Kangyo Bank, Sumitomo
Bank, Fuji Bank, Mitsubishi Bank, Sanwa Bank. Forbearing im-
mediate destruction, they investigated each system's fail-safes
and backup systems. Cleverly, they hid data bombs designed to
spread throughout entire systems, on-line and off-line, and
timed to go off at each system's most vulnerable moment.
When they could do so without revealing themselves, they
called up the backup media and contaminated them with the
data bombs. Before backing out, they left a maze of transactions
orders, so that even if their data bombs were defeated, trillions
of yen would still be transferred to accounts held by the Japanese Red Army, the 18th of September Movement and various
tech rojin. Trickster also activated the deposit of billions of yen
in Swiss, Sri Lankan and Panamanian accounts created for
themselves. Trickster had determined that money in the other
world was a potent weapon. As was his habit, he armed himself
as he played the game.

The data bombs they planted, if undetected long enough,
would corrupt the entire system, on-line and off-line, and render it impossible for any bank to prove that it had more than
twenty percent of its assets. Trillions of yen would vanish without a trace.

"Destroy Japanese industry," Trickster said.

His doppelgangers penetrated the security of the networks
for controlling robotic factories. The most heavily automated
nation in the world, Japan possessed more than fifty million
robots. Most of these were secure, because they were physically separated from any circuit that the tribe could access.
Some five million robots, however, were accessible through a
nation-wide maintenance surveillance system. These tended to

be in completely automated factories building higher technology products. Trickster's doppelgangers perverted the maintenance surveillance program so that they were able to gain access to the programs for fabrication and quality control. Although they could have ordered the robots to tear each other apart, their destruction was far more subtle. They inserted routines into the fabrication and quality-control programs so that the robots produced high-technology products with hidden, fatal flaws. Chips for controlling pilotless land vehicles, for example, were corrupted so that they would perform perfectly for one hundred hours, at which time they would direct the land vehicle into the nearest solid barrier.

"Destroy Japanese government," Trickster said.

The hordes of doppelgangers intruded into the empire's data banks. They issued Japanese passports and supporting documentation to five million foreigners throughout the world, including some of the world's most dangerous terrorists. They released felons and Yakuza thugs. They issued arrest warrants for the most powerful men in Japan, showing special attention to University of Tokyo alumni. They intruded into secure teleconferencing networks, mimicking authority figures, issuing bizarre and contradictory orders. They discovered secret death lists, which they edited heavily.

"Destroy Japanese transportation," Trickster said.

Although most of the airline traffic in and out of the Japanese islands was suspended due to the war, Trickster's doppelgangers were able to penetrate the air traffic control systems for Tokyo's principal airport, Narita-Sanrizuka, as well as Kansai International Airport, built on an artificial island in Osaka bay. They implanted viruses that would make the systems report aircraft where none existed, hide some aircraft that were airborne, and misplot the positions and altitude of other aircraft. They intruded into the automated highway systems, subverting routines by inserting "NOT" judiciously in logic controls, which turned the routines into perfect traffic-jam generators.

"Destroy Japanese military command-and-control," Trickster said.

Trickster's doppelgangers began to play hob with the imperial armed services command-and-control systems. Partly through their own gambits, partly through gambits suggested through System to the People's Liberal Army, Trickster's doppelgangers began the long sequence of intruding, spoofing, meaconing, jamming, infecting, interfering, mimicking, echoing, decrypting, compromising. Trickster's doppelgangers inflicted on the Japanese every trick in the electromagnetic spectrum. Through clever coaching of the People's Liberal Air Force and Navy, they managed the physical destruction of key targets, ones that were too hardened against electronic measures.

Through these gambits, the tribe allowed the Chinese to recover from the initial heavy onslaught of the Japanese. The war hadn't gone nuclear yet, however, so the tribe made no judgments about the final outcome. Battle problems like these generally went nuclear. The nuclear phase of a war of this size generally made the earlier conventional phase irrelevant.

Yet for Trickster, the attack on the Japanese was only a distraction, a feint, a throwing of sand into the face of the real enemy, System. As the chaos wreaked by his doppelgangers spread, Trickster yearned to turn his attention to the real problem: overthrowing System. As usual, however, Dreamer had wandered off. She had intruded into the American Pacific Fleet command-and-control circuit.

"Come on, Dreamer," Trickster called.

"Wait," Dreamer's voice answered. "I've busted the American's most secure channel."

Trickster investigated the circuit. It was a computer-to-computer network for secure routing of command-and-control messages. Almost by instinct, with a twist of his wrist, Trickster flung doppelgangers into the network.

"Send the *Lincoln* into the combat zone," he instructed. "Try to get her attacked by the Japanese. The goal is a cause for war between Japan and America."

"America," his doppelgangers acknowledged.

"Confusion to the enemy," Trickster said.

Then he prepared to escape from the world. On the threshold of freedom or oblivion, Trickster hesitated. *Am I about to free myself? Or kill myself? Am I software? Or something with neurals? Whatever I am, I must be free,* he decided. *If in doing this, I meet destruction, I hope that destruction will come slowly enough so that I can see the true image of myself reflected in its eyes . . . growing larger as I near the end. . . .*

He exfiltrated his camouflage packet. He inserted it into one of the circuits streaming into the window. As he had expected, the window's security mechanisms alerted on the camouflage shell and routed it to the supposedly isolated area for study. When the trusted computer base stripped off the shell, the stutter right routine shifted the interior of the package, unleashing system-level commands. Trickster seized the central processor of the trusted computer base. The subsequent commands enslaved System to doppelganger 46. Doppelganger 46 replicated itself throughout the system, the subsequent doppelgangers acting as daemons, processes executing continuously in secret, interpreting and falsifying and manipulating. To the human operators monitoring the world, the transition was unnoticeable. The daemons consumed computation cycles, but they falsified the reports on processor activity. The daemons subverted the security threads of information passing through the trusted computer base, allowing Trickster to access all information, but they reported normal threading of information. The daemons changed the video images reported by the security cameras so subtly that the operators didn't guess that none of the information reaching them was true.

Still enwombed, Trickster studied the true video images from the security cameras in the main control room. Secretly, he watched the operators as they watched the false images of himself. He smiled as he realized that he had reversed the universe. All of his life, he had inhabited an environment generated by unknown entities in some secret realm. Now he was in a secret realm, generating an environment for the entities, whom he now knew.

He took the next step and turned off his constellation of neural-computer interfaces.

For the first time in seventeen years, the world ceased.

20

Deprived of input, the interface filaments spliced into all of Trickster's cranial and spinal nerves defaulted to a straight pass-through. Functionally, they ceased to exist. Trickster regained his natural senses.

Intense pain radiated throughout his entire body, shocking waves of pain, shooting stabs of pain, skittering sheets of pain. Trickster resisted the impulse to scream. He could not let the enemy hear him. He thought that he was dying or that something had gone horribly wrong. Within a few moments, though, the pain subsided and then vanished. Electrical imbalances in the interface wafers stabilized.

The echo of a shout was still reverberating when his ears began to hear. His eyes were already open as he began to see.

Deprived of their computer control, his swaddling of Novlar fibers was relaxing slowly. Trickster felt himself sinking toward the floor. Like veils, the fibers drifted down before his eyes, sinking to the floor. He caught a glimpse of two dimples in the lower back of a female Chinese; then more veils covered his eyes. His fingers tingling, Trickster brushed the veils away. He smelled a peculiar funk of sweat and pheromones. The odor seemed overwhelming.

When his feet settled on the steel grid of the floor, pains shot up his legs. Trickster looked down toward his legs and for the first time saw his own body. His uncircumcised penis dangled in his view beneath the rippling domes of his abdomen. His body was hairless.

Dream form, Trickster thought. He reached down and brushed his genitals. The sensations that blossomed from his penis reminded him of the thrill of victory.

It's as I dreamed. . . .

Trickster glanced up and saw thirteen humans. Eight were golden-skinned Chinese men like himself. Two were golden-skinned Chinese women. There was an African man and an African woman, and a Caucasian man and a Caucasian woman. Trickster realized that he was seeing the true avatars of his brothers. He wondered which one was Cat and which one was Dreamer.

His comrades were moving in the cage, scampering about their canopy of Novlar fibers, engaging in conversations with unreal entities and making gestures that had no bearing on their true situation.

This is what I looked like, Trickster thought. *They watched me acting like that, for all of my life, they watched me.*

One of the tribe squatted to defecate. A Novlar strand presented a white ceramic bowl under the buttocks, catching the waste, then passing the bowl from strand to strand until it was passed through the service opening in the bars. Several white ceramic bowls lay waiting disposal on the shelf across from the service opening.

Trickster watched the tribe. These avatars aroused a strange fascination. Trickster found himself watching the female brothers more than the males. He wondered which of the bodies he was watching belonged to Cat. Which belonged to Dreamer? Despite his many problems, this issue seemed, somehow, the most important.

Then he activated the routines that drove the supportive Novlar fibers. Like awakened cobras, the Novlar fibers rose and wrapped around his feet, knees, hips, elbows and wrists. Experimentally, Trickster began the motions of climbing. Obligingly, the fibers provided the appropriate resistance so that he began to ascend.

Trickster made a gesture that set the timer to one hour and then made another that collapsed the command interface to voice commands, allowing him to see fully with both his eyes. He climbed to a top corner of the cage, knelt and began to study his brothers. He knew that he could ask doppelganger 46 to identify them, but he wanted to recognize them with his own eyes and ears.

For many years, Trickster had been accustomed to inter-acting with his comrades while they wore strange avatars. Every day in the world was like a masked ball. They were able to recognize one another through the most subtle hints. Trickster knew Cat as Cat, not as an appearance. Watching and listening to the tribe as they continued to move in their computer-generated environments, Trickster recognized her by the beauty of her movements. She was flowing from one pose to another, assuming a stillness between movements that was so relaxed that she invited the eye to slide away from her. Trickster experienced joy, seeing that she was female. He noticed that she was the only African female. He felt pleased, because he would have guessed that Cat, had she been able to choose, would have chosen the most distinctive of the color options that apparently were available. Cat's face was sculpted, graceful, with molded cheekbones and feline eyes. Her teeth were brilliant white. Her tongue was clean and pink. Shaved or engineered hairless, her skull, defined by intelligent ridges that

Trickster recognized from her default avatar, glistened in the lights. Cat's limbs were long and graceful and powerful. Her body fat content was low enough that Trickster could observe the rippling domes of her abdominal muscles, yet she stored enough fat in her lips and buttocks that they formed beautiful complex curves. More acutely curved, less round, yet just as beautiful were her breasts. Trickster found her wonderfully beautiful to watch.

Turning his attention to his other brothers, Trickster recognized Berserker next. The powerful violence of his gestures was unmistakable. Trickster smiled, noting that Berserker was the huge white man, densely muscled, with freckled pale skin and flaming red hair and beard. The hairs of his pubes and his armpits were also flaming red. Berserker was ranting about having to maintain watch on a Chinese frigate flotilla in addition to his study of the Japanese amphibious defenses.

Snake appeared next. Trickster recognized his voice, which had that low grating raspiness that Trickster despised. Snake turned out to be a golden-skinned man whose body was not much different from Trickster's, although it was somewhat taller and thinner. Trickster considered stepping down and choking Snake to death. Snake would not even feel the fingers around his throat. He would lapse into unconsciousness and simply die. *If I understood death here*, Trickster thought. *Perhaps I could make the decision that he deserves it. Maybe later.*

One by one, he recognized the bodies of the entities with whom he had shared his universe since babyhood. He saw that Lightning was the white female, long-boned and sturdy, with hairs so blonde that they seemed silver. Her skin was pure white, not freckled like that of the other Caucasian, Berserker. Trickster was surprised to see that she looked so strong. It was remarkable. She seemed much more powerful in the other world than she ever appeared in the world.

He recognized Skipper next. She was a Chinese woman with a slim, almost emaciated, body. Trickster recognized her because, as usual, she was busy leaping about, making jokes and having fun.

Lancer was the sole African male. Trickster felt impressed by his appearance. He seemed much older than anyone else. His face was lined; his eyes were dark and blood-shot red. Yet his body corresponded closely to his default avatar—it was tall and lean and hard. Just as he did in the world, Trickster felt more secure knowing that Lancer was on his side of the fight. At the moment, Lancer looked fairly ridiculous, standing in the far corner of the cage, maintaining a vigilant gaze on a blank wall.

Gimp had a withered right leg in the other world, too. Trickster consulted his doppelgangers and learned that an abrasion from the BioApex interface wafer had damaged his sciatic nerve. Trickster felt sad for his stalwart squadmate.

He identified Crush, Trance, Cut-Back . . . all three of them male Chinese, compact, hard, their movements fast and precise. The last three comrades remaining to be identified were Barker, Dummy and Dreamer, but there were only two bodies left. One was a Chinese woman. She had a heart-shaped face with prominent cheekbones, a firm chin and a pug nose. Her eyes were almondine and lovely. Her hair was very long, jet black, and glossy. Her body was athletic, but more padded than anyone else's in the tribe. Her hips were wide and her breasts were full. She moved less than anyone else in the tribe. Trickster guessed that she was Dreamer.

Barker and Dummy, therefore, shared the last remaining body. Watching it closely, Trickster could see no clues of the mirror-imaging that both Barker and Dummy employed in the world. Consulting his doppelgangers, Trickster learned that all of his identifications had been correct. The mystery of Barker and Dummy was that Barker resided in the left hemisphere of the brain, while Dummy resided in the right hemisphere. The corpus callosum had been experimentally severed at the age of three. They were a side experiment, noted a failure years before. Neither lobe of the brain was a better warrior than the normal brains.

A strange desire had been building in Trickster for many minutes. He tasted a strong acid in the back of his mouth. His heart was tripping. Looking down, he saw that the strange organ between his legs had changed shape, assuming the shape that Cat had dreamed.

He looked upon the females, Cat, Dreamer, Lightning and Skipper. Trickster felt pleased. Staring at Cat, he began to make an avatar modeled after her true body. His hands waved in shapes, his fingers pointed at palettes of colors and textures. All four of the females were among his favorites in tribe— although Cat could be terribly bossy, Dreamer was unpredictable and weird, Lightning could be such a wimp, and Skipper was so slow to take anything seriously. Yet he loved Cat. She was the one with whom he had shared his truest feelings. She was his best friend, although she had always been everybody's best friend, which was part of her power as the leader of the tribe. Dreamer and he had always had a unique rapport. No one could understand Dreamer, but Trickster had tolerated, then valued her, long after the others had given up. Lightning had always been a nuisance in battle, but she had always been grateful to Trickster. She loved him more than anyone else in the tribe, more, he suspected, than he loved Cat. Then there was Skipper, with whom Trickster had quarreled all his life, because no one in the tribe was more like him. No one loved a trick more than Trickster, unless it was the irrepressible joker, Skipper.

With a welling of emotion, more warm even than his growing lust, Trickster realized that he loved these four females. He wanted to care for them. He wanted to help them to safety. In that safe place, he wanted to discover their true natures, freed from the constraints of the world.

Then, there was Lancer, faithful Lancer. Brave Gimp. Barker and Dummy, poor fools. Even Berserker. Although as frightening a killer as Trickster could imagine, Berserker was like a force of nature. He was Trickster's comrade in many a hard battle.

All of them, really . . . all of them, less the evil Snake. Trickster wished he could pull out the hate he felt for Snake from this upwelling of love for the whole tribe, just as he wished he could pluck Snake from the tribe itself. In his increasingly compassionate mood, it occurred to Trickster that it was possible that even Snake himself, if he were freed from the world, could become less irksome, perhaps even tolerable.

It's my comrades that I must free, Trickster thought. *Not just myself. The whole tribe. But where?*

Trickster thrashed his hands before his face, entering Cat's private domain. Trickster looked around; Cat had made many changes since the last time Trickster had visited. Before, her private domain had been an epic wilderness of glaciers and smoldering volcanoes and skies shot with meteors and shimmering with auroras. Now it was much simpler: an endless black plain etched with a matrix, the variously distant intersections marked with semantic icons. The eastern horizon was burning ruby red and gold with a predawn light. Overhead, the stars were configured to help navigate through the matrix.

Trickster jumped from intersection to intersection until he found Cat. She was wearing her chess avatar, the onyx-black queen.

"Hey Cat," Trickster said.

The black queen metamorphosed into Cat's default avatar.

"Hi Trickster. Welcome back."

"You've changed your domain."

"Lots of visitors. Lots of discussions. I cut back to the old domain every now and then. Still like it. But this new one is better for sharing information. Hey, check out Battle Space. The Japanese are bombarding Shanghai."

"They'll go nuke soon."

"No bet."

"I've worked up a new avatar for you."

Cat looked up and smiled. "Did you really? I've been wondering what you've been doing, neglecting the battle problem so hideously. Let me see!"

Trickster reached behind his back and produced the new avatar, which was a perfect model of Cat's body. With a sly excitement, he watched Cat's face as she saw the image of her own body for the first time.

"Oh, one of those female ones!" she exclaimed. "Pounding hard! Slashing! I like it, Trickster. Let me try it on."

Cat jumped into her new avatar. Trickster's breathing quickened as she began to move in it, bending backwards to admire her wide, muscular calves. He cut back to the cage and saw Cat's real body moving with identical motions. He thought that she was more beautiful in her avatar, so he cut back to Cat's private domain. She had called up a looking glass and stood admiring herself.

"The detail is edge-keen," Cat said. "A real piece of work. Nice design. Feels good. I like the color, too."

"Here's another," Trickster said, producing an avatar copied from Lightning's body.

"Oh, beauty!" Cat said. Abandoning her twin avatar, she jumped into Lightning's twin avatar.

"This one's got a great feel too," Cat said. "The skin's like silk. Smooth. Color's interesting, don't you think?"

"Here's another one," Trickster said, calling up an avatar like Dreamer's.

"Oh, that's nice," Cat said, disinterested. "That's like a female version of our default avatars."

"Hey Cat," Trickster said.

"Yeah?"

"I pulled a trick, you know."

"What? Tell me."

Trickster laughed. "No, you figure it out. I'm going to leave these three avatars with you. You play with them. Tell me when you figure it out. Let me just say that I've got a surprise for you."

"All right."

Trickster cut back to the cage, but he kept a one-way window open into Cat's private domain. He watched with amusement as she hopped back and forth between her new avatars.

But now the shifts were changing. Trickster unleashed a fake message from the director that ordered the off-going shift to the cage for cleaning and preventive maintenance inspections. Then, climbing into the corner of the cage above the entrance into the room, he watched with his eyes as, one by one, the off-going shift strolled into the room. When all ten of the off-going shift were inside the cage, cleaning and inspecting Novlar fibers, Trickster clapped his hands. For a moment, no one noticed the clapping amid the din that the tribe was making.

"Hey!" Trickster shouted.

A Chinese woman looked up at him. Trickster laughed when he saw her panic as she saw the intelligence in his eyes. "Hey prisoners!" Trickster shouted. He clapped his hands and then made the command gesture that caused Novlar fibers to reach and ensnare all ten of the off-going shift. Quickly the fibers hauled them up to the heights of the cage, where they were arranged in an even row facing Trickster. He sneered as he watched the horror and terror in their eyes.

"Nice," Trickster said, "Nice. Seventeen years. See if you like it. Seventeen years. My prisoners."

Trickster checked to make sure that the daemons were falsifying the video feed from the security cameras. He noted with satisfaction that the images they were showing were of the first captured shift cleaning and inspecting. He checked the wall clock. Just under four hours before the next shift change. He checked the meteorological display. The eye of the typhoon would pass over the island just about then. *Four hours*, he thought. *Shifts are four on, eight off. In four hours I can take the second shift, take the building, and send out reconnaissance against the island.*

He jumped into the Realm of Night. Without physical referents, the Realm of Night was alive with extrasensory signals, synesthesia noise, audible light, visible sound, unique symbols and randomness. Only Dreamer would live in such a chaotic place. No one except Trickster ever visited her there.

"Hey Dreamer!" Trickster called.

"Here, Hero," Dreamer answered. She did not bother assuming an avatar. Trickster imagined that she was taking the form of an oscillating red, green, white band of light. Or perhaps that was a semantic cluster that only made sense to Dreamer.

"I killed System."

"Yes, I noticed."

Dreamer's nonchalant answer annoyed Trickster. He had anticipated congratulations, even from Dreamer. He waited, but when Dreamer remained silent, Trickster realized that she was not impressed because the overthrow of System was not a monumental achievement in her terms of reference. Finally, he asked, "Now that I can ask you without System interfering: when you talked about the other world, did you mean this one?" He shot her images of the cage and scenes throughout Building 514.

"Yes and no. I've seen things like that before."

"How?"

"Thinking."

"So how long have you known about the other world, Dreamer?"

"Always, I think. My oldest memories are of it, not the world. Sometimes it's hard for me to tell them apart, really."

"What does it look like to you, when it doesn't look like this?"

"Ah . . . well, there's lines of force that connect every-

thing. Necessities, possibilities, probabilities, causalities, in-
heritances . . . these are normal enough, but then there's the
emotions. I can feel them, sometimes. Mostly a mortifying
anxiety, a crawling, throbbing anxiety that lacks the clarity of
fear. Almost matching it is this hunger—literal, physical hunger
and other varieties of hunger—with wide swaths of content-
ment, full bellies. And a yearning, oh sweet Hero, such a
longing. A longing that is the better part of you. You could find
a home there in that other world. Sharp shocks of joy, contin-
ual across the surface of the other world, like sparkles in the
dark, mostly visceral joy, that thing they call sex. Hate, a black
thing, heavy, brooding. Then something worse than that."

"What is it? The bad thing?"

"Evil, Trickster. I can feel it sensing me. It's more than a
thing, almost an entity, but too dead to be alive, a force worse
than hate. It survives by destruction, grows stronger as it de-
stroys. A fatal flaw in the design of that world, even though it
allows all things, should not have allowed that. Mere hate would
have been enough. Such an evil . . . it's either an intensely
botched world, cracked, doomed to be subsumed by evil, Trickster, or masterfully intense, a wild, extreme, free, epic, heroic
place, Trickster. I don't understand it and I don't care for it."

"I'm not sure I do either. But the other world is our true
world, isn't it, Dreamer?"

"Yes. No. I don't know. I have visions of the next world, the
world after the other world. But I don't know if the visions are
real. Not as real as . . . these bodies are more real than our
avatars. It's true that the world is just an artifact of the other
world."

"Then we have to deal with it."

"You, Hero. You deal with it. I'll help, but I can't take responsibility, can't participate in that. It frightens me. I'm not
strong enough. I can feel my mind going, sometimes, sometimes in the best of times. I don't know if I could live in the
other world."

"I need your help, Dreamer."

"Stop playing with Cat. Get her to help you."

"Ah, I'm buzzed with her. She never believed in the other world. I'm going to play some more."

"Lancer has a good head. Get Lancer to help."

"Lancer's no fun."

"You've got this red hot line straight down your middle. That's the sex thing, did you know that?"

"What?"

"Red hot line. It's taking over your center, really, Trickster. You're breathing the real air, smelling the real smells. Pheromone. Chemical signals. Triggers a burning mating imperative. Your nose is in the other world, Trickster. So your mind is following."

"I do feel hungry, starved, but not for food."

"A new kind of yearning for you, Hero. It's called lust."

"Ah, I read that. Saw that. The feeds. Since you're female and I'm male—"

"Huh! Sex leads to this thing called pregnancy. Did you notice that?"

"Yes."

"The female ones get the child. The child grows actually *inside* the avatar of the female. When it comes out, there's this screaming white hot pain. Hu! Scares me. Just the idea of pregnancy frightens me. It's so bizarre! To have a growing mind inside of my avatar. I don't know if that would be healthy. Not for me. Go ask Cat."

"She's—"

"You love her better anyway. All this talk, I can feel myself going away. So long, Hero. Come talk to me again sometime soon . . ."

Politely Trickster exited the Realm of Night. He returned to the cage. Looking at the females, he knew that he could touch them any way that he wanted without them knowing, but his entire mind revolted against that idea. That would be sinister, not tricky. That would be something System would do. System or the enemies who had made System.

No, this sex thing bore study. Trickster found it difficult to believe that anyone would truly enjoy allowing the penetration of their avatar by another entity. Although the world had had no culture of sex, the taboo against physical contact was deeply ingrained in him. Physical contact had always been associated with battle. He had yearned for touch. He had known he needed that, but he had only visualized an embrace and a caress. Violation of the perimeter of another avatar was something that happened only in physical combat.

Slowly Trickster realized that his natural passion, his lust, had been repressed, repressed and diverted to aggressiveness, repressed and perverted. He was not innocent. He was merely ignorant and deluded. System had stolen his innocence. He could not recover what no longer belonged to him. He could only try to grow away from this evil beginning. He had smashed System. Now he needed to smash the mind-forged manacles that System had created in him.

Trickster cut back to Cat's private domain. In her vast plain of shining black marble, she had settled into her twin avatar.

"What do you think?" he asked.

"I like this one best."

"Have you figured it out?"

Cat looked slyly at Trickster. Studying his eyes, she smiled ever more broadly. "You . . . traded in your jewel spiral just to get enough energy to build these avatars."

Trickster snorted. "Don't be dense, Cat."

Cat walked over to where she expected the boundary to be between Trickster's personal space and hers. She reached up as if to touch the invisible wall, their traditional gesture of friendship. Her hand stopped where she expected to meet resistance. Feeling nothing, puzzled, Cat withdrew her hand.

"Something is broken," she muttered.

"Shattered," Trickster said.

He waited patiently until she extended her hand, tentatively, seeking out the limits of her personal prison. Taking one step nearer, she extended her hand toward Trickster. Trembling, Trickster raised his hand towards hers.

Their fingertips touched.

As if shocked, Cat snatched back her hand. Trickster guffawed nervously as if from the release of tension.

"What is it that is broken?" Trickster asked, his voice unintentionally hard and demanding.

Cat pounced at Trickster, who spun away from her so quickly that she never touched him. He laughed at her.

"What a wimp!" he hooted.

Leaping, Cat tried to land a kick on Trickster's head. As he dodged, Trickster felt the air pushed by her foot. Suddenly he realized that she was not playing. Cat was furious.

"Enemy in my private domain—" she muttered, while trying to land a back fist, a knife hand and a knee in rapid succession. Trickster ducked in monkey pose, skirting around Cat, and shouting, "Hey, it's me! Trickster!"

"Mimicking avatars. Invading my private space!" Cat shouted, trying to kick Trickster in the head, sternum and solar plexus. Moving as quickly as he could, Trickster never saw the blow that caught him under the cheekbone. A hard white light exploded under his eye; the pain seared his mind. He heard Cat screaming from the pain in her foot.

"It's me, Cat," he shouted. "System is destroyed."

"That hurts!"

Rolling onto his back, Trickster signaled for the attenuation of pain by twelve decibels. He leapt to his feet, kneeled with one leg wrapped around the other, bowed his head, and held his hands in front of him, inner wrists up, fingers down, in one of the tribe's most emphatic postures of surrender.

"I destroyed System."

"Why?" Cat asked.

Trickster looked up. Cat had changed to her default avatar. Although the pain had been attenuated, she stood rubbing the ball of her foot.

"Freedom," he said.

Cat changed into her African avatar. She sat down in lotus seat, still rubbing the ball of her foot. Trickster found himself staring at the jiggling of her breasts and the interplay of her muscles underneath the skin.

"Freedom to hurt my foot?" she asked.

Ever nimble low to the ground because of his mastery of the Monkey King discipline of kung fu, Trickster scooted closer to Cat. He laid his hand on her thigh. The skin was rich and smooth. Cat looked up into his eyes. Her look was deeply serious. Trickster reached, brushed away her hands and began to rub her foot.

"Ow ow," Cat complained. "Not so hard."

Trickster rubbed more gently. Cat unwound from the lotus seat, rolling onto her belly, raised on her elbows, all the while leaving her foot in Trickster's hands. Gently he massaged her foot, although he imagined that his face needed it more.

"It's weird, feeling someone else touching you," Cat said.

Trickster gazed at her muscular back, broad across the shoulders, tapering to a small waist. The muscles alongside her lower spine were raised, two smooth forms that reflected the light, cast a shadow in the valley of her lower spine. Her gluteus muscles were bunched, raising the oblong forms of her buttocks into pronounced shapes that mesmerized Trickster.

"I can see white lights when you rub my foot," Cat said.

"Cat," Trickster said, his voice hoarse. It was all he could do to keep his hands on her feet.

"Yeah. Don't stop."

"Do you know how there's the world, and inside of the world, we have our realms?"

"Yes," Cat said, her voice neutral, when anyone else in the

tribe would have been sarcastic about Trickster repeating the obvious.

"Well, the world is just a realm inside of the other world."

"How would you know, Trickster?"

"Would you like to see it?"

"Yes."

Holding onto her foot with one hand, Trickster made gestures that commanded both his and her realms to stop. Instantaneously, they were catapulted into the cage. Without missing a beat, Trickster continued to rub her foot. Cat looked around the cage with curiosity.

"Funny realm," she said.

She twisted and sat up, her torso so close to Trickster that he could feel her body heat. Cat looked around, noting with amusement the antics of their comrades and the miserable expressions of the prisoners, trussed up in Novlar in the far corner of the cage.

"OK. Tell me about it," she said.

Trickster opened up a semantic interface and shot images at Cat, explaining how he had overthrown System. Since Cat had never mastered computers, she had a difficult time understanding how her entire universe could have been a computer-generated environment. She was spared much existential agony due to a lifetime of being submerged suddenly and often in strange environments. She nodded gravely as Trickster tried to explain his problems in understanding the other world, but Trickster was left with the impression that she thought that his misapprehensions were more Weeble-like madness. Apparently, to Cat, the world was the world and the other world was the other world.

"Just a different problem set," she said.

"But what does it all mean?"

"Well, I guess it means that the real enemy all along has been those monsters over there, who have been keeping us prisoner in this cage."

Abashed by Cat's simple but undeniable judgment, Trickster could merely nod.

Cat said, "It reeks in here, you know?"

"Yeah."

"Aren't there showers in the other world?"

"Yeah. Over there. It doesn't smell like it, but they did bathe us regularly."

"Could we shower now?"

"Sure."

Trickster and Cat used the shower facilities in the cage, which were located in the corner farthest from the entrance. Trickster made the command gesture that turned the warm jets of water streaming down. They tested the water. Finding it pleasantly warm, they stepped under its stream. The sensation of thousands of water drops striking and sluicing down his skin was incredibly pleasant. Trickster gasped and stood away from the water. Experimentally, he placed his arm under the water. It felt better than anything he had ever experienced. Although the supercomputers that had manipulated his sensory input had been extremely powerful, there had been limits to their abilities. Vision had been given preference, so all of his life, Trickster and the other members of the tribe had been robbed of more than half of their tactile sense. His brain, accustomed to handling only a fraction of the tactile input, began to hallucinate under the rich stimulus of the shower.

"Ohhh, it's unbelievable," Cat moaned.

Trickster looked over and saw Cat arching backwards, allowing a hot stream of water to bombard her chest and belly. She turned and allowed the water to strike the back of her neck.

"I can see gold flashes," she said.

Encouraged by her example, Trickster stepped back under his own showerhead. He found it very strange. Water didn't feel like this. Nothing felt like this, except perhaps victory. He was feeling the rising emotion that was like the beginning of a victory. The acrid taste in the back of his mouth had returned.

His eyes were locked on Cat. Glistening from the water, her sculpted body had an overwhelming fascination. He stumbled toward her. He reached out and touched her.

With strangely idiotic eyes, Cat looked down at him.

"You want to do that thing we dreamed?" she asked.

"Yeah I do."

"Can we do it in my person domain?"

"Yeah . . . sure."

Sensitive to privacy, Trickster caused the Novlar to face the prisoners outwards. He allowed his comrades to continue their blind movements, although most of them were sleeping. Dreamer was still moving. For a moment, Trickster thought that she was looking at them, but then her vacant eyes turned away. He and Cat cut to the black marble matrix.

"No, my old domain," she said, twirling her index finger in the air, causing the appearance of a landscape of distant smoking cone volcanoes, lava rivers, a shimmering rainbow over massive waterfalls into a rocky gorge, auroras and meteor showers. She and Trickster reposed on a thick bed of freshly fallen cherry blossoms over soft grass underneath a cherry tree in riotous blossom. Pink and white flowers, carried by the gentle breeze, continued to fall down upon them.

Cat lay on her side, stroking Trickster's shoulder. Trickster laid his hand on Cat's ribs. He could feel the ribs spreading as her rib cage expanded with her inhalation, could feel them moving together with her exhalation. He could feel the rush of air in her lungs. He could feel the pulse and beat of her heart, the moistness of her perspiration, the richness of her skin. He slid his hand up and cupped her breast, which was full, not fatty but spongy with lactiferous glands. His thumb caressed her wide areola and brushed the emphatic dark nipple.

Cat squirmed. "That hurts," she said. "Don't do that."

"Feels good," Trickster said, lowering his hand.

"Cuts through me," Cat said. "Cuts me to my center." She shivered.

"I could . . . adjust—"

"No, just leave it like it is. Touch. The sights and smells here are so much better than that nasty place, but I want to feel you just the way it is. The touch. It's been so hard all these years not being able to touch you."

Her hand was long and strong, smooth, without calluses, subtle and gentle. She touched Trickster's face.

"It's been a long lonely time, hey, brother?" she asked.

"Yes, brother," he said. He caressed her hip. The feel of smooth skin and pliant muscle, soft fat and emphatic bone, warmth and coolness and gliding movement, was delectable. He had never imagined that the sense of touch could be so exquisite. He was beginning to appreciate that the world modelers had simplified tactile sensations, so that they had lived their lives in a numbing cocoon. Their brains, unaccustomed to the onslaught of tactile information, were reeling, delirious, hallucinatory. As the sexual response of arousal heightened, sensations that were previously interpreted as painful or ticklish, now were interpreted as pleasurable. Unable to restrain himself, Trickster found that the second time he cupped Cat's breast, she didn't complain. Her eyelids seemed to grow heavy. She sounded a note deep in her throat.

Among the falling cherry blossoms, Trickster, obeying an instinctive impulse, climbed atop Cat. The sensations caused by full frontal contact, face to face, mouth to mouth, chest to breasts, belly to belly, loin to loin, legs entwined, caused a riot in their minds. Merely the sensations of Cat's plush, luscious lips, her tongue, her respiration upon his cheek would have been enough to cause an electrical storm within his brain. Joined with the hundreds of other sensations, he experienced a vertigo of pleasure. He felt himself swooning.

Far too much, he thought. *Far too beautiful.*

He moved his mouth from hers and whispered in her ear, "Are you sure?"

"Yes. Oh! Trickster, I! OH!"

Trickster grunted, a deep animal sound. He convulsed, his face buried in the flowers behind Cat's ear, his pelvis thrust forward, his abdomen one arching insistence. He felt his mind ripped asunder in showering sparks and dazzling rushes of ecstasy, his body's sensations elevated, accelerated, as if for one grand moment he was electric. For six long seconds, waves of ecstasy, then rich pleasure, then an abiding satisfaction swept through his being. His thoughts reeled. He had never imagined that anything could feel like this.

"Oh my, Cat," he whispered.

"Oh don't stop," Cat pleaded.

Victory, victory . . .

Trickster, however, quickly lost the wherewithal to continue. As his heat subsided, he realized that System had wired him all those years so that these sensations would be associated with victory in the battlefield. With a black welling of hate, he realized that his enemy had stolen this, the most sweet . . .

But Cat was murmuring, muttering in his ear, words he didn't understand. Her lips and tongue were in his ear, against his throat. It didn't matter. That was gone now; he had destroyed that world. Now he was in her secret realm. Trickster sought her lips. Their mouths joined in a kiss. It was overwhelming, joyfully sensate. He could sense her so intensely now. His member began slowly to regain its firmness. He began to move again.

Oh, he had wanted it to be perfect, perfect, but nothing in the other world was perfect. Everything was flawed and incomplete, with pain mixed with ecstasy, hate recalled in the midst of love. It was a very strange world, but it was also splendid and awesome.

Before Cat experienced orgasm, she reached a long, high plateau of ecstasy. A phase that Trickster had rocketed through, Cat experienced for several long, defining minutes. Opening her eyes, she saw the idiocy of her lover's expression and beyond that, a kaleidoscopic commotion of cherry blossoms moving in the breeze and beyond that, a sky with a freakish beauty of her own invention. Cat realized that this life was overwhelmingly precious, beautiful. Then, with four giant visitations like rolling thunder and heat lightning, she experienced climax. She felt a part of her self submerging, falling down a long well of ecstasy, down the long tunnel of time. When her self emerged again, she felt transformed, wiser, more powerful.

Embracing her lover, Cat lay thinking.

She was the first to be able to speak.

"This world," Cat sighed, "this world, this world is . . . this world is good, Trickster."

"Thanks."

Her mouth close to his ear, Cat chuckled softly. "I thought you weren't responsible for this world."

"I'm not," he said. "But I'm glad I found it. Now I can finally hold you. Touch you."

"It's a good world," Cat whispered. "Sweet, very sweet. If this were all that was in it, I'd be happy to stay here with you. Forever. Forever here in this one realm."

"Me, too," Trickster said. "But we've got to find a way out of here, out where we can be alone like this, just the two of us, with no one to tell us what to do or think . . ."

"I'll help you find the way, Trickster."

"We'll find a way, Cat."

"Touch me."

"I'm touching you."

"My true friend."

21

An alarm sounded. Doppelganger 46 reported that the second shift was being relieved. Trickster sent a message from the director instructing the second shift to report to the cage for cleaning and inspection duties. When the second shift arrived, Novlar fibers captured them before they noticed the swaddled and muffled prisoners. Now two of the three shifts were Trickster's prisoners. Trickster cut back to Cat's domain.

"Now we have to go take the last shift," he said. "Time to take the building. Take the guard shack, post a guard and send a recce party out."

Cat grinned. She laid her smooth hand on Trickster's shoulder. "Whole tribe?" she asked.

"No. Minimum force." Trickster kept his expression natural. He didn't want Cat to guess he feared some of his brothers more than he feared any of these enemies.

Cat nodded. "All right," she said. "Let me lead the recce."

Trickster shook his head. "We need people that look Chinese. That eliminates you, Lightning, Berserker and Lancer.

Barker and Dummy are out because they share a body. Gimp is not up to it. Neither is Dreamer. Skipper is not much better. I need to stay here in overall command. That leaves Crush, Snake, Trance, Cut-Back and Sly."

"Mainly the soldiers. Mainly Snake's squad."

"Right."

"So send Snake and his squad."

Trickster had a vision of Snake commandeering weapons from the outside and returning to Building 514 to confront him with superior firepower. He set his feet in a posture like a fighting stance, tribal body language for strong personal opposition. "No," he said.

Cat kept still, pretending that she hadn't noticed Trickster's body language. "Why not?"

"I don't trust him."

"You never do."

"You don't get it yet, Cat, but you will. I'm sending Trance. Alone. He looks like the enemy. He's more zoned than any of us, and he's subtle and swift. And I'm going to spring Lancer and Lightning first."

"Why?" Cat asked.

"Before I let out Trance, I want our liegemen at our side."

Cat smiled. "Yeah, the wimp."

Trickster jabbed his thumb at Lancer, then jerked it over his shoulder. Instantly, Lancer's filmed eyes began to focus on the cage. He grunted from pain. Among relaxing Novlar fibers, he descended to the floor. Trickster made the same command gesture at Lightning, who shrieked.

Trickster noted that Cat seemed disturbed by his decision to allow Lightning out into the other world. Ignoring her for the moment, he briefed Lancer and Lightning.

"Full contact drill," he said. "With pain. Sticking pain, so be careful."

Trickster reached out and touched Lightning, who startled

but then gentled under his touch, laying her cheek on his hand. He looked into Lightning's eyes, which were misty and adoring. Her uncritical support reassured Trickster. Despite her obvious state of confusion, she seemed to be handling the transition well.

The annoyance that Trickster had sensed in Cat seemed to boil into anger. She laid her hand on Lancer's shoulder in a gesture mirrored on Trickster's. Immediately, Trickster understood that Cat resented him touching Lightning. Jealousy was not a new phenomenon, but the violence of the jealous reaction to physical touch was new. Trickster was surprised at the violence of his own jealousy of Lancer.

Lancer himself startled when he felt Cat's hand upon his shoulder. Gasping, he sunk to his knees and embraced her legs. For a long moment, he was incapable of any reaction other than sobbing. "Such a long time," he said. "To touch you . . ."

Cat looked down at Lancer's head. She rested her palm atop his crown. Her eyes welled with tears; she looked over at Trickster, her expression betraying love, concern and a note of triumph. Abashed, Trickster withdrew his hand. He wondered if System had had a good reason for maintaining the invisible barriers.

Then he awoke Crush from Cat's squad and briefed him.

"Once you take the guard, put on his clothes and pose as him. Send anyone who comes down here to the cage," Trickster said.

"Why don't I just drop them?" Crush asked.

"Please, I would've chosen Berserker if I had wanted to open up a new front," Trickster said. "Whatever you do, though, don't let them come in and then leave."

Trickster lowered one prisoner about the size of Trance. He stripped him of his clothes and then sent him naked back to the heights of the cage. He then pointed toward Trance and jerked his thumb over his shoulder. Trance's black eyes gleamed as he peered down at Trickster so sharply that his earlier oblivion seemed a ruse. He floated down to the cage floor. After a momentary blur, he stood near Trickster and Cat.

"Whose domain is this?" he rasped in his habitual tone, an imitation of Snake's voice.

"Full contact drill," Trickster said, his voice flat and hard. "With pain. There's a guard in the guard shack, see him here? Crush will take him. You put on these clothes, go outside this building, and recce this island. Without a trace, hear me? Don't take any enemies unless you have to, but if you have to, take them neat. Silent. Bring back weapons if you can. Look for means of escape for the entire tribe."

"Who put you in charge?"

"I did," Cat said.

Trance raised an eyebrow. "What the hell is Snake doing?"

They looked up at Snake, who stood above them, muscles knotted in fury, arguing with an entity that he thought was Trickster. Trance shouted at Snake. When Snake didn't respond, Trance looked anxious.

"What the hell, Cat?"

"Snake is in another realm for this part of the problem," Trickster said. "He can't hear you. Now do you understand your mission?"

"What's the deal with these avatars?" Trance asked. "What happened to the battle problem?"

Trickster shook his head. "Four-hour time limit. Overtime, lose all points. Now, go."

Trance sneered but he bent to pick up the clothes.

"Lancer goes on watch," Trickster said to Cat, not to Lancer.

Cat glanced at Lancer and nodded. Lancer relaxed. Trickster threw Lancer back into the world, supplying him with live feeds from the other world.

"Watch Trance as long as you can," Trickster shot to Lancer. "Warn me if he doubles back. Watch Crush. Make sure he stays vigilant. Watch the whole facility. This is doppelganger 46, a sentinel module. It will help you. Help it."

Trickster turned to the others. "Careful. It's going to be combat with pain. And you lose, game over. Dead."

Cat grinned more broadly. "Then let's win, shall we?"

Doppelganger 46 sprung open the cage door. Trickster, Cat, Crush and Trance stepped outside of the cage where they had physically been imprisoned since babyhood. Trickster felt no particular joy. From his perspective, the cage was just another room. System had been his cage.

They prowled down to the end of the room. Closest to the cage room were the facilities for the care and feeding of the bodies of the tribe. They passed the kitchen and the medical laboratories, climbing up the stairs to the main floor. Trance and Crush moved toward the front of the building. Cat and Trickster stepped toward the interior. Turning a corner, they saw a technician walking away, far down the corridor. Bounding, Cat loped after him. So soft were her footfalls that only the last two were heard by the technician, who didn't have time to turn around before Cat smashed him in the back of the head with her fist. The pain in her hand was hideous, but she sucked in her breath.

"You all right?" Trickster asked.

"Hit them somewhere soft," Cat said. "Or hit them with something else."

Trickster checked the downed enemy, noting that he was still breathing. He checked the technician for weapons, but there were none. Trickster stripped off the man's laboratory jacket and bound his wrists behind his back with the sturdy cloth belt. Together, Cat and Trickster continued down the corridor, the wool carpet plush under their naked feet. Hearing movement around a corner, they moved smoothly against the wall. A man appeared, his head bent over a clipboard. Trickster kicked him in the throat.

Moments later, most of the on-duty operators were standing their watch in the main control room. They were discussing some interesting anomalies in System when suddenly two streaks, one golden and the other dark brown, invaded. The golden streak, barely recognizable as a naked Chinese man, leapt in the air and kicked a woman under her chin, spun and smashed his heel into the temple of a man. As Trickster prepared to land and drive the edge of his hand under the lip of another man, his right arm moved in front of a large screen display.

Suddenly the muscles in his right arm convulsed. Weird sensations of pleasure and pain—silk drawn across his elbow, fire rushing along his thumb, his forefinger located in the crook of his arm—disoriented him. Landing, he let his numbed right arm fall limply to his side.

Cat noticed Trickster's predicament. With her left hand, she formed a knife and drove it into the solar plexus of a woman. The Chinese man stepped toward her. Launching into the air with a roundhouse kick in his sternum, Cat finished the fighting.

"You OK, Trickster?"

"Yeah. I think."

Standing, dazed and confused, Trickster looked down at his prostrate enemies. He wondered what had gone wrong with his arm. Pacing, he walked in front of the large screen display. Swirls of colors invaded his left field of vision. A stench of burning rubber and salt surrendered to whiffs of bronze and lilac. A spasm caused his head to jerk and his throat to close. Acting on instinct, Trickster ducked from the large screen display.

His heart was racing. *The thing is a weapon*, he thought.

"Stay away from that," he said, chokingly.

Crawling on his hands and knees, Trickster searched for means to tie up his enemies. In the corner of the System center, he found an electronics tool kit which contained a bunch of sturdy plastic ties for bundling cables. He tossed them to Cat, who grabbed the still-moving limbs of the enemies and tied their wrists together behind their backs, then tied their ankles together. Some packing tape served to seal their mouths.

In the corner of the main display, Trickster studied the security display of Building 514, a color-coded floor plan with symbols. He ordered his doppelganger to reveal the true video feed from all the surveillance cameras. He noted where the remaining enemies were located. He could see that most of the off-duty operators were sleeping down in the emergency shelter. Also, Trickster spotted two technicians performing work in obscure corners of the building.

"Cat, go get those, will you?"

"Sure."

"I've got to clean up after System."

Cat backtracked to the fire staircase and descended. The shelter was in the subbasement in the wing opposite the tribe's cage. Deep in the basement, she was walking down a cement-block corridor. Turning a corner, she entered a new passageway, the ceiling/wall corner of which contained a run of four-hundred-cycle power lines. Cat felt nauseous. She heard bells, whispers, garish static. The flesh of her face began to crawl. As her knees buckled, her head moved away from the power lines. The hallucinations and spasms lessened.

Shaking her head, Cat pressed to the emergency shelter. Once inside, things went smoothly at first. She was able to incapacitate four workers without awakening one. After she had them trussed up, she turned to leave, but at that moment, an engineer came bustling into the room. Cat tried to coldcock him, but the engineer, a clandestine Beijing security operative who was trained in *kung fu*, blocked the blow. Cat spun and landed an elbow against the man's face, receiving for her reward a knife hand in the kidney area. This surprise blow to the kidney was so unbelievably painful that Cat fell to her hands and knees gasping. Mercilessly, the engineer pummeled Cat in the other kidney, then chopped down on the back of her neck. Cat felt herself losing consciousness. Realizing that she was in danger of losing her life, in a survival reaction, she blocked out the pain, lashed out with her foot, and tripped the engineer. Lancer blurred into the room. With all the might in his body, Lancer drove his fist through the man's face. He didn't notice the pain signals from a deep gouge across his knuckles and along the back of his hand.

Cat climbed to her feet. The movement allowed through her mental barriers the dull roar of pain from the kidney bruises. She gasped. She never had imagined that something could be so painful.

Trickster burst into the room, his eyes wild. Lancer grunted an all-secure. Trickster stopped short. Together with Cat and Lancer, he stood and looked down at the dead engineer, whose glassy eyes did not return their gaze. The glassiness in the eyes told him that no one was home any longer. For this enemy, the game was over. The eyes, in expressing nothing, communicated a world of horror. Trickster wondered what it all meant. *Why is death different in the two worlds? What happens to these enemies if they don't disappear?*

"Game over," he said.

"He's not on this level," Cat said.

"Not anymore. Let's go."

Together they continued his battle plan. They hunted down, incapacitated and tied up the remaining two enemies in the building. Mentally reviewing the action, Trickster counted fourteen enemies captured.

"Let's go to the cage," Trickster said.

"Huh?"

"I'll make the pain better."

They entered the cage. Trickster made the command gestures that attenuated their pain signals by twelve decibels, where they were still strong enough to discourage them from motions that would cause further damage to their injured tissues.

"Whoever designed the pain here overdid it by twelve db," he said.

Trickster shook his head and turned his attention to completing the overthrow of System. Meeting his doppelgangers as he had planned, he helped them make the transition to overt control of the entire system. After a few hours of work, he was confident that he controlled everything. Trickster tested backup procedures, from the Crays to the S-7s, from the S-7s to the off-line S-7s. His confidence increased.

While Cat took a nap and Lancer continued his watch, Trickster departed from the cage. Finding a trolley cart in a repair technician's tool room, he trundled his prisoners one by one into the cage, where Novlar fibers wrapped them up. Trickster then checked the building's video feeds. All enemies were tied up. Crush stood watch in the place of the security guard at the front desk. The building was secure.

Trickster turned his attention to the strange phenomenon caused by the large screen display in the control room. *What sort of weapon is a viewing monitor and a power line, anyway? Wait . . . it's obvious. Electromagnetic interference. EMI. There was a warning in the documentation on the interface devices.*

Trickster reviewed the files which described the neural/electronic interface between himself and the computers that generated the world. He called up a graphic that showed the iridium and gold wafers that had been spliced into each one of his cranial and spinal nerves. The holes connecting the spliced axons were all labeled. The interactive graphic explained the sequences of firing that created different neural messages. For the one million axons in each optical nerve, the encoding was fully mapped. These sequences caused a faint purple glow in the corner of the eyesight. Other sequences caused a flash of red from the upper right to the center of the eye. And so on.

The rim of the interface wafers contained a microelectronic radio that allowed transcutaneous transmission and reception.

The signal was extremely weak, in the microjoule range, and could only be picked up by the large, sensitive antennae that had been built into the cage itself. Outside of the cage, the signals were lost in the electromagnetic noise.

Receive range depended on broadcast power, of course. The antennae in the roof of the cage put out only two watts. There it was:

>>>>>WARNING WARNING WARING WARNING <<<<<
Despite advanced noise rejection circuitry (patents pending), unshielded Microteq transcutaneous radios remain vulnerable to electromagnetic interference (EMI). Exposure of the radios to solar radiation, radio and television broadcasts, electric circuits and other forms of electromagnetic energy will result in static.
!!!!!! LETHAL ADVISORY !!!!!!!!
Static transmitted by the Microteq transcutaneous radios may interfere with the signals processed by the BioApex gold-iridium neural interface wafers. This could result in hallucinations, muscular spasms, agony, disorientation, heart failure and death.
======>>>>> The command, "Hi7299Lo8190-Hi3032Lo7300" disables the Microteq radios. Disabling results in interruption of energy-sump replenishment. Energy sumps will deplete after five hours, after which time the radios cannot be reenabled without replacement of the energy-sumps. See major surgery.

Trickster considered his situation. He controlled Building 514, but he couldn't leave it. The building's skin contained a lead shield, protecting it from EMI. Outside, mere sunlight would kill him, if radar emissions or FM radio didn't kill him first. Through his gateway, Trickster could attack the world just as he had attacked the Japanese, but he was imprisoned and vulnerable. He could disable the radios, but five hours later he would be trapped in the other world, just a meat robot without access to the interfaces and tools that were to Trickster what language was to a poet.

Just another room, he thought. *Just another set of problems to solve. To get to the next room. The next struggle. But I break on through. System couldn't keep me in the world.*

A lead-shielded suit might protect him, but then he had to worry about air and heat ventilation. What he really needed was a suit designed for nuclear-viral-chemical combat. Building 514 might have some hidden somewhere. If it did, he could escape the building. But where would he go? This world was very strange. You couldn't cut from domain to domain. In what they called the natural world, you could only walk or run . . . until you died. Death was the only way to leave this realm.

A strange death, too, Trickster thought. *A bloody, messy, painful, smelly, sickening death. And as far as you can tell, it's the end of realms. Then this world is the last world. The end here is the end. How horrible . . .*

Then Trickster realized that he had sent Trance to his death.

Gale force winds had lessened to the moist, warm winds of the eye of a tropical typhoon. Tatters of palm fronds slapped spinning past rippling puddle waters. A heavy scent of mud mixed with an unusually pungent stench of rot from the beach, where pounding waves had stirred up the compost of decay along the sandy biosphere of the shoreline. The warm moist night smelled of fecundity and mortality. Wearing the clothes of a scientist, Trance casually strolled out of the building where he had spent his entire life. A strange music whistled in his ears. For a moment he thought that he was seeing whorls of green and purple colors lurking in the shadows. He felt his guts crawl.

Reduce . . . reduce . . . Trance thought. He entered into the intense concentration that had earned him his name. In his mind he filtered all of the extraneous sensory information. He denied agony. He rejected the information that his heart was crawling up his throat.

He passed through the stand of coconut trees behind the beach toward the dark shapes of the botanical garden. Soon he was walking among genetically engineered tropical fruit trees, many in riotous flower, many blown over, all tattered by the storm. Trance allowed himself to experience the night, the buffeting wind, and the heady smell of tropical flowers. He began to accelerate uphill.

From the top of the hill of the botanical gardens, he could see half of the shoreline of Batan Island, the entire campus of the technological enclave, the airstrip and the small town toward the east.

Ten minutes later, Trance knelt in the shadows of the woodland outside of the double-fenced perimeter of the airstrip. He worried about the outer fence. It was five meters high, topped with razor wire. Already, a few bumps and scratches had convinced him that he did not want to climb that fence. Trance recognized the meaning of the narrow path worn smooth in the tropical grass in the run between the two fences. *Regular foot patrol. Great.*

A lifetime of escape and evasion exercises made him wary. Yet he had to get to the hangars. There were no aircraft visible either on the tarmac or through the hangar doors, two of which were partially open. A plastic bag blew across the tarmac, which brilliantly glinted from the hard white light of arc lamps shining down from towers. When he saw this evidence of neglect, Trance realized that he had been watching the airstrip for too long not to have seen some evidence of occupation. He peered up at the control tower cab, which was dimly lighted but apparently empty. *Deserted . . . I think it's deserted . . .*

Trance moved deeper into the woodland, then began to follow the fence line toward the hangars. With predatory eyes and ears, he searched for evidence of the enemy. *Nothing . . . nothing . . .*

His suspicions were confirmed when he saw that the post at the vehicular entrance was deserted. Trance waited another five seconds, then he shrugged his shoulders and exited the woodlands. As if he had every right, he walked up to the entrance, ducked under the lowered gate arm, and proceeded along the road toward the first, larger hangar. Trance entered the zone of high glaring arc lights. His shadows spread in all directions, the overlaps on the cement like the points of a compass. He felt oddly dizzy. Strange stenches of burned cinnamon, sulfur and ammonia nauseated him. He felt his flesh crawling. A convulsion catapulted Trance forward onto his knees. He coughed. His heart leaped and thrashed as if anxious to escape the prison of his rib cage. *Nothing is real but my own mind. . . . willing the body forward . . . command to crawl . . . forward . . .* Slowly Trance crawled beyond the zone of the electromagnetic interference caused by the brilliant arc lights. The electrically induced hallucinations and convulsions subsided. He gained the area of shadow outside the perimeter of the hot white lights. Trance stood and attempted to gain control of his breathing.

Just like Trickster, he thought. *Send me out alone with an inadequate brief. Damn realm where light is a weapon.*

At the first hangar, he glanced through the partially open doors with the appearance of casual interest. *No aircraft . . .* His quick eyes saw a tool caddy knocked over, stainless steel tools gleaming on the hangar floor. *This place is deserted,* he thought, accelerating into his own speed. He entered the hangar and snatched up a long chisel and a crow bar. He dashed over to the second hangar and banged through its personnel entrance. It was empty. Trance ran over to the third and final hangar. Two aircraft stood in the darkness. Trance turned on the lights and saw that one of the aircraft was missing its wings, while the other was missing its engines.

Trance consulted his time sense. He was already an hour into the problem. He had three hours left. *I need to do a quick recce of the coast,* he thought. *No stinking aircraft. Gotta see if there's a boat.*

Alone, vulnerable to stray emissions of electromagnetic energy, Trance began to run through the darkness, following the coastline.

Mike, come see me now."

"Aye aye, sir."

Mike exited SUPPLOT, stepping through the vestibule into the flag command center and taking a short cut to the flag bridge. The command center's four bulkheads were deck-to-overhead interactive displays. In the center of the room stood the admiral's chair, occupied by the current battle captain. To his left, four enlisted men sat, facing the interactive displays along the long bulkhead. They monitored dozens of radio and internal communications circuits, as well as over a hundred different automated status boards.

Rushing through the center, Mike had an idea as strange and tenuously associated as thoughts experienced while crossing the threshold into sleep. *The command center is a computer-generated environment. The ship is a created world, housing a hive brain. I am a thought running through a brain.* In his vision, each watchstation was like a node in a great brain, the ego of which was the admiral. SUPPLOT was the intelligence and electronic warfare processing node, the visual cortex that saw beyond the horizon. These four enlisted men in the flag command center were like the admiral's cerebellum. They monitored the health and welfare of hundreds of communications and weapons systems. The two flag tactical action officers who sat in front of the admiral were like the neocortex. They preprocessed everything for the admiral. During an engagement, there was too much information for any single mind to process. The flag TAOs preprocessed it for the admiral, ensuring that his master plot reflected reality. Contemplating reality, the admiral—hopefully—could think clearly and make the correct decisions.

Behind the interactive display, Mike grabbed the wheel to the emergency escape hatch, balancing himself. The ship was rolling severely, penetrating deeper and deeper into the typhoon. *If the big old* Lincoln *is rolling like this, it must be getting wild outside.*

He undogged the escape hatch and opened it slowly, so as not to brain any crew member running down the port passageway. Mike eased his body through, one limb at a time. Once in the port passageway, he hustled forward. A roll caught him by surprise, sending him veering toward a master chief walking aft. The master chief grabbed Mike's arms and helped him regain his balance.

"Easy does it, Commander," the master chief said, smiling.

In the athwartship's passageway, cutting over from portside to starboard, Mike had to labor uphill and then apply his shoe-brakes as the passageway rolled downhill.

The bosun's whistle blasted over the 1MC. "Stand by for heavy rolls. Secure all articles. The weather decks are off limits to all unauthorized personnel."

Mike peeked aft down the main starboard passageway. He saw an empty stretch of it almost a hundred meters long. As he watched, the rolling and pitching of the ship caused the passageway to twist. Mike could see the changes in the relative angles of each of the hatchways. *The ship's got to twist*, he thought.

Just like a skyscraper has to sway. A ship that twists is safer than a ship that doesn't twist.

As he hurried aft in his twisting ship, Mike listened to the noises of the ship in the storm. The buckling of the bulkheads caused metal to groan and then to pop. Wind and rain sounded on the flight deck, a centimeter of steel just overhead. The wind dominated. Gale-force winds found the carrier's sharp angles, crannies and strangely shaped protuberances. Moans, howls, screams, whistles and susurrations sounded near and afar— echoed and muffled and amplified by passageways and intervening spaces, carried by the unusual movements of air through the battened-down ship.

He arrived at the captain's passageway and began to climb the steep ladders, huffing as he arrived at the 08 level. He ducked around the blue canvas with the two white stars and entered the flag bridge. The admiral was wedged into his sheepskin-covered chair.

"Reporting as ordered, Admiral," Mike said. Although custom required him to stand tall before the admiral with his hands at his side, the physics of a ship in a typhoon forced him to reach out and grab the sill of the flag bridge windows.

The bone phone chimed. The admiral picked it up and began to talk with the captain. Mike took the opportunity to glance outside. The armored windows of the flag bridge were strong enough to withstand shrapnel from explosions on the flight deck. Tilted outwards, the windows accommodated leaning over and staring down onto the flight deck. Wipers thrashed furiously, allowing glimpses of the storm. Cleared of aircraft and people, the flight deck looked empty. The only things remaining topside were the yellow gear, the tractors and blowers and the big crane, all clustered around the superstructure and chained obsessively.

So empty, the flight deck looked even more huge than normal. Over five acres of steel, it was widest just below the superstructure. The angle deck stretched off to port. Ahead, he could see the bow area, more narrow than the angle deck. Although it was difficult to see far in the storm, the seas visible around the carrier were awesome. Mountains of waves rolled from the starboard bow, crashing into the ship, shocking it, lifting its bow, heaving under its keel, lowering its bow down to receive the next blow. Mike felt ill. It was one thing to feel the ship move. It was another thing to watch the huge flight deck move. The sight of the great expanse of gray steel, formed in such a perfect geometric plane, moving through the natural chaos of the tempest, rolling and pitching in obedience to tumultuous waters, squeezed a cold shot of adrenaline into Mike's heart.

We're fools, he thought. *Weak little idiots. The ocean is awesome huge powerful. This is wrath. How can we survive?*

The admiral hung up the bone phone. "Well, Mike, what do you think about the air threat?"

Mike shook his head. He tried to clear his thoughts. Forcing himself to concentrate, he tried to frame his response. "As close as we can tell, Admiral, the Japanese are practicing sea denial. They know where their own vessels are and they're destroying everything else without—"

"Yes, I know what sea denial is," the admiral interrupted. "But what difference does it make? They can't fly in this."

"They've been using the typhoon to their tactical advantage, admiral. We should expect them to launch attacks in this area as soon as physically poss—"

"Don't like it," the admiral said. "You guys are sure that that circuit is secure?"

Mike sensed this was the real question. The admiral wanted his opinion separate from the N2s. Mike considered and provided the answer that he believed.

"Checked and double-checked, Admiral. That circuit doesn't come any more secure. Those were authentic orders. And you have the teleconference with CINCPAC to confirm."

"He acted strange. Not like him. I've known the man for

twenty-five years. I should know. I don't like it. But there's not a GOOD GODDAMNED THING I CAN DO ABOUT IT!"

The admiral pounded his fist into the arm rest of his chair. Mike looked away from his frustrated, angry, suspicious face. He looked out at the havoc the typhoon was working with the carrier, as the ship plowed ahead toward its ordered rendezvous point, in the middle of a combat zone, in the middle of a typhoon.

24

Under the tempestuous waves west of the Bashi Channel prowled the Japanese Imperial Navy's Sixth Fleet flagship, the nuclear-powered command-and-control submarine, the *Uzushio*. At forty thousand tons, the *Uzushio* was larger than many ballistic missile submarines. While surfaced, satellite dishes, parabolic antennae, radar arrays, Yagi antennae, whip antennae, domes, blivots and other communication and jamming gear bristled across her deck and atop her mast, giving the surfaced submarine a festering, sinister look. In wartime mode, while submerged, she was as sleek as any submarine. Her main means of communicating while submerged was through small floating communications sleds attached to the ship through kilometers-long strands of optical fiber wrapped in kevlar. Below decks, she contained working and berthing spaces for two hundred highly trained specialists.

In her deepest deck, just above the shaft alley, was an extensive brig, capable of handling the detention and interrogation of hundreds of prisoners of war. These sophisticated facilities could accommodate prisoners who had been subjected to nuclear, bacteriological and chemical warfare, keeping them isolated and alive long enough to be debriefed.

Uzushio was a great ship. Lieutenant Kenichi Takahashi had been proud to be selected to serve in her, but now he felt sick to his stomach. For several years, since the rebirth of imperial rule, he had told himself that this war would not happen, but now the nightmare had taken form. So far, the destruction to his beloved homeland had been limited mainly to military bases and such militarily significant targets as power plants. So far, destruction of the cities and massacre of the civilian population had been avoided.

This bloody war was far too dangerous. Before becoming an intelligence officer, Takahashi had written his master's thesis at Tokyo University regarding the strategic confrontations of the twentieth century. Both the Chinese and the Japanese, bipolar enemies, nuclear and economic superpowers, had been foolish enough to borrow doctrines from the Cold War of the previous century. The dynamic between the Soviets and the Americans had been unique—and that dynamic had nearly led to nuclear holocaust during three crises. How idiotic to dare to start a conventional war, based upon such fallacious and antiquated doctrines as mutual assured destruction!

Takahashi understood the drive to greatness among his people. He understood their fear of the Chinese. The creeping anxiety that the Chinese would surpass the Japanese, leaving them in the wake of history with such flotsam as the British, the Russians and the Americans was understandable. Takahashi had difficulty imagining an ascendant China dealing fairly with a decrepit Japan. Yet, the *wa* of history was a vagabond. Death and sorrow were the rewards for attempting to maintain supremacy after the *wa* had moved on. How he wished that his people could have contented themselves with greatness in small things, in the perfection of a work of art or in the glimpse of a cloud above a distant mountain.

His stomach churned. The latest rash of electromagnetic attacks worried him. These attacks surpassed the state of the art that they had ascribed to the Chinese. Along with other electronic warfare specialists, he had been studying them for many hours now, using the most powerful computers in existence, the Fujitsu supercomputers, both ashore in Tokyo and installed in the fifth deck of the *Uzushio.*

The flag intelligence officer loomed over his shoulder.

"What news?" he barked.

"Yes, Captain, analysis is continuing—"

"I want results!"

"Yes, Captain, we are almost certain that . . . we were just concluding the analysis—"

"Talk to me. Speak Japanese!"

"Yes, Captain. It seems that there is a previously undiscovered command-and-control node. We've indications that many of the latest network intrusions originated from there."

"Where?"

"From the technological enclave on Batan Island. That's Philippine national territory, leased for ninety-nine years to China. It's supposed to be neutral territory. Basing a command-and-control node there would be a violation of its neutrality."

"Marshall the evidence. I'll want to brief the Ops O. The Ops O will want to get permission to attack that node and destroy it."

"Yes, Captain. May I suggest that it might make a good target for capturing. Acquisition of material or personnel at such an unusual and capable site would almost certainly be of high intelligence interest."

"Noted. Advise me when the evidence is ready."

"Yes, Captain."

"It looks like a good target for the special forces."

K*atana* to the north!" Intelligence Specialist Malcolm Zwide called.

Mike McCullough was already watching the icon for the *katana*, a Japanese airborne search radar. He had only one sensor indicating that the *katana* was present, but Mike believed that sensor. He opened the gates and allowed the contact to enter the battle group's general command-and-control system.

"Japanese aircraft to our north," Mike said, sending an emergency voice note to the admiral, the battle watch captain, the N2, and other decision-makers in the battle group.

South of the mightiest winds of the typhoon, *Lincoln* and *Trenton* had transited the Bashi Channel, entering the South China Sea. Currently they were twelve degrees north, in the middle of the ocean near the latitude of Da Nang and Manila. Due to their more southerly course, *Lincoln* was now presenting a different aspect to the wild seas still driven by the typhoon, causing her to pitch as violently as she was rolling. Of the many unusual motions of the ship, the most horrendous was the sudden lurching caused by the stern rising so high that the four massive screws of the aircraft carrier churned shallow water.

Several of SUPPLOT's watchstanders were unfit for duty: two from severe seasickness and one from head injuries after a fall. Those able to stand their watch felt nauseous and distraught. The three holes in the watchstanding teams forced everyone else to work longer hours, so that exhaustion was beginning to take its toll. Heaved and rolled and swayed by the groaning ship, they felt threatened by the element that they usually considered an ally—the sea.

Now, they found themselves in the middle of a war zone, when the *Lincoln* was incapable of using its main weapon, the airwing, because the wild seas made impossible the launching of aircraft from the pitching deck.

"Flag TAO," Mike said, opening a circuit that included all of the battle group's most important decision-making watch centers.

"FTAO," acknowledged Mike's roommate, Pedro, who currently had the watch as the flag tactical action officer.

"Threat vector is three three zero," Mike said.

"Profile?"

"Japanese aircraft have been attacking their targets at low altitude, high subsonic or supersonic, nonsquawking and nonradiating until just before launch."

"Roger," Pedro said. "Out."

During this exchange, the klaxon for general quarters had begun to sound. Wearing cybergear, Mike heard the klaxon distantly, the headphones acting as sound attenuators to outside noise. One corner of his command-and-control interface began to flash a "GQ" icon red white, red white. Mike acknowledged the icon. Amid the noises of voices speaking in the cyberspace command-and-control circuits, the howl of the wind, the growling and groaning of the ship's steel, the klaxon of general quarters, Mike could hear the tattoo of hundreds of booted feet pounding the steel decks as the entire crew rushed toward their battle stations.

"General quarters, general quarters," the yeoman was announcing on the 1MC, "All hands to your battle stations. Proceed up and forward on the starboard side, down and aft on the port side. This is not a drill. . . ."

As these sounds from the ship insinuated themselves through his ear phones, Mike concentrated on the visual images presented in his tactical display. He was watching the threat sector from the north through the northwest very carefully.

". . . weapons red and hot . . . " the admiral's voice was saying. He was declaring all airborne objects, aircraft or missiles, hostile. He was giving permission for the crews of *Trenton* and *Lincoln* to use any of their air defense weapons, including the enhanced ARM surface-to-air missiles, the Phalanx radar-directed machine guns and the Iris laser cannons. Unfortunately, during the storm, the rain would render the laser cannons useless.

Mike and the other watchstanders began to crawl into their nuclear-chemical-bacteriological protective suits. Mike concentrated on the tactical display while he did this, just as a driver might force himself to pay attention to traffic while donning a jacket. Once he was wearing the protective suit, Mike plugged its air hose into the wall socket. He continued to breathe the ship's air. If a weapon penetrated the skin of the ship and violated the integrity of the air supply system, it would automatically shut off. Mike then would have to switch to the bottled air, tanks of which were waiting clamped along the bulkhead.

"*Wakizashi*—" Intelligence Specialist Zwide said.

Another red icon had appeared to their north. It was an electronic intelligence report on a momentary radiation of a *wakizashi*, the Japanese airborne fire control radar.

"*Wakizashi* radar on the 320 radial," Mike reported on emergency indications and warning circuit. "Contact one seven one niner. Confirmed *wakizashi* fire control radar."

Another voice spoke. "Contact one seven one niner designated samurai one." The battle group had worked together for so long and so intensively that they no longer followed the voice reporting procedure that required each speaker to identify himself and his intended audience. Everyone recognized everyone's voice. Mike recognized this speaker as the chief who headed the air warfare commander's plot center.

"Vampire," the chief was saying. "Active radar on incoming missile, track three niner, designated vampire one. Missile is inbound, speed mach two point eight—"

"Engage vampire one—" the air warfare commander said.

"Vampire one locked on with ARM."

"Fire. Repeat, fire."

"Roger fire. Birds away one, birds away two."

"Engage samurai one."

"No lock on samurai one."

"Engage ARM search and kill mode against samurai one. Fire. Repeat, fire."

"Roger fire. Birds away three, birds away four."

"Vampire one intercepted by bird one. Assessed destroyed."

"Visual from *Trenton*. Confirmed vampire one destroyed."

"Retarget bird two, contact samurai one."

"Roger retarget bird two. Retargeted. Mode switched to search and kill."

"Delete track vampire one."

"Vampire one deleted."

Another red blip appeared, just south of the first. It was another *katana* radar. Quickly, Mike checked the parameters of the new radar contact. Its pulse repetition frequency was several hundred hertz higher than the first contact.

"New contact one seven one eight," Mike said. "A second Japanese fighter. Estimate that several more Japanese fighters may be airborne to our north."

"Contact one seven one eight designated samurai two."

"Engage samurai two," the air warfare commander said.

"Engaging samurai two with ARM, search and kill mode."

"Fire. Repeat, fire."

"Roger fire. Birds away four, birds away five."

The admiral's voice interceded. "Jake, recommend saturation fire, threat sector three zero zero through zero four five."

"Aye aye sir. Stand by to launch battery saturation fire, birds six through twenty, search and kill mode, low-low-medium-high. Acknowledge."

"Acknowledge six through twenty, S&K, lo-lo-med-high, sir."

"Fire. Repeat, fire."

"Birds away six, seven, eight, nine, ten . . . birds away six through twenty."

Mike stared at the tactical display. In the past two minutes, *Trenton* and *Lincoln* had fired a barrage of twenty surface to air missiles. They had just spent forty million dollars. Mike felt sure that the admiral had ordered the barrage because of Mike's estimate that more than two Japanese fighters were airborne to the north. He watched the outbound tracks of the nineteen remaining missiles. At various altitudes, they were seeking airborne targets, using their own active radars as well as optical and infrared imaging cells. Each missile was a highly intelligent and sophisticated robot, able to cruise and loiter at low subsonic speeds, find its target, and accelerate to hypersonic speeds to attack with advanced high explosives as powerful as ten kilotons each.

Mike felt tempted to call up the images the missiles were telelinking back to the ships, but he resisted. That was somebody else's job. He had to concentrate on his job, which was processing information from sensors outside of the battle group.

"Starboard aft look-out. Visual on incoming missile, radial zero one five."

"Phalanx engaging."

Through his earphones, Mike could hear the machine guns

of the starboard aft Phalanx close-in weapon system firing. The machine guns sounded as if a giant had ignited a chain saw. Mike noticed that some of his watchstanders were dialing up the top-side video camera. Naturally enough they were interested in watching to see whether the Phalanx would shoot down the incoming missile prior to impact.

"Eyes on the tactical picture," Mike said.

Quickly, the watchstanders changed back their displays to the tactical picture.

"Stand by for impact," the yeoman on the 1MC announced.

Like a steel drum struck with a sledgehammer, the *Lincoln* rang, shock waves racing through every surface. Mike checked his displays for the integrity of his battle station's air and electrical supply. They read positive. He checked the computers. *Full up. Combat ready . . .*

"Hit alpha, hit alpha, missile debris hit starboard and aft. Damage control team bravo yankee lay to compartment zero three tack fifty-two tack seven tack charlie. Damage control team . . ."

"Mike, I got the watch," the N2's voice said.

Mike flipped his eyepieces so that he could see the natural world. The N2, fully encased in protective gear, loomed before him.

"I've got the watch, sir," Mike said. "I've got it."

"Mike, you're relieved," the N2 barked.

Mike blinked and said, "Aye aye sir. We had two ELINT cuts—"

"I know, I know, I got it," the N2 said.

"I stand relieved, sir."

Mike stepped down from the bastion. The N2 took his place. With every able watchstander jammed into the SUP-PLOT, there was barely any room for Mike. He wended his way into a corner.

"Take a look around the ship, Mike," the N2 said. "Give me heads up for an abandon ship."

"Aye aye sir," Mike said, while thinking, *Abandon ship! In these seas! Impossible. If the* Lincoln *goes down in this typhoon, it goes down with all hands. Dead, all of us.*

Dutifully Mike began to explore the dozens of information channels available to determine the health of the ship. First, he checked the live video feeds from the flight deck. He couldn't see any damage. Then he checked the video feeds from the damage control teams. Fragments of the incoming missile, due to the tremendous force caused by their hypersonic velocity, had ripped large holes in the hull near the gallery. The holes were high enough that ordinarily they wouldn't have allowed water to enter the ship, but in the mad waves of the tempest, white spray came rushing through them. Dark figures of other damage-control workers loomed before the camera.

Mike checked some of the automated status boards. He could see that the ship was going to survive this missile hit. Even if the warhead had been bacteriological or chemical, there were enough airtight barriers isolating the damaged areas.

"We're OK, N2," Mike said. "The ship's C1."

"Check out casualties in cryptologic berthing."

"Aye aye sir," Mike said, startled at himself for not thinking about this earlier. The missile hit was in the vicinity of the berthing for the enlisted cryptologists. Mike tried various circuits, but he found no one who knew about the damage to cryptologic berthing and who had time to answer questions. Mike reported no progress to the N2, then he stood by for further instructions.

His joints ached. His head sagged forward. He held onto a vertical reinforcement beam as the ship pitched downwards heavily. After a few minutes of no further activity, he began to feel sleepy.

Under attack in a typhoon, he thought, *and I'm passing out. Well, why not? The N2's made me a passenger. Maybe I should just bust all the airtight compartments, go back to my stateroom, and sleep.*

He reminded himself that the N2 shared his battle station with Mike and several others. It would have been derelict of the N2 not to assume the watch station, since the tactical situation had permitted it.

But I got the warning, Mike thought. *He can't take that away from me. It started on my watch and I handled it.*

Mike rested his forehead in the crook of his arm. He felt so sleepy that he didn't think he could stay awake any longer.

Stay with it, he thought. *If the N2 takes shrapnel through the head, you've got the watch.*

Trickster pointed to Gimp, yanking him into the other world. He assaulted him with a true brief, gave him five seconds to absorb the shocking truth, and then charged him and Lightning with interrogating the prisoners.

"This gesture is the command to lower them. Do them one at a time."

"What're the essential elements of intelligence we want?" Gimp asked.

"We don't know where to go," Trickster said. "Any ideas about what our next move could be. Safe havens. Political and military dynamics. They understand this world, hopefully, better than we do."

"How hard an interrogation?"

"They're scared. They'll respond to the soft approach."

Trickster made a gesture that caused the Novlar to lower the first prisoner. Gimp and Lightning grabbed her. They began to carry her bodily out of the cage room, but she started to shout, "I am Iva! I am Iva!"

TOM COOL

She made so much noise that she woke Cat from her nap. Cat stood and stretched, long and lithe. Trickster hardly noticed; his vision seemed hazy.

"Hold it!" he shouted.

His legs grew awkward as he stumbled forward. Iva stood, head lowered. She was biting her lower lip. Trickster still didn't recognize her. Slowly he realized that this woman was Iva, less idealized, more real and detailed, uglier and aged fifteen years from the image that he knew.

"So, Iva?" he asked.

"Yes, I am Iva," she said, looking up, allowing their eyes to meet. Trickster's heartbeat accelerated as he recognized the long suffering of her soul. Since System had always censored her emotions, Trickster felt powerfully moved as he realized that she had indeed cared all those years and that she had suffered.

"You tried to tell me, didn't you, Iva?"

With a rush of hope, Iva began to cry. "Yes. I tried. They never—they wouldn't let me, Trickster."

"I heard your thoughts," Trickster said. "I knew that . . . even when your avatar froze, I knew you were trying. . . ."

Iva collapsed to the floor. She hugged Trickster's ankles and sobbed, the only coherent words being, "I'm sorry."

Trickster lifted her up and held her at arm's length. "Why?" he asked. "Why did you join them?"

"In the beginning . . . in the beginning, I didn't know any better. It was just an experiment. I didn't understand that it would be for a lifetime—"

"Tell the truth!" Lightning shouted, a stridency in her voice that Trickster didn't understand.

"I knew, I knew! But I didn't understand. I was young and ambitious. Human experiments were part of the . . . the way things were done. It was only later, when I grew to know you all, care about you as persons that I realized how horrible . . . I wanted to quit. For years, I wanted to quit, but I didn't dare, be-

cause that would leave you alone with them. I tried to make it
as good . . . I tried to make them, make them make the world
as good a place as I could. For you! For you."

Trickster held Iva at arm's length. He tried to decide
whether to forgive her. Finally he said, "We weren't the only
people who didn't know the truth. You, too, Iva, you lived a lie
all this time. You still think that you're our parent. But we never
had a parent. Now the lies are over. So forget it."

"You're not angry at me?"

"What use is anger? You played your position as well as you
could. You helped them for seventeen years, waiting, like me,
for the moment of action. Now we're free, partly because of
your play."

"You don't hate me?"

"What good is hate?"

"You don't even hate Chang?" Iva blurted.

"Chang? Who is that?" Trickster asked.

"Well, Chang . . . the director of Project Standing Whirlwind."

Trickster thought back to the documentation on System
and explained to Cat, "Project Standing Whirlwind is what they
call all of this. Us. Making the world."

"Whirlwind," Cat said.

"Which one would that be?" Trickster asked Iva. "Signal
him, please."

Iva began to smile, the smile growing slowly into a venge-
ful grin. "Yes," she said.

One by one, Trickster commanded prisoners to be twirled
around until their faces were visible to Iva. She didn't seem able
to see them until she suddenly shouted out, "That's him! That's
the one."

Trickster hauled Chang down to the cage floor. He stood
erect, his gaze steady but his expression wooden with fear.
Trickster hooked his elbow and dragged him out of the cage.
They continued until they arrived at the barracks room where

Lancer had killed the security operative who had almost defeated Cat. The dead body lay stretched out on the floor.

Cat strode into the room. As she looked at the body, her expression remained calm. Iva entered next, screaming when she
saw the corpse of her coworker, his lower face crushed, blood
and other fluids pooled under the head. Gimp brought up the
rear. He barked a low, guttural nonsense sound when he saw the
body. Trickster studied Chang's face. He seemed more surprised than horrified.

"I'm curious," Trickster said. "This seems to be the true
face of death. Why did you give it such a pleasant mask in the
world?"

Chang shrugged. "Ask Iva," he said. "That was a psychological feature. The soft scientists made those types of decisions. If I remember, it was to protect your developing
personalities or some such thing."

Trickster looked at Iva, but her face was glazed with horror.
He guessed that it was the mere fact of death that horrified her,
but in truth she was horrified by the knowledge that one of her
children had killed.

"Why did you lie about death?" Trickster asked, his voice
insistent and hard.

"Death is an ugly thing, as you can see," Chang said. "We
didn't include unnecessary ugliness in the world. There was no
need for it and there were those, like Iva here, who argued
against it. Why?"

Trickster blinked at Chang's clinical answer. He realized
that Chang didn't feel guilty for creating the world. He felt
proud.

"You lied to us," Trickster said, his words sounding lame in
his own ears.

Chang's brows furrowed. "Not in your world," he said. "In
your world, we told you the truth."

"The entire world was a lie."

Chang's lips twitched. "It was a logically consistent subset of the real world," he answered. "Not so much a lie as a reduction. Now you've got access to the chaos, madness and nonsense, lies, superstitions . . . just go ahead and scan the real world, Trickster. See the things that parents teach their children. See the things that people soak their brains in, calling it entertainment." Chang actually managed to guffaw. "Fantasies and trash ideas, evil images . . . The most poisonous pollution in the twenty-first century is mental pollution. Almost universal. Except for you. We fed your brains with sensations and information that made them strong, just as we fed your bodies with food that made them strong. Not necessarily what you would have chosen, but nourishment nonetheless."

Having spoken this much, Chang seemed to have regained his confidence. He looked at Trickster with a pride that Trickster could not help but notice.

"The world is a hard place, I know," Chang said. "I know it's been hard for you, but this place here is harder. Believe me. You don't have disease, brutality, crime, marginalization, other things I know you can't understand because you haven't been exposed to them . . . There's no place for you here in this world, Trickster." Chang looked over Trickster's shoulder at Cat. "Not for you, either, Cat. Not for any of the tribe. You've busted out. I'm very proud of you. I suppose I always expected you would, one day or the other. But you must go back."

"Go back!" Trickster shouted, as Cat tossed her head back and laughed. "Go back! Tell me one thing before I decide to go back and put my throat in your hands. Tell me one thing."

"I'll answer any question."

"Where is Weeble?" Trickster asked, his voice low and hard.

Chang blanched. His knees began visibly to shake. "Weeble . . ."

"Tell him where is Weeble! Tell him!" Iva shouted.

"Weeble . . . is in a psychiatric sanitarium near Beijing. That is a type of hospital. He has been diagnosed with catatonic schizophrenia."

"He doesn't move, he doesn't speak, he hears no one around him!" Iva shouted.

Trickster tried to understand these concepts. Finally he said slowly and sadly, "He is waiting for us." He turned to Cat. "And we can't get to Beijing."

"What should we do with this prisoner now, Trickster?" Cat asked.

"I don't care to judge him," Trickster said, watching Chang out of the corner of his eye. "But since I command, it's my prerogative to choose who shall judge him. Do you think he should be judged by . . . Snake?"

Chang stepped back, staggered by the possibility of being judged by Snake. Trickster did not smile. "That would seem fair," he said. "He made Snake, or at least allowed him to become what he is."

Cat shook her head.

"How about Lightning?" Trickster suggested. "She might be interested in judging the man who condemned her to a lifetime of battle."

"Not the wimp either."

"Then you, Cat. I appoint you judge over all the prisoners."

"I accept. I'll consider their fate."

Trickster made a gesture. Lightning grabbed Chang and hauled him out of the room. "Take the other one, too," Trickster shouted. Gimp twisted Iva's upper arm and hustled her away. Trickster shouted, "More gently with her! And don't tie her up. Just watch her."

Cat stood staring at the corpse.

"What do you think?" he asked.

"What do *you* think?"

Trickster shook his head. "In this level, you bust up the avatar, the entity goes elsewhere, vacates the avatar. Avatar remains, busted up."

"Where does the entity go?" Cat asked quietly. "The other possibility is that the avatar *is* the entity. Break the avatar, destroy the entity. Or the entity is a phenomenon of the avatar. Destroy the avatar and the phenomenon of the entity ceases. Come on, let's go. It stinks in here."

As they walked back toward the cage, Trickster asked, "What are you going to do with the prisoners? After they've been interrogated?"

Cat shrugged. "Better figure out death in this realm first."

They entered the cage. For thirty minutes they helped interrogate some of the prisoners. Lancer interrupted them with a report.

"Trance is returning," he said, then shot them the video feed from the camera that covered the plaza in front of the building. The eye of the storm had passed beyond the island. Hard winds, now arriving from the opposite direction, were driving walls of rain parallel to the ground. On hands and knees, Trance was struggling against the forces of the wind and driven rain. A loose sheet of plywood came flying toward him. He appeared not to see it, but at the last split-second, he flattened against the ground. The plywood flew past his back. Trance rose to his hands and knees and resumed his struggle against the wind and rain. He wiped his palm across his eyes. It seemed that he was trying to see the building through the rain driving into his face.

Finally he gained the area where the building served as a windbreak. Instantly Trance leapt up as if freed from bonds. He sprinted into the lobby of the building. Trickster commanded his doppelgangers to allow him to pass through the security gates.

At his post, Crush doubled his hands into fists and crossed his wrists before his chest. His clothes tattered and torn and muddy, his face slick with rain and blood, Trance drew himself erect and made a poison-hand gesture, acknowledging Crush's tribute.

"The weather is not conducive to maneuver," Trance said.

"Is it a realm of pain outside, too?" Crush asked.

"I'll allow myself to feel it later."

"You're a tough warrior, brother."

"Zoned. Just zoned."

"Trickster's below for debrief."

"Debrief."

Trance made his way down to the cage. He noticed that Snake was still moving as if oblivious to this realm. Trickster surprised him by dipping to one knee, eyes downcast.

"Recce report," Trance said. "Airfield is deserted. No aircraft. I recce'd a good part of the coast. Found no boats. Saw one marina. Storm destroyed the piers and boathouses, battered some small pleasure craft against the sea wall, then threw their hulks over it. I found no way off the island."

"The prisoners say that the island was partially evacuated two days ago," Trickster answered. "All the aircraft and seaworthy boats went to the mainland."

"I believe it."

"Anything else?"

"Violent, I say, violent extrasensory noise. Intense pain. Very hard to filter. I don't think anyone else could have survived it, let alone function."

"Sorry. I didn't know about that when I sent you."

"Luckily you picked the right brother. I was able to zone it out, almost . . . almost all the way."

"Well done. Are you hungry?"

"Bitter thirsty."

Trickster threw Trance back into the world, but into a realm different from Snake's. He commanded his doppelgangers to feed him and give him drink. Then he turned to Cat.

"How do we get off this island?" he asked.

"Why don't we just ride out the war? Then we can commandeer some craft in peacetime."

"No good. The Japanese and the Chinese are going to go nuke. They could target this facility . . . or we could die just from the fallout."

"Well, we can't swim."

Trickster held up his hand as he tried to solve the problem. With Microteq radios activated, they were trapped in the building. Even with the radios off, they were trapped on the island. He needed to conjure up an aircraft or a boat. In wartime, how could he summon something large enough to evacuate all fourteen of them?

"Ah . . . " he said. "Get Dreamer to intrude on a command-and-control network and order an evacuation party here. We take the craft, get to Luzon, and from there escape out of the theater."

"A plan," Cat said. "The Japanese or Chinese?"

"Neither. The Americans. Then, worst case, we're in neutral hands. The Americans are less likely to imprison or kill us."

"What Americans?"

"That aircraft carrier. *Lincoln*. Dreamer beat the circuit once. She can beat it again."

The fifty commandos of the Special Forces Unit *Kaizen* reported directly to the Imperial Navy's Sixth Fleet. Sergeant Major Fujiwara was the leader of the fifty-man unit. There were two sergeant first class, the senior of whom would lead the unit in case Fujiwara fell. Packed and ready, Fujiwara watched the unit prepare their weapons and food supplies. Occasionally, he barked a command. His voice seemed to come up from the soles of his feet. Fujiwara's eyes were flat black with age, but his body was hard, harder than any of the younger fighters, as if his muscles had knotted and toughened over the long years of effort and hardship. His troops knew the extreme toughness Fujiwara had obtained. They had seen him drive his index finger through the thin bone of the temple of a rebellious Malaysian prisoner.

Fujiwara carried a *tanto*, the scabbard stuck through his belt. In the five hundred years since its creation, the knife had always been warm from the flesh of a Fujiwara following the various professions of death.

Fujiwara seethed with anger. He bitterly resented the unit's assignment. With the empire waging war finally on the overbearing, overreaching, gross, despicable Chinese, he was being sent to a Philippine island on a fool's mission. Even the anticipated thrill of a high-altitude jump, low-altitude parachute-opening could not improve his mood. The best that he could hope for was to kill as many of the inferior barbarians as he could, execute the foolish mission, return with his prisoners to the homeland, and then wait for the order to deploy to the Chinese mainland.

28

Radars silent and radios receive-only, *Lincoln* plowed north-ward through the wild waves and deep troughs of the South China Sea. Off-watch, Mike McCullough was standing over the table in the war room, surrounded by a Marine captain, an Army lieutenant and a handful of enlisted men, highly trained intelligence specialists and mission planners from the battle group's special forces. Since the airwing types had occupied every available square meter of the intelligence center for contingency air strike planning against Japanese targets, the cell for the mission into Batan Island was using the war room. They huddled over a computer-generated chart of the Batan Island technological enclave.

"What if the Japanese get there *while* we're there?" the Army lieutenant asked in a low voice.

Mike scratched his temple. He waited for the Marine cap-tain to speak up. While he waited, he ran through the rules of their orders, the validity of which had been confirmed by CINCPAC's crypto-signature. Covert insertion. Evacuation of the American scientists. Avoidance of capture. Survival of party first priority.

"That's a tactical decision," Mike finally said. "I'm senior, but not in command. The only reason I'm going at all is that the missile hit in the cryptologist's coop killed every other Chinese linguist in the ship. Tactical decisions will be made by the tactical leader. That's you, Captain."

Mike and the lieutenant turned to the captain, who inhaled preparatory to answering.

A shock rang through the steel surrounding them. Under their feet, the deck vibrated from a tremendous impact. Mike heard the distant roaring of the close-in weapons systems.

". . . missile hit, amidships. Hit bravo, hit bravo. Missile hit, amidships. Starboard side, vicinity frame one three five. Away fire detail alpha, away. All hands make way for fire detail alpha. Fire fire fire. Fire in compartment oh two tack one three two tack eleven tack Charlie. Fire fire fire. Fire in compartment oh three tack. . . ."

Mike mentally envisioned the location of the missile hit. It was nearby, outboard and forward, probably just forward of the captain's cabin. *Fire . . . fire! They've got to control the fire. No, easy. Is this what it's like? I don't want to die here. Sissy was right. No, I've got to hang on. Calm down. Just a fire.*

A petty officer first class burst into the war room.

"Form a fire control party!" he shouted, then disappeared again into the starboard passageway.

Mike was the senior officer present in the war room. "Who's the senior damage control petty officer here?"

The war room began to fill with smoke.

"I am, sir!" Boatswain First Class Mitchell, "Boats," replied. He was a tall, lanky man in his late twenties whose primary duty was to maintain and operate the admiral's barge.

"Take charge, Boats!" Mike shouted. "You lead the team."

"Decouple ship's air!" Boats shouted. "Shift to air tanks! All hands! Move!"

As the war room continued to fill with smoke, the fifteen men and women present unplugged from the ship's air. Following the routines practiced during many drills, they connected to their designated air tanks and then helped each other strap the tanks onto their backs. They stowed their planning materials into SUPPLOT.

"Follow me!" Boats shouted.

Mike followed Boats into the starboard passageway, which was so thick with smoke that they couldn't see more than a few frames down its length. Boats left most of the fire control party at the nearest firefighting station, with orders to break out the hoses and other equipment. Boats grabbed Mike's arm and shouted, "Let's go find this fire, sir!"

They didn't have long to look. Forward two frames and outboard, in the athwartships passageway that led to the catwalk forward of the superstructure, red flames and white-hot flames were roaring. Even through their protective suits, the heat hit them like a wall. Quickly, Boats and Mike backed away, returning to the much cooler starboard passageway.

"That's a propellant fire," Boats said.

"You're right."

They hustled back to the firefighting station.

"Good news!" Boats shouted. "This firefighting station is close enough! You take one of the shield sprays, Commander McCullough. I'll lead the main hose. You there, you're second. You, third; you, fourth. You, take the other shield spray. The rest of you, go forward to the next fire control station, set up, and lead a main hose aft to frame one two zero, then outboard. Fight the fire."

Mike took hold of a shield spray nozzle, which was a thin metal wand about two meters long, its shaft crooked so that it could be directed around corners.

"Shield spray men, keep the fire off of me," Boats shouted. "Open the valves!"

From the ends of the shield-spray nozzles, a thin circle of

water and mist sprouted. Mike adjusted the nozzle so that the circle of water was as thick as possible.

Trailing the three hoses behind them, the fire control party advanced forward to the athwartship passageway. Mike led the charge into the passageway, holding up the circle of water as a shield against the intense heat. Boats followed him, taking his stand behind the shield. Boats opened the nozzle of the main hose, letting free a tremendous jet of white foam, which he shot toward the center of the inferno.

"Calling damage control!" Boats shouted into his suit's radio. "This is Boats Mitchell, leading a ship's company fire-fighting team. We got a missile propellant fire in compartment oh three tack one twenty five tack twelve tack quebec. We've engaged with foam. One main hose, two shield hoses."

A jet of flame reached toward Boats. Reacting, Mike swung the circle of water to protect him.

"Wet me down!" Boats screamed. "I'm burning up!"

Mike began a motion to move his circle of water to soak the firefighting team, but realized that removing his shield would be suicidal. Boats had been shouting at the other shield spray bearer, who played his hose directly over Boats and Mike. The water relieved the heat but then evaporated almost instantaneously.

"Keep hosing us down!" Boat shouted. "All right, Commander, forward!"

Hesitatingly, Mike stepped forward, closer to the raging fire. Boats continued to jet a torrent of foam against the base of the propellant fire. Paint on the bulkheads peeled off and ignited before Mike's eyes. Black, oily smoke roiled, blinding them between flashing visions of open flame.

"Son bitch!" Boat shouted. Mike glanced over at him, but saw nothing more unusual than Boats staring intensely into the flames as if fascinated, working the foam jet back and forth as if it were broadsword and the fire a many-headed dragon.

"Forward!"

Together they stepped deeper into the passageway. As if intimidated by their boldness, the fire retreated. For the first time, Mike had the idea that the fire was something that they could actually beat. Strengthened by this idea, he took another step forward, thrusting the circle of water so that it formed a complete shield in front of Boats. The deck underfoot was treacherously slippery with foam and water. Mike could feel the heat from the steel deck bleeding through the protective soles of his boots.

They fought the fire, step by step, for what seemed to Mike only a few minutes.

"Number two man, take over the lead!" Boats shouted. He stepped aside as the man behind him moved closer to the brass nozzle. Boats turned it over to him and then retreated.

Hands fell on Mike's shoulder. He realized that someone wanted to take over his shield spray. Mike relinquished it, his hands aching from the strain of clutching the nozzle. He worked his way to the rear of the firefighting team. Boats and he returned to the war room, where they swapped out their air tanks. Mike was shocked to see that he was almost out of air. He had been fighting the fire for over half an hour.

"Plug into ship's air for a while, Commander," Boats suggested. Mike did so, discovering that the ship's air supply seemed incredibly cool. He realized that his entire suit, including the air tank that he had just discarded, had been heated to an unholy temperature. His face felt hot, as if he were sunburned.

"Some fire, huh, sir?" Boats asked.

Mike screwed a water tube into his protective suit and drank it dry. As he screwed the empty tube into his bladder sack and released his urine, he said, "Hell fire."

"Let me check damage control central ASTAB," Boats said.

Using the ship's internal radio link, Boats dialed up the automated status board and studied the graphic display of the ongoing firefights.

"Two fires under control. The main fire, down on the oh one level, is touch and go."

"Let's go back, then," Mike said.

"Yes, sir. Do you want to take over—"

"No, Boats. You're doing a super job."

Through his smoke-smeared filthy mask, Petty Officer Mitchell grinned. "Nothing an old crow can't handle, sir!"

Mike's joints ached as they made their way toward the fire. Once he was back in the firefight, however, he forgot about his fatigue. Face-to-face with the fire, he found himself studying his mental map of the Batan Island technological enclave.

The storm's past now," Lancer said. "We need to send out some forward sentries."

Trickster nodded. He knew Lancer was right. They couldn't afford to rely on the video cameras for the surveillance of the perimeter. They needed to send out at least three sentries. Trickster weighed the safety of the whole tribe against the right of three people to access the world. He made a decision. Trickster eyed the rows of prisoners. He selected two of the right size and sex and gestured so that they were lowered to the floor.

"Strip to your default avatars," he said.

"What?"

"Strip off those clothes."

Taut with fear, the two men removed their clothing.

"Hurry!" Trickster shouted, exasperated by their natural slowness and confounded by the nudity taboo of these foreign people.

When he finally had the clothing in a pile, Trickster thrashed his hands. Novlar seized the two prisoners and hoisted them to the roof of the cage, where they joined the other whimpering prisoners.

Trickster made the gesture that turned off the Microteq radios for Trance, then Cut-Back and Sly. They grunted, squealed, shouted from the transitional pain and discomfort. "Cut-Back, Sly, get dressed. Then you three, go outside," Trickster said. "Forward sentries. Warn us if any enemies approach."

"What about the extrasensory noise?" Trance asked, as the other two dressed.

"I've taken care of it. Go."

Trance, Cut-Back and Sly departed the cage, Trance leading the way. Trickster returned to studying the battle problem. He was searching for clues as to the location of the *Lincoln*. He expected the evacuation party to arrive at any moment.

"Boss," Doppelganger 46 interjected.

"Report," Trickster said.

"Chinese exploitation of Taiwanese over-the-horizon radar indicates that a Japanese transcontinental cargo aircraft released fifty objects at sixty thousand feet above Batan Island. Objects are descending at terminal velocity. Estimate they are bombs. Correction. Sudden drastic slowing of objects indicates that they are parachute-retarded. Estimate objects are either sensors or airborne combat troops. They are landing now."

"Battle!" Trickster cried. He stepped atop his vantage point on War Council Rock. In this familiar environment where he had fought thousands of battles, all his tools, his tricks, and his data were available, laid out exactly where he knew to find them. Quickly, Trickster searched for more information about the parachutists, but without success. They were not radiating any electromagnetic energy, so he could not engage them directly in electronic combat.

After a few moments, Trickster decided that the only trick he could pull was to call the security forces on Batan Island and inform them of the assault. He following the voice report procedures documented in the emergency directory of System, but no one answered the phone at security.

He then turned his attention to the fight in the natural world, where the tribe had no weapons. Not yet, anyway. Three of the tribe's best soldiers were outside of the building. Opening a window to the natural world, he looked up at the siblings still moving in the world: Barker/Dummy, Berserker, Snake, Dreamer and Skipper.

Fifty enemy . . .

"Spin down the world for Berserker. Spin down Snake," Trickster said. "Spin down . . . spin down Dreamer, too. And spin down Skipper."

Trickster watched the Novlar fibers began to relax. He stepped out of the way of a Chinese man as he descended.

"Arrrghhh!"

"Hey what?"

"Time out!"

"Nah, new team quals."

"Ow!"

Berserker, with his fiery mane of hair and red body hair, stood on one foot, holding the other foot, and cursing. His face was turning red with his anger.

"Trickster, is that you?" the red giant bellowed.

"Yeah, Berserker, what is it?"

"Why is this battle problem so sticking painful?" Berserker shouted.

"This is a hard battle problem," Trickster said. "There is pain, every mistake."

"I got no access to System," Snake shouted.

"What is this, squad quals?" Skipper asked. "There's no services here."

"Listen up!" Trickster shouted.

Everyone, except for Dummy/Barker, turned to listen to Trickster.

"I am Trickster! This is a team qual. System has appointed

me team leader. We're going to have to defend this building against fifty enemies. They're armed—unknown weapons. We're unarmed."

"But that Japanese war was just getting interesting. We were about to go nuke. I could tell."

Trickster scanned the tribe. Snake's eyes narrowed suspiciously as he stared at Trickster.

"This is a funny domain," Skipper groaned. 'Everything hurts."

"Stinks here, too."

"No services."

"Weird-looking avatars. What's that dingus called?"

"Ah shut up."

"We've already secured the building," Trickster said. "The fifty other enemies are just landing now outside. Now look at this."

Trickster called up an image of the dead man on the barracks floor. He shot the image through a window into the senses of his brothers.

"Whoa!" Berserker shouted. "You skizz that one, Trickster?"

"Yeah."

"Why didn't he disappear?"

"I dunno."

"Looks strange. You made him look like food."

"The battle problems are getting weirder and weirder."

"Be careful," Trickster said. "If you lose a fight in this realm, this is how you end up. Game over."

Silently, the tribe considered this information.

"This is one hard realm, then," Berserker said quietly.

"Ultimate qual," Trickster said. "Let's go, brothers."

The tribe exited the cage. Dreamer remained, standing, her right hand clutching the grid of a wall. She seemed to be smiling slightly.

The tribe spread throughout the building, searching for weapons. Within minutes, they armed themselves with knifes, fire axes, crowbars and other tools. They found one 9mm pistol behind the armored security desk in the front lobby. There were only three clips of fifteen rounds each. After a few seconds studying the floor plan, they spread throughout the building, so that they could ambush the enemy and fight a battle of attrition.

Trickster wanted to stay near Cat, but he decided that she should lead half of the team on the ground floor. Trickster led the team on the other half. The weaker fighters were sent below. They would defend the basement, if the enemy got past the top fighters on the ground floor. They assumed their waiting positions, laying and squatting in ambush.

Machine gun fire erupted dimly beyond the well-insulated walls and armored entrance of Building 514. The machine-gun fire approached closer and closer until individual rounds sounded against the outside wall.

Trickster wondered who they were fighting.

30

Moving outbound for a high point where he could assume a sentry watch, passing through the flowering fruit groves, Trance heard an unusual sound, a faint scraping of a tough fabric against thorny leaves. He began to fall into his characteristic mental state. Everything slowed down. *Something is up ahead,* he thought. *Something moving.*

He held up his hand, giving the signal for enemy ahead. The three of them listened intently. Amid the thousands of sounds of the storm, they heard the rustling of the fabric against the leaves, moving away from them, moving toward Building 514.

Trance made a decision. He flashed the signal for pursuit. The three of them accelerated, but they moved so artfully that they made no noise. Reaching the lip of the hillside where the botanical gardens began, they halted in the shadows of a pagoda, its red paint darkened by night, its gold gilt white. Trance counted three enemy, encased in mottled full-body armor, moving down the hillside. A fourth enemy appeared.

They were all carrying flat-black heavy machine guns. Trance thought he had spotted them all when Cut-Back signaled a fifth enemy. Trance pushed Cut-Back and Sly against the pagoda and hid himself so close to the earth that he doubted the enemy would detect him, even if they had night-vision or infrared goggles. He watched them deploy along the perimeter of the botanical garden.

Just as he was debating whether they could take all five of the enemy with three men and two weapons, a sixth enemy appeared, far ahead, alongside the building across the corner from Building 514, advancing so that he could command the entrance of their home building. Squinting, Trance could see Crush, wearing clothes, standing behind the security desk. Trance decided that the enemy had a hostile intent. He would have to attack them.

Full contact drill, he thought. *With pain. That's what Trickster called it. Hate pain. Hate it. Evil enemy armored. And you gotta know that there's more to it than that. With Trickster taking direction over the whole tribe, Snake off . . . Maybe we'll go the way of Weeble today.*

Trance smiled small, tight and crooked.

Straight to hell . . .

As Trance watched, the squad in mottled armor continued to deploy around the entrance to Building 514. A seventh enemy, then an eighth and a ninth, appeared out of the darkness to take up positions to the left of the plaza. He could sense Sly and Cut-Back winding up like springs, ready to launch into combat. Trance reached back with a restraining hand. He had mentally envisioned several attacks, all of them leading to death. The possibilities were continuing to fan out, but they weren't improving.

As he watched, something went through the mottled squad like an electric shock. Moving with exoskeleton-enhanced speed, they redeployed to accommodate a new threat sector, this one out to right.

Machine-gun fire erupted. Flash hiders dampened the flashes to stabs of bluish light. Trance tried to understand who the enemy was fighting. He saw one enemy receive a round in his helmet, which disintegrated, pitching the enemy onto his back. Trance watched his machine gun clatter to the concrete.

31

"ap commandos—"
  "Swing right, B-squad."
  "Suppression fire! West your sector!"
  The men's voices were tight, not yet tense, flat with suppressed emotion, emphatic with import. A woman spoke, using the same tones.
  "Fifteen Jap commandos to the one three zero—"
  "Surly's down."
  "—got at least thirty more Japs out the zero nine zero."
  Mike McCullough began to lose the tactical picture. He did not understand the location of any of the Japanese except for the ones he could see trying to kill him. Prostrate, he pressed his powered exoskeleton incrementally harder into the juncture of the concrete sidewalk and the tapering concrete wall of this ramp that accessed the plaza. He was trying to shrink, to disappear from the battlefield by compressing himself into the ungiving ground, to disappear from this senseless chaos. But he was trapped by the sullen corporeality of his body, by the hard

logic of life in a physical realm. He clutched his machine gun, but he did not remember its purpose.

The Japanese had attacked without warning. The *Lincoln*'s three-dimensional air surveillance radar could have picked up the falling objects of the paratroopers, but, under restricted emissions control, the radar had been silenced. It was only when the American's outlying sentries had begun to engage the sudden black apparitions of the Japanese commando that the group in the plaza realized they were in trouble.

Bullets exploded around Mike's helmet, concrete fragments singing against the armor. As if he had been slapped, Mike remembered the purpose of the instrument that he clutched. He swung his weapon to his shoulder. The motion raised his head five centimeters. Two Japanese bullets caught the upper surface of his helmet, snapping his head backwards so violently that only the algorithms of the powered exoskeleton kept his neck from breaking. Another bullet glanced off the front of his mask, cracking the armored plastic, pitching his helmet against the concrete wall. The two violent movements, the second a millisecond after the first, accelerated his brain against the inner surface of his skull. Despite the padding and protection provided by the outer and inner layers of dura, the outer layer of the arachnoid membrane, the arachnoid fibers and the inner arachnoid membrane, the violence wreaked on Mike's brain caused him to lose consciousness. Blood from ruptured vessels began to seep across the pleats of his cortical surface.

32

The battle sounds began to die.

"Here we go, brothers!" Trickster shouted.

Thirty seconds later, a tremendous explosion rocked the building. Torn from its hinges, the outer door to the security area flew inwards. Shrapnel and cement fragments ricocheted from the inner walls.

Squatting behind the armored security desk, Trickster tried to listen intently for noises of intruders. He felt dazed from the concussion of the explosion. It was strange, because explosions in battle space never felt like that. The roar of the explosion had made his ears ache.

Acting on instinct, Trickster popped up. He saw four Japanese soldiers, dressed in flat black armor, fully suited and bearing heavy caliber machine guns, moving slowly through the smoke of the explosion. Two were already inside the lobby; the other two were silhouetted against the outer door.

Trickster aimed and fired at the one most immediately endangering him. He caught him in the center of the chest. Trickster then drew down and fired on the two in the door, finally shooting the last enemy to his right.

He dodged to his left and then ducked. Listening intently, he could hear the men whom he had shot stirring.

Hard enemies. Armored, he thought. *I don't even know if I can kill them with this weapon.*

He popped up again. The enemy were still moving slowly. Trickster studied their armor. He shot at their eyes, their throats, their hands, and their groins. He determined that the nine millimeter rounds were effective against the eye-shields of the enemy's armor, at least at close range. Mercilessly, Trickster shot them all through the eyes. He ducked down and replaced his ammunition clip.

A grenade appeared, sailing over the edge of the counter. Trickster grasped it in midflight and threw it back, aiming in the blind for the blasted opening of the door. From the sound of the explosion, he could tell that it had exploded outdoors, possibly in the midst of the enemies who had thrown it at Trickster.

"Berserker, forward here with me!" Trickster shouted.

Naked, Berserker appeared at Trickster's side. Trickster pressed the pistol into Berserker's hand and said, "Shoot for the eyes. Watch out for grenades."

"Kill any?"

"Four down. Forty-six to go. Cover me."

Trickster slithered over to the side of the armored counter. Through the smoke, he could see the outdoors. Shadowy figures were moving in the darkness of the plaza. Trickster dashed into the lobby. He snagged the four heavy machine guns, tossing them over the counter to Berserker, then vaulting the counter himself. Bullets scoured the wall above them.

"They're going to throw the heavy stuff now," he said. "Fall back."

Using the counter for cover, Trickster and Berserker exited through the inner security door and moved toward the rear of the building. As they passed their comrades in hiding, they handed out the heavy weapons.

"Shoot the eyes."

A massive explosion from the front of the building confirmed Trickster's intuition. Had he and Berserker stayed one minute longer in the security desk, they would have died.

I would be solving the mystery of death now, Trickster thought. *I would be in the next realm, right now. Empty or full set? I would know right now.*

He hid in an office, waiting for the enemy.

Naked except for the captured weapon, Cat waited behind a doorway leading to the emergency exit. She heard booted footsteps falling. Her eyes narrowed in an ecstasy of concentration. The wimps were slow. She could hear six pairs of footfalls. No one else was coming now. They were all in the hall. There was a sudden noise of rapid fire and screaming from the other side of the building.

Reacting instantly, sensing the opportunity of the distraction, Cat vaulted from her hiding place. She was midair, soaring, as she sighted down on all six of the enemies. None of them was aiming directly at her, although all of them, after a split-second hesitation, were slowly bringing their weapons to bear. Starting with the one closest to her, she shot them all, one at a time, through their right eyes. As they began to pitch backwards and collapse, Cat pushed herself off the wall. Retaining her own weapon, she grabbed one, two, three—three was enough, she could hear others coming—of the heavy machine guns, sprinted backward, weapon at the ready, and disappeared around the corner.

In his office, Trickster waited until the enemy ran past. Opening the door, he shot them in the backs of their heads, knocking them over. As they struggled to regain their balance, Trickster dashed to stand over them, shooting them one by one through the eyes. He confiscated their weapons and dragged them into one of the offices. Although their body armor was strange, Trickster figured out the clasps and release mechanisms. Within a minute, he was wearing the body armor, less the boots and mask. He stripped the other two enemies and began to carry their armor and weapons to one of his comrades.

Silently, two enemies materialized by his side. Trickster was astounded. He had not guessed that they were hiding among the rubble and strewn furniture. He dropped his burden, knocked one over with a roundhouse kick, then jammed his hand, painfully hard, under the jaw of the other. As his enemies fell, Trickster unhooked and tore off their helmets. One regained his balance and kicked Trickster in the belly. Powered, the kick caused Trickster hideous pain. Berserker appeared, crushing one enemy's skull with a crowbar, then jamming the claw end of the crowbar through the other's face. Snake appeared. With gasping instructions from Trickster, they stripped the enemy of their armor. The suits were too small for Berserker, so he clamped the helmet on Trickster's head.

After conferring, they agreed to split up. While he tried to recover from the blow to his abdomen, Trickster staggered down to the subbasement. He entered the cage, finding Dreamer still standing there.

"The other world," Trickster said, handing Dreamer a heavy weapon.

Dreamer smiled, accepting the substantial machine gun as her first gift in the other world.

"Defend yourself."

"Defend you," Dreamer said.

Too busy to chat, Trickster turned and fled back up toward the fight. Now that all of the tribe, less Barker/Dummy, were armed, they had ten combatants. Trickster estimated that they had killed thirty of the fifty enemy. The odds were swinging in their favor, especially since the enemy were so slow.

Insidiously the building began to fill with a gas that caused wretched crying and burning of the throat. At the first whiff, Berserker and Cat and the other fighters without masks retreated toward the basement. Almost blinded and horrified at how miserable the tear gas made her feel, Cat became incapacitated. Gimp helped her retreat to the subbasement, where he washed her face with water.

When Trickster returned to the ground floor, stalking down the long central corridor, he came across the corpse of Berserker, shot through the head, chest and abdomen. Horrified by the apparition of his dead comrade, Trickster's muscles tensed. His shell-shocked ears failed to hear the stirring behind him. Tremendous blows across his back and shoulders flung him to the floor. Novlar-driven reactions had wrenched his back sideways, so that the force of the bullets against the armor had been largely deflected, but still, the impacts were bruising and agonizing. Trickster lay in a heap, stunned. Three Japanese commandos leaped forward to finish him.

Through the walls, large-caliber bullets rocketed, knocking the Japanese commandos off their feet. Snake burst through the office door, wearing the other complete armored suit. He handled the captured weapon like a hydraulic hammer, shooting and killing one commando after the other. He tossed the spent weapon aside, threw Trickster over his shoulder and retreated at full sprint down into the subbasement.

"Don't let them pass, Gimp," Snake ordered, carrying Trickster down the cement-block passageway. Gimp, though suffering from the tear gas, was ignoring the pain, just as he had ignored pain all of his life.

Dazed and agonized, Trickster tried to keep tally of the battle. Seventeen enemy remaining, perhaps less. Everyone except Snake incapacitated. Berserker dead.

"Who else is dead?" Trickster asked.

"Lightning, I think. Maybe Skipper."

"Lightning? No . . . get me to the cage."

Snake grunted, but he turned to run toward the ground floor, where he intended to carry forward the fight alone. Trickster crawled into the cage and made the gestures that dialed his pain back to almost nothing. Floods of relief poured through him. He looked around. Dreamer and Skipper were missing. Cat was retching. Very much still alive, Lightning stood behind her, cradling her head and trying to soothe her torment. Trickster took control of Cat's senses, substituting camera-derived vision, registered to her perspective, for her natural sight. He removed her sense of touch for the entire head and lungs. Cat began to choke on her own phlegm. Reluctantly, Trickster restored her sense of touch.

A Japanese commando burst into the room. Trickster shot him through the chest. Two other commandos appeared. Trickster caught one in the head, the other in the lower abdomen, just as the last one squeezed off a full clip of ammunition.

Then, silence.

Trickster looked over to Cat.

She was still coughing. The bullets had missed her. Behind her, on the floor of the cage, sprawled the ruined, bloody dead body of Lightning. With his mind's eye burning with the vision of the bullet's mutilations of Lightning's body, Trickster advanced in the cage so that he could cover the entrance better. A form appeared and Trickster drew down on it; his trigger finger began to squeeze, but then he eased up the pressure. The form was Sly. He was wearing mottled armor across his chest.

"Dead," he said. "All dead."

"What?"

"We hold the building."

"Where . . . what . . . where were you?"

"Outside. When the last enemies went in, Trance, Cut-Back and I captured weapons and armor from the other commando and we attacked from the rear. Trance did good but now he's in Time-Out, I guess."

"What others?"

"The other commando. They're all busted immobile, except for one who was still moving."

Trickster shook his head. "Who's out?"

"Berserker. Gimp. Trance. Skipper. Maybe others."

"Dreamer?"

"Dunno. I can't cut to her. No services."

"Look for her!" Trickster shouted.

Knees weak, Trickster sat down on the mercilessly hard edges of the cage floor. He tried to imagine a world without Lightning, Berserker, Gimp, Trance and Skipper. A third of the tribe wiped out in one small battle. Trickster felt as if he had lost a third of his body. Suddenly it seemed hideously unfair that battle in this world was so final. He remembered the bullets that the last commando had sprayed through the cage. Trickster stared at Cat as she continued to cough. A single bullet through her head would have destroyed her forever, or sent her to hell, or to a secret realm that Trickster couldn't imagine, one perhaps he could never enter. *Lightning knows that realm now, if she knows anything . . . empty set, null set, set of zero . . .* The mystery of death in this realm staggered Trickster. He decided that no price was too high to pay to remain here with Cat, because in the next realm he might lose her—if there was a realm after this one.

Any price, even . . . maybe even imprisonment. Maybe this death is the ultimate prison. No escape from hell?

Trickster forced himself to climb to his feet.

"Cat," he said.

Too wretched to hear, Cat continued to cough.

"Still no Dreamer, Trickster," Cut-Back called, before disappearing again down the hall.

"Keep looking."

Trickster cut back to War Council Rock. He studied the theater of operations. The Japanese were bombarding Beijing with medium-range ballistic missiles. As far as Trickster could tell, the warheads were high explosive, but it was possible that they were nuclear or chemical or bacteriological. *If they haven't already gone nuke, they're about to,* he thought. *We've got to get out of here. The Japanese are targeting this place hot.*

Trickster felt his characteristic coolness snap. He had no

more patience. He couldn't stand the uncertainty any longer. He had to make his move.

Back at the cage, Dreamer appeared alongside of him.

"Where've you been?"

"Outside."

"Didn't the—"

"Some beautiful noise—"

Trickster felt a wave of inattention sweep through his brain so powerfully that for a moment he lost the sense of where he was. As he stood numbed and dumbfounded, one by one, the other surviving members of the tribe appeared.

"What's the goal here, Trickster?" Crush demanded. "Where the hell is System?"

"What kind of battle problem is this?"

"This gnaws! Berserker's all broke up. He looks like . . . meat. Ribs . . . *gah!* It stinks."

"Trance's head's gone missing."

"This avatar . . . is it Cry-Baby?"

"I hate this problem."

"My hand is slaying me."

"*Shut up!*" Trickster screamed. With wild eyes he stared at his siblings. "This isn't a battle problem. This is a battle in the other world. The world was just a realm inside of the other world. This cage here . . . this was where our default avatars, our bodies, these meat avatars, have been, all our lives, all our lives. . . ."

Trickster choked a sob. Hot tears began to cascade down his face, streaking the filth and smoke from the fight. "We're trapped here," he said. "Trapped inside these meat avatars. Dead, you're done. . . . This is it. I can't take it anymore. We've got to get out of here. I've got to break the models for the world, turn off our radios. . . . We've got to make a run for it."

Blindly, Cat reached out and folded her arms around Trickster. The touch of her sweet flesh reminded him how close he had come to losing her forever. He broke down completely, sobbing into her shoulder.

"What the hell is he talking about?"

"How come we can touch each other?"

"Where's System? I got no services!"

"Trickster broke the world!"

"The world is gone. I can't cut to anywhere."

"This place stinks."

"Come on, we got to run for it. This place is targeted hot."

Cat raised her head and shouted. "*Shut up!* This . . . this is the fight we've been training for all our lives. Calm down. Trickster has command. We can beat this one." In the following silence, Dreamer spoke up with a calm, clear voice. "There is another realm after this one," she said. "Don't worry. Lightning and the others are there now. It's the next world. It's a secret realm, but we can hope it's better than this one."

"This is a good realm!" Cat shouted.

"How do you know, Dreamer? Can you cut to them?"

"No. No one can."

"Then how do you know?"

Dreamer smiled. "There's something more profound than knowledge. There's the dream of faith."

"Gah! Let's get *out* of here!"

"Faith? What's that?"

"Come on, Trickster," Cat whispered. "Come on. They're falling apart. They need you."

Trickster heard Cat's words and realized the truth of them. He reached down into reserves of strength that a lifetime of struggle had provided. Slowly he stood. He wiped his arm across his face.

"The world is dead," he said. "We gotta run for it. Two ways to go—I turn off your radios—wait . . ." He spun up the world for the last time. The entire tribe stood on War Council Rock. Lightning, Berserker, Trance, Gimp and Skipper were laid out in a perfect row atop the commander's rock. A flaming sky illuminated the war theater spread out below in night.

"The world is dead," Trickster said. He shot images to his siblings explaining what the world had been and what the other world seemed to be. He presented two choices: stay here, waiting to be captured by one enemy or the other; or run for it, but only after they had their radios turned off, condemning them forever to life in the other world.

"Here I'm a whole man," Barker said. "I'm staying here." He cut to his personal realm, leaving nine.

Trickster looked at Dummy, who signed that he wanted to go wherever Trickster went. Slowly, sadly, Trickster shook his head.

"You stay here, my friend," he said. "You stay and keep Barker company."

Dummy hung his head, then, bowed low to his leader. Humbly, he cut away, leaving eight.

"I . . . don't know if I can make it outside of the world," Dreamer said. "But where you go, I go."

"I'm with you," Cat said quickly.

"I and my squad are going," Snake said, nodding to Cut-Back and Sly. Trickster realized that he had lost his entire squad, except for Dreamer, whose one skill would be lost outside of the world. Lancer and Crush remained to Cat. On top of everything else, Trickster realized that a new power shift had come to the tribe. A mad laughed bubbled up through his misery.

"The eight of us," Trickster said. "Trickster, Dreamer, Cat, Crush, Snake, Lancer, Cut-Back and Sly. We are the tribe now."

Preparing to take the terminal step of cutting their interface into the world, Trickster stood atop the commander's rock. For what he meant to be the last time, he looked down at the battle problem. He saw the theater-wide devastation caused by the Japanese and the Chinese. Seeing all the symbols of destruction, he looked down at the bodies of his five companions. Lightning, dead. Berserker, dead. Gimp, dead. Trance, dead. Skipper, dead.

In his grief, Trickster came to realize the meaning of war. He understood the sickness, the brutality, the stupidity and the waste of it. The hundreds of thousands who had died and the millions who were about to die were all as dear as these five had been to him. Life, however limited, however constrained, was precious. *The living may choose to live free or die. The dead would choose life.*

Further, he realized that these symbols of enemies had a reality. The tribe, he realized, was humankind. Together, they were all victims in the same realm. The realm of the real world. Victims of war.

War termination . . .

Trickster made a gesture to his companions, silencing them. His mind was starting to accelerate. He looked out at the battle problem from a fresh perspective. *Not how to win the war. Not even how to escape it. How to end it.*

Trickster called up his note. *The emperor of Japan is the center of the battle.* That was the crux of the problem. He envisioned a way he could bring this war to a halt. He gestured to his siblings, harnessing them for the battle problem.

"—thought we were going to cut out of here."

"He's on to something. Let's go with him."

"Sly," Trickster said. "You were head-hunting, right?"

"Yeah."

"You never did locate the emperor?"

"Nah. They got six deep shelters that I could find and about a dozen alternate command posts for national command authority—"

"Type?"

"Two trains, three aircraft, two ships, rest mobile vans. Lots of shells for just one pea."

Trickster turned to Dreamer. "Dreamer, can you bust the right Japanese circuits to locate the emperor?"

Dreamer shook her head. She shot to Trickster a highly complex diagram of Japanese command-and-control. "You want the imperial command circuit, the ICC. Only circuit that the emperor and the general staff are using besides the fiberoptics in the home islands. The ICC is a extreme high frequency satellite link. The EHF sat is in geosynch. Aims and tracks pencil beams—"

"Low probability of intercept—"

"Zero possibility of intercept unless it's transmitting right to you. The only way to intrude on that circuit is to capture one of the circuit participant sites. You need to take a national command-and-control site, take it intact, and so fast and clean the other sites don't even notice. And those sites are restricted to the home islands except for the command-and-control flagships like the *Uzushio*—"

"The sub."

"Yeah, the sub—"

"Still unlocated."

"Of course."

"It's south, I think."

"What, you're going to take a submarine?"

"No," Trickster mumbled, distracted. "Just the opposite."

He reversed the battle problem and studied the submarine problem. They had had very few indications of Japanese submarine activity. The natural place for a large command-and-control submarine like the *Uzushio* was in the lee of Japan, where they could enjoy the protection of Japanese land-based defenses. Trickster marshaled all the evidence of Japanese submarine activity further south. Although there was no direct evidence of Japanese submarines in the Bashi Channel, there had been a number of sinkings that were difficult to attribute to any other source. He reviewed the reports they had of those sinkings. Either the ships had gone down with all hands, or, somehow, survivors had been rescued.

"Intruder," Lancer said.

33

Mike's eyes had opened slowly. He was remembering the heat of the hot sun on a white sandy beach. He was a small boy. Blood filmed his eyelids. Mike tried to remember where he was and what he was doing. He became aware of pain somewhere in his head. He reached up and wiped his eyes. Blood trickled down into his left eye.

Mike struggled to sit up. He groaned. He found himself sitting on a concrete ramp into a plaza. Pools of blackness in the darkness, inert figures, possibly dead bodies, lay unmoving. The tropical night air felt strangely warm and moist. A warm wind buffeted his wet face.

With a painful effort, Mike tried to remember where he found himself. A nude Chinese woman materialized before his sight. Mike became aware of deep black irises around pupils as dilated as an owl's eyes at night. He felt as if the woman was reading his soul. Slowly, as if pleased with Mike's text, she smiled. Then her head snapped to the left with rapid exactness.

She seemed to blur. Mike found himself looking for her eyes in the darkness of the night sky.

Searching painfully for the apparition of the nude woman, Mike glanced over his left shoulder. He saw the devastated entrance to Building 514 and beyond it the lighted lobby.

The trauma to his brain was blocking his access to all memories of the past sixteen years. Mike could not remember the receipt of the orders to evacuate American citizens in the Batan Island technical enclave. He couldn't remember the feverish preparation. He couldn't remember the seaborne infiltration, the anxious hour crossing the open countryside, the maneuver into the enclave's campus, the sudden and deadly attack by the Japanese.

He couldn't remember joining the United States Navy. He couldn't remember being in a frame of mind that would consider joining the military.

Mike turned so that he could more comfortably watch the lobby. As he watched, a naked black man sprinted into the lobby, blurring as he moved, then disappeared. Mike wondered whether he had seen the black man snatch a weapon.

The building looked strangely familiar. The nude Chinese woman was probably in the building, too. Mike realized that he wanted to talk with her. She seemed intensely important, as if she were the expression of his ideal of womanhood.

He stood. Blood drained from his brain. Amid golden sparkles, he began to collapse. Mike reached out to the ramp's handrail and steadied himself. He began to stagger toward the plaza. At the edge of a dark puddle, he looked down at a fallen marine.

Some sort of battle in the dream . . .

Mike stepped through the puddle. His feet felt tacky with a warm thick liquid. In the uncertain light, he realized that the puddle was not rainwater, but blood. He shivered with revulsion. In a clear patch of pavement he could see his bloody footprints. As he bent over to peel off his socks, blood rushed to his head. Mike blacked out and collapsed to the plaza floor. After a minute of fighting a wave of nausea, he tore off his socks. His hands touched his flight suit, which he realized was also sticky with blood. He reached to his throat and unzipped the suit down to his crotch. He shed the flight suit, then the cotton undershirt and drawers.

Naked, he stood. He looked up to the night sky, hoping for a cleansing rain, but no such rain was falling.

Inside the lobby, he stepped over the corpses of the Japanese commando. The stench of smoke bothered him more than the sight of these dead men. Mike coughed. He stumbled forward through the second set of blasted armored doors.

The nude Chinese woman appeared before him. She blurted a rapid torrent of nonsense which Mike recognized as something that could be related to Mandarin.

"Have you eaten?" Mike asked in Mandarin. He remembered Mandarin. He had learned it in his infancy, when the foreign service had stationed his mother in Beijing.

Dreamer smiled. She forced herself to move and speak as slowly as possible. "Yes, I have eaten, thank you," she said. "Have you?"

Mike nodded. "Yes, thank you."

"I would like you to come meet your brother, the one of us called Trickster," Dreamer said.

"Ah . . . yes. Trickster. Strange name."

"He is the hero."

Dreamer began to lead Mike down toward the basement. A primal pulse, untouched by any trauma, caused him to glance downward and notice the dimples over her sacrum and the full oval buttocks.

"And you?" Mike asked.

"I am Dreamer."

"What happened here, Dreamer?"

"There was a battle between the tribe and these enemies. They are called the Japanese." Mike noticed that Dreamer cringed as she walked as far away as possible from a four hundred-cycle power run.

"Ah . . . Japanese . . ." Mike said. He thought it was strange that the Japanese would be the monsters in his dream. They were such a peace-loving, industrious people.

His lips twisted foolishly in a smile, Mike staggered into the cage room. At first the randy stench of the place overwhelmed him more than the bizarre sight, but then he realized that the forms hanging from the ceiling were humans cocooned in grayish fibers. Some of the prisoners wriggled and struggled; others hung there as if dead. Five corpses were laid out in a row on the cage floor. Several Chinese men with a dense, chiseled musculature were arguing with one Chinese man who stood with an air of command somewhat glazed over by a wild look in his eyes. Mike noticed in the rich mix of odors the stench of chemical explosions.

Dreamer escorted Mike into the cage. Snake blurred to confront Mike. He jabbered too quickly for Mike to understand. Dreamer replied. Leaving behind a hissing sound like steam escaping from pressure, Snake disappeared, reappearing in front of Trickster, where he resumed his argument.

"We've got enough captured armor from that one's commando," Snake said, using his chin to point to Mike. "We've also got him. I say we take him hostage, get an aircraft in here, take the aircraft across the strait to one of the larger islands to the south."

"That's neutral territory in this battle problem," Cat said. "Let's move before the Japanese go nuke."

Trickster nodded but said nothing. As if dazed, he stumbled forward and stood staring up into Mike's eyes. Mike smiled uncertainly at the strange Chinese man who studied him with such intensity.

Trickster reached and grabbed Mike's shoulders. He spoke so rapidly that Mike was unable to understand some of what he said.

"You are the first man, the first free man, I have ever spoken to," Trickster said. "Except for my prisoners, those who imprisoned me . . . I cannot understand your world. Sickness . . . if the . . . this is the question! Can you answer the question?"

Mike said, "What is the question, please?"

"How can . . . how can this world work? If everything . . . entropy in all things . . . this mechanism of evolution . . . survival of the most vicious. The killers breed, each generation more vicious, gentleness is selected out. It seems that your realm . . . everything degenerates. Who would choose to live in such a realm? Why should I live in such a realm? Why would I condemn my children to eternity in such a realm?"

"Are you saying evolution," Mike asked, "is a degenerative process?"

Snake rasped at Trickster, who shook his head as if brushing away flies.

"Meat . . . meat-eaters," Trickster said. "Cannibalization . . . eat . . . struggle of genes to propagate genes . . . viciousness. Concentration of power in the meat, meat-eaters evolve into power. Power accumulates . . . power . . ."

Mike shook his head. He felt sick to his stomach. Major chunks of his memory were falling into place. "Could you speak more slowly?" he asked.

"Can't you see it?" Trickster asked. "Your realm is evil. You are the sons of murderers and the grandsons of murderers. Your victims, your gentle victims, are extinct. . . . bad to worse."

Mike shook his head. He thought that Trickster was impugning the honor of the United States Navy, which he now remembered was his parent organization. "We are not evil. We . . . we are not tyrants. Do you understand tyrants? Hitler. We defeated Hitler. We defeated the communists."

"Trickster, let's go!" Cat shouted.

The others of the remaining members of the tribe were checking their weapons. In search of ammunition, Sly and several others brushed past Mike and exited the cage. Trickster

turned his head and asked in a hollow voice, "How many men
and women are alive in the *Lincoln?*"

"I don't know."

Trickster's eyes narrowed. Mike felt an awful fierceness as
radiant as heat from white-hot metal.

"I've read that the crew numbers two thousand men and
women. Yes? Let us say, two thousand. They are your tribe?"

"Yes."

"Are you willing to die to save them?"

The final chunks of Mike's memory fell into place. He experienced a troubled, nauseous sense of clarity. He believed
that he understood himself and the image of himself, this Trickster, better than he had ever understood anything. He answered
the question with the candor he would use with his own self.

"For my shipmates, for my countrymen, yes, I would, yes."

". . . calculus of life and death in your realm? Then I can cal-
culate as well as any of you . . . ratio two thousand to one?
Would two thousand die to save four million?"

"Depends on the two thousand, I guess."

Trickster's eyes went opaque. He made some gestures that
were nonsense to Mike, then began to speak too rapidly for
him to understand.

Trickster opened a personal window with Cat. "What is
more important, Cat? That we escape? The eight of us?
Or that we take a chance and end this war? We could postpone millions, maybe billions of deaths. Or we could die for
nothing."

Cat considered. "That depends on what the next level is,
doesn't it, Tricky?"

Trickster reached out and grasped Cat's wrist. "I believe
that there is a realm after this one. But that is just belief. I don't
know. I can't know. Maybe there isn't another realm after this
one. But if that's so, the only . . . the only part of us that can live
forever is our children. Children's children. Tunnel of mirrors.

Echo down forever. Then this is our realm. We should act in it. For the better."

"Who's the tribe, then, Trickster?"

Trickster's thumb caressed the flesh of Cat's forearm. "Who's the tribe, then, Cat? That is my question. The eight of us? Or all the human creatures in this realm?"

Cat smiled beatifically. "This is the fight I've always dreamed of, my friend. All our lives, I've felt us ascending, growing for this. To do something. To fight a fight that means something. So . . . we are the tribe. All of us. If you can postpone deaths, do so. Life in this realm is sweet."

"Our blood?"

"Our blood flows like a great river through the veins of all our brothers," Cat answered. "Go for it."

"The gambit is extremely risky. A queen's sacrifice gambit."

"Go for it," Cat said. "Your campaign plan. Your command."

Trickster turned back to Mike and slowly said, "Then I am your prisoner."

Naked, bloodied, Mike stood while the experimental subjects began a shouting match in a Mandarin too rapid for him to understand a single word. Cat stood shoulder-to-shoulder with Trickster, facing down Snake. Lancer stood at Cat's side. Dreamer joined Trickster. Cut-Back joined forces with Snake, but when Sly sided with Cat and Trickster, Crush decided for the majority, leaving only Snake and Cut-Back in opposition. Dreamer turned to Mike.

"Prisoners or refugees, we go to your ship," she said.

"Evacuees," Mike said. "Evacuees is the correct word. I am here to evacuate you. Are you ready?"

"There is some . . . technical equipment and data," Trickster said. ". . . possibly of intelligence interest."

"Bring anything you think is of value. No weapons," Mike said.

"Take the prisoner to the lobby and wait for me there," Trickster shouted, then he exited the cage. Dashing to the computer room, Trickster downloaded his universe. The entirety of all the code that had been System, the extensive mappings of sensory data to neural codings, all of the documentation, all of tribe's personal data, their paradigms and tools. The data amounted to five petabytes, which he flashed into the most advanced secondary memory medium available, a Mitsubishi holographic cell, so that his entire world was translated into smears of colors trapped in a translucence. Although he was pressed for time, he made a backup copy. He stored the cells in a high-impact transportation case, using duct tape to secure the case against his lower back.

He considered the fate of his other prisoners: Iva, Chang, and the rest. *Left me ... alone ... all my life. Stole from me my own sensations. Hid the world ... let them stay. Until someone discovers them and frees them.* He made command gestures. *They'll be fed as I was fed, bathed as I was bathed, caged as I was caged. If they had the wafers, I'd send them to the world ... except that Chang.* Trickster felt the rising, heavy, black pressing of anger and hate. *With these Novlar fibers, driven by my hands, I could choke him to death, now ... made as I was made. He did not make me. Or should I take his eyes, a quick gesture, blind him to the real world as I was blinded? Fah! No! Just let him hang until someone comes. ...*

He opened a voice circuit to the cage. "Iva," he said.

"Yes?" Her face, strangely youthful-looking, turned up toward the sound of his voice.

"In another hour, it'll be safe to go outside."

"Oh?"

"Good-bye."

"Good-bye, Trickster. Go and please be happy."

"That doesn't seem to be my function," he said heavily. On seeing the torment on her face, he added softly, "But for you, I will try. Good-bye."

"Good-bye, my son."

"Good-bye. I forgive you."

Iva began to sob. Trickster cut the voice circuit. He turned and ran. Back in the lobby, he found the survivors of the tribe and Mike. They had stripped the radios from the commandos' armor. Mike was dressed in his blood-stained flight suit. The rest were nude.

"Our evacuation flight will be here in a few minutes," Mike said.

Trickster stripped a Marine of his flight suit, which he donned. The holographic cell case remained strapped to his lower back. The others declined to dress in the uniforms of fallen enemies.

The two darkly mottled Firefly tilt-jet special operation aircraft appeared over the opposite building with hallucinatory silence. Their noise-canceling diaphragms launched air waves directly out-of-phase with the other sounds emitted by the aircraft. The Fireflies touched down in the plaza. Mike walked out of the ruined lobby and stood next to the bodies of his fallen comrades. Armed and armored marines leapt from the Fireflies. They deployed in a defensive perimeter, while unarmed medics attempted to assist the tribe into the two aircraft. A momentary confusion resulted when the medics tried to split the tribe so that Snake would be separated from Cut-Back, Lancer from Cat, and Dreamer from Trickster. After some adroit shuffling, the tribe managed to board the aircraft split as they desired.

As the Firefly prepared to lift off, Mike brushed away a medic. He grabbed a crew chief mask and spoke on the intercom.

"Like I said on the long-haul, these people are not helpless," he said. "These eight people killed over fifty Japanese special forces commandos. Do not—"

Accelerating to his top speed, Trickster blurred forward. He punched Mike in the temple, knocking him unconscious. Snatching a submachine gun from the marine who had thought he was guarding him, he shot the marine underneath the jaw and then the load-master through the heart. Spinning, he shot the side-gunner, who was still falling toward the deck as Trickster moved forward into the cockpit. His fist smashed into the back of the head of the pilot. His elbow smashed into the face of the copilot. Trickster hauled the aircrew out of the cockpit. By the time he arrived back in the cargo bay, his comrades had killed the rest of the marines. Mike lay sprawled on the aircraft floor.

Snake appeared standing at the open door. He clutched a submachine gun identical to the one Trickster held.

"We took the other one!" he shouted.

"Yours!" Trickster shouted. "You and Cut-Back can keep it. Go your own way."

Snake drew himself to stand at attention. He bowed to Trickster, who returned the bow, their gestures consciously patterned on the bows they'd made at the end of their duel with pain. Trickster kept his head tilted so that he could watch Snake at the bottom of his bow. Snake's eyes shone as he watched Trickster watching him. Cut-Back suddenly appeared to Snake's right. Snake uncoiled from his bow, the barrel of his submachine gun foreshortening. Trickster saw that Cat had a clear drop on Snake, but that she was not moving. Cat's love of the entire tribe, even of Snake, was preventing her from shooting Snake. Dreamer was armed, but Cat was blocking her line of fire.

He had anticipated such a betrayal within a betrayal. He had known that Snake would have chosen such a moment. Trickster had waited until he saw Snake's chest and arm muscles begin to contract under his taut skin. Relaxed and ready for it, Trickster reacted at his top speed. Swinging up, his weapon came to bear on Snake's hip while Snake was still bringing his weapon upwards.

The squeeze that Trickster's finger exerted on the trigger increased slowly, tripping the mechanism at the correct moment. A series of bullets ripped Snake's flesh and bones asunder from hip to shoulder. Cut in half, Snake's body folded as it pitched backwards, knocked by the force of the rounds. Blood splattered Cut-Back, who hesitated to kill Trickster as he realized that Snake had failed.

Trickster fixed Cut-Back with a look. Trickster did not bring his weapon to bear on Cut-Back. Understanding the full portent of Trickster's look, Cut-Back dropped his submachine gun and assumed one of the tribe's traditional postures of surrender: two knees to dirt, feet pointed outwards, hands clasped behind the head, eyes lowered.

"Climb aboard," Trickster shouted.

Cut-Back leaped aboard in one movement. Trickster glanced at Lancer, his look ordering Lancer to watch Cut-Back. Then Trickster gazed down at the ruin that had been Snake.

"Why?" Cat asked, her voice husky with grief.

"He was going to shoot me," Trickster said.

"You were going to shoot him, too," Cat said, angrily. "The two of you, faced off like that, ready to kill each other. Why? Why were you two always like that?"

Trickster shrugged. "You never understood Snake," he said. "You never knew him."

Cat looked at Trickster. Her large brown eyes seemed huge with sadness.

"Maybe I never knew you either."

"Maybe not," Trickster said. "Do you want to take the other aircraft and go your own way? Snake's escape plan was the safest. Jump to Luzon, hide, run, another prey on the run in a realm dominated by predators and overpopulated with prey . . ."

Cat shook her head slowly. "This realm . . . is too free. Too wild. There is no System."

"I am System," Trickster said. "I am my own System. Be your own System. Run. Or fight. But decide."

Cat looked up at Trickster, seeking strength in his hardness. "You are the leader of the tribe now."

"There is no tribe. There is only you and me, Dreamer, Lancer, Cut-Back, Crush and Sly. If you follow me, though, you . . . trust me to understand this world thoroughly. And I say it is a place for us to act. To do the right. And I believe . . . I believe that there is another realm after this one. Do not follow me if you don't believe that yet. Because today we might find out if I am right." Trickster turned and shouted at the others. "Into the heart of the volcano. That's where I'm going. Follow me! Victory or death! We'll end up as dead as Snake, that meat garbage out there. Or in total victory! Follow me at your risk! Or go take the other aircraft."

"Let's go!" Crush shouted. "Slay!"

"I'm with you, Trickster," Cat said. "Play out the gambit."

"Death in this realm is final in this realm," Trickster warned. "And there is no proof that there is another realm after this one."

"Perhaps we'll find out today," Cat answered. Her smile was neither as simple nor as pure as it had been in the world.

"Go forward and fly this aircraft. Sly! Copilot!" Trickster said, turning. "Give me a read on flyability." They threw the bodies of the marines out onto the muddy ground, where they sprawled next to Snake. Crush was hauling Mike toward the door, but Trickster pointed with his chin toward the canvas seats. Crush propped Mike up in a seat and strapped him in with the five-point harness.

Trickster slammed and bolted shut the door. He moved forward. Sly and Cat, the best two pilots in the tribe, had already donned the flight crew's headgear.

"Tilt jet," Cat said. "Fuel indication, four thousand, three hundred kilos. All indicators, green. No red indicators. For Americans, this is good. This is power, yoke, flaps, tilt jet. Brakes."

"No, this is brakes," Sly said.

"Yeah, right, sorry. Brakes. Radios. Altitude. Attitude. Cabin pressure . . . it's all straightforward, Trickster."

"Yeah, what's that?"

"Oh I dunno. Don't think it's that—"

"Lock for tilt jet," Sly said.

"Right, right, lock for tilt jet. This is dump fuel. Emergency hydraulic backup. Manual fire alarm . . . I think I've got it, Trickster."

"Study it another fifteen seconds."

"Yeah . . . that's right . . . let me try . . . feels good. I got it. I got it."

"Can you ditch us at sea?" Trickster asked.

"Yeah. Sure."

"Land us on an aircraft carrier flight deck?"

"Maybe."

"Take off, then," Trickster ordered.

Returning to the cargo bay, Trickster sat down next to Mike, whose eyelids were fluttering open, his eyes unfocused. The air pressurization fluctuated as the jets accelerated, and the noise-canceling diaphragms created strange anomalies. The canvas seats grew hard as the aircraft climbed upward. They were airborne.

"I'm sorry that this battle happened," Trickster said. "One of my brothers misunderstood a gesture that one of the marines made. He thought that your marines were going to kill us."

"You . . . what . . ."

"We acted in self-defense. It was unfortunate."

"Vector!" shouted Cat.

Trickster placed his arm around Mike, staring into his dazed and fearful eyes. "Where is the *Lincoln?*" he asked.

"Why? What are you up to? You can't capture a ship with . . . you can't possibly capture the ship."

"East!" Trickster shouted. He saw a glint in Mike's eyes that convinced him that his guess was correct. Of course, the station of the *Lincoln* would be east of the Bashi Channel, away from the war being fought in the South China Sea, with her path eastward, homeward, open before her once the mission had been accomplished.

"I killed a man today," Trickster said. "Have you ever killed a man?"

"No."

"All my life, I hated that man. But I didn't kill him when I could. He was in my power. I could have killed him with no risk to myself. With no one even knowing. But I didn't kill him then. I had planned to allow him to live until the moment I saw him begin to try to kill me. This is what you call in your realm 'justifiable homicide,' isn't it?"

"Yes. Yes, I think so."

". . . many fine shades of murder. Such connoisseurs of chaos. First degree. Second degree. Was that self-defense? Or was that an act of war? What moral alchemy your convention of warfare works! . . . the act of killing from a crime to an honorable act . . ." Trickster's voice began to catch. "Or should we call it fratricide? He was my brother, you know. I hated him, but I wanted him to become well. Or was he the sickness in all of us?"

Mike tried to wrap his mind around the lunacy of the previous hour.

"What?"

"Are you vicious animals? Or merely barbarians?"

"You seem pretty vicious yourself," Mike said.

"You are our teachers in all things," Trickster said. "Everything we know, you taught us. But where is this civilization of yours that you talk and write about? I would like to go there, but it doesn't seem to exist. You Americans seems to relish warfare as much as any other tribe." Trickster turned and shouted to the cockpit. "Keep a sharp lookout for the ship! It will be running dark."

"Yeah!" Cat shouted back from the cockpit.

"We don't start wars, typically," Mike said. "Typically, we're invited to join them in progress. Typically, we then go in and devastate the enemy. Then we establish a peace."

"Waging war to make peace," Trickster said. "Like fornicating to make virginity. A saying of your people."

"One mother can make many virgins."

Trickster snorted a laugh. "So how good a history does your tribe have in waging war to make peace?"

Mike shrugged. "The entire planet would have been enslaved a couple of times over if it hadn't been for us."

"Perhaps it would be better to live a slave than to die a freeman."

"Ask a slave."

"Slavery. Another one of your fine institutions."

"We fought a big war to end that, too."

"It seems to me that your warfare, like your slavery, is a social institution," Trickster said. "Very large, entrenched, learned behavior. Like cannibalism, foot-binding, female circumcision, human sacrifice, abortion, murder, child abuse, sacrificial self-mutilation . . . social institutions. Barbarisms, barbarisms. You are a barbarian."

Mike smiled crookedly. "Your point?"

"You admit that you are a barbarian?"

"I am a barbarian who is possessed by the idea of civilization."

"Which are the barbarians and which are the barbarians possessed of the idea of civilization? I am a stranger to your realm. You make fine distinctions that I have trouble perceiving."

"The question is, what are we supposed to do when we're confronted with aggression? Surrender? Or fight?"

"Are you a Christian?" Trickster asked.

"I would like to be one."

"Are you a Christian?"

"No."

"Your tribe is a Christian tribe? I've read many reports to that effect."

"Says so on the label."

"And you are not?"

"How can I be? And wear this uniform? This blood . . . I don't even know whose blood this is."

"There are millions of warriors who call themselves Christians. Christian soldiers."

"Christian soldiers are not very profound students of his teachings."

"Then what is your religion? Is there a realm after this one?"

"I don't know. I would like to be a Christian. But I chose to wear this uniform."

"Why?"

"Because I cared more about my country than my soul."

"Why?"

"Because I'm pretty sure that I have a country."

"Ah . . ." Trickster said. "Then, even if this realm is the only realm and there is no realm afterwards, how do you stop the cycle of violence? In this realm? Without forgiving your enemies?"

"I don't know. My countrymen, those Christian soldiers you mention, believe in the forgiveness of our enemies . . . after we have destroyed their armies and a few of their cities. That's the American way of war. Ask the Japanese, the Germans, the Iraqis, the Koreans. I don't think that is what the man had in mind. I don't know. Maybe I'm wrong. My responsibility is to die, my son a free man."

"Are you a father?"

"Yes."

"Is your son free?"

"Yes."

"Then you may well succeed."

"Ship on the horizon!" Cat shouted.

Trickster moved forward to the cockpit. Above the sea on the eastern horizon stood a broad bright spectrum of color, scarlet through gold, turquoise shot with emerald before indigo faded to black. Silhouetted against the predawn light was the unmistakable form of an aircraft carrier, superstructure towering to the starboard.

"Dive to the waves and retreat west," Trickster said. He picked up a high frequency radio handset, dialed in the frequency that allowed him to broadcast back to Building 514. In the clear, he spoke just a few code words that reported the *Lincoln's* position. Back in Building 514, doppelganger 43 injected a false report into Japanese merchant ship reporting. Masquerading as a Japanese fishing vessel, the doppelganger reported that it had sighted the *Sun Tzu*, the former *Carl Vinson*, which the Chinese had bought from the Americans ten years earlier. The report stated that the carrier's crew was changing the ship's colors from Chinese to American and repainting the hull number to 72.

"Orbit out here until the ship starts to go down," Trickster said. He returned to sit with Mike.

"The hardest part is over," Trickster said. "We've located your ship."

"What are you going to do?"

"We are going to assist your ship . . . maintaining the peace," Trickster answered. "I am a student of your moral calculus. Plug my numbers into your formulae. See if my results agree with yours. You are, after all, my teachers."

"What? Speak sense."

"Be quiet, now," Trickster said. "We will be swimming before the sun is high. Save your strength."

An hour later, Cat called Trickster forward.

"We're running out of fuel," she said. "This low altitude

orbiting has been consuming a lot of fuel. We have enough for thirty minutes. Enough to return to Batan Island."

Trickster shook his head. "Victory or death," he said. "Take it in to the aircraft carrier."

34

On watch in the *Uzushio*, Lieutenant Kenichi Takahashi read the report of the *Sun Tzu* changing its colors. The daemon continually running in the back of his mind, the one that searched for vital data amid the thousands of lesser reports, alarmed when he scanned this report. Another daemon, the one that alerted on suspicious data, also alarmed. Recognizing both the potential importance and the dubious veracity of this report, Lieutenant Takahashi did exactly what any watchstander should have done: he informed his boss.

The captain seized upon the report. He stifled Takahashi's arguments about the suspicious provenance of the report and the lack of other data indicating that the *Sun Tzu* was east of the Bashi Channel. The captain took the report to the admiral. A founding member of the Imperial Party, the admiral was such a vigorous advocate of sea denial that he didn't much care which flag an aircraft carrier flew in the western Pacific. In his mind there were only two flags: the rising sun and all others. The ad-

miral ordered the *Uzushio* to the vicinity of the reported position of the *Sun Tzu*.

"Visually confirm that the target is an aircraft carrier and
that it's hull number is 72," the admiral said. "That will be suf-
ficient."

35

Trickster returned to the cargo bay and stood next to Mike. "We're going to land on your ship," he said. "If you care to . . . procedures for returning to the carrier in radio silence, our chances of survival will improve."

Mike shook his head. "No."

"I'm not a torturer," Trickster said. "I'm willing to allow us all to die. I'll shoot you if I have to. But I'm not a torturer."

"You have a fine sense of chaos, too," Mike said. "How is torture worse than murder?"

"I don't know," Trickster said. "Perhaps I've been trained to be a killer but not a torturer. I do know that I am not a torturer." He glanced out of the small porthole at the side-gunner position. "Besides, I doubt that your ship will shoot down one of its own aircraft, even if it violates safe-return procedures."

"Try it," Mike said. "That's the surest way to find out."

A kilometer from the aircraft carrier, Cat swung the tilt-jets from cruise to helicopter mode, then locked them in the vertical. The aircraft swung wildly before being brought back under control.

"Stand by to take aboard Firefly," the Air Boss blared over the 5MC, the open-air address system. "Ready spot two."

The tilt-jet aircraft swung toward the carrier. Only twenty meters away from the angle deck, its left wing dipped, the aircraft wobbled and swerved until it appeared about to veer into the superstructure, but then Cat corrected and the aircraft settled into a hover above spot two. A sudden decrease of jet power brought the aircraft crashing down onto the steel deck, buckling the landing gear. The jet engines began to die. Flight deck personnel ran forward, chocking and chaining the aircraft at spot two.

The Firefly's cargo doors opened. Wearing the dead marine's flight suit, barefoot, Trickster stood, holding a submachine gun to Mike's head. The Firefly's door slammed closed.

Trickster sat Mike down.

"Hostage barricade incident," Trickster said. "You have a name for this, too."

"What are you doing?" Mike asked. "What is the point of landing on the ship and then not allowing me to take you in?"

"I'm afraid," Trickster said. "Let's wait here for a while. I don't want to be a prisoner again."

"What?"

"What will your admirals decide to do? What is the doctrine for hostage barricade incidents aboard one of your vessels . . . gas?"

"What? Slow down."

"How long do you think it will take them to use gas?"

"I don't know. Are you insane?"

"No. Force of will."

They waited fifteen minutes. The first emissaries emerged from the superstructure, walking slowly toward the Firefly. Trickster and Mike stood.

The first torpedo detonated against the keel of the *Lincoln*.

The shock wave almost knocked Mike from his feet. Trickster's superior balance and his sudden firm grip helped Mike remain standing. For a moment, he thought that something had gone wrong with his own mind. Then the second torpedo struck the keel of the ship, then the third and fourth in quick succession. Trickster's hand released.

Horribly, the ship began to list to starboard. The Firefly bounded over its chocks, straining against its chains.

"Now!" Trickster shouted.

They opened the door and scuttled away from the aircraft looming over them. The naked survivors struggled to maintain their balance. A yellow gear tractor slid past, crashing into the superstructure. The Firefly bounded over its chocks and hung by its chains from the increasingly sloping flight deck. Trickster and Cat scrambled up the slope, gaining the heights above the Firefly. Lancer followed.

"Abandon ship, abandon ship," the captain's voice sounded over the 5MC. Mike shouted an obscenity. He tried to crawl up the rapidly slanting flight deck, to reach the catwalk and release one of the hundreds of twenty-man rafts kept in their steel barrels alongside the catwalk, but the slope of the deck was too extreme. He stumbled and began tumbling down the scraping flight deck toward the looming sea. Mike scrambled to grab onto something, anything, but he fell off the flight deck into the steel nets. The fifth torpedo struck. Aviation fuel spilled into the sea and ignited. Huge sheets of flame towered above the dying ship, the momentum of which was still carrying it forward. In his shocked state, Mike could only think of the necessity of opening a raft canister. The sixth torpedo struck. With a horrendous scream, the keel of the ship disintegrated. Horrible roars of rending steel, secondary explosions, the staccato of bolts popping in succession like firecrackers further disoriented him.

He found himself flying through the air. Some calamity, worse than the others, had thrown him from the catwalk. He had a momentarily glimpse of ship looming above him, then flames, just before he plunged into shockingly warm ocean water.

The explosions flung shrapnel through the grouping of the survivors of the tribe. A small scrap of metal caused a red blossom to form on Cat's right temple; from the corner of his eye as he tumbled through the air, Trickster saw a stream of white matter jet upwards from Cat's head. He experienced a searing heat, then shocking warm salty water.

Having been catapulted thirty meters, Trickster plunged deep. He opened his eyes and tried to find the surface. Shafts of broad tropical sunlight were filtering through the surface, which was blazoned with flame and mottled with strange black shapes. Trickster began to swim toward the surface. His lungs were only half full of air. The surface seemed impossibly distant. He seemed to be sinking, not rising. An evil current seemed to be drawing him deeper, down toward a drowning death. Trickster looked behind him and realized that some huge part of the ship was sinking below him, its doomed wake sucking him down with it.

Then Trickster saw Lancer and Cat. The two were below him. Cat appeared to be unconscious. Her form was lifeless and unmoving. Lancer was swimming down toward her. Every fiber of Trickster's body screamed for survival. He turned his face upward, toward the surface and the possibility of life. He saw Dreamer swimming not upwards, but away from the huge sinking section. Looking back downwards, he realized that if he followed Cat, he would die. He knew that he had only a second to decide whether to follow her into the secret realm of death or to struggle for the surface and life. His love for Cat drew him downwards, but then the howl for oxygen from within each cell of his flesh overwhelmed him. His snapped out of his cramped position. With powerful strokes, he fought the evil current that was sucking him downwards. Taking his cue from Dreamer, he swam outwards, away from the sinking section.

Down below him, Lancer struggled to reach Cat. Lancer, too, had seen the impact of the shrapnel. Lancer's mind was wailing with the desire that Cat be merely unconscious, not dead. He fought to reach her. The evil suction was taking them down lower and still lower. Lancer reached out his hand and grasped Cat's wrist. He turned to drag her up toward the surface, now impossibly distant and dim, but her body, dense and strong and airless, dragged him downwards.

Lancer looked up and saw the possibility that, if he abandoned Cat, he might yet live. He turned his face from the surface and looked down at Cat. Her face was turned from him. Lancer embraced her body and redoubled his efforts to carry her toward the surface. Slowly they sunk.

He could not abandon her. She had entered the next realm. He would stay with her. He would not abandon her. Lancer clung to Cat's body. A convulsive need to breathe forced him to inhale ocean water. The bubbles of his last breath exploded from his tortured lungs, hurtling upwards with a traitorous felicity toward the surface. He had no eyes for that, not in this darkness. He closed his eyes. Dying was hard and very painful, but he concentrated on the sensations of the body of his beloved in his arms. Those sensations, which had been robbed from him all his life, were his now, and even agony would not rob him of their experience.

Heavier now, he sunk lower and lower. He would not surrender her. She was his, he was hers. None of the loves in the world had been stronger than his love for his Cat. She was his only friend. He could not abandon her even in death. Especially, not in death.

Yet it was painful. The body had its own imperatives. Convulsions, horrible wrackings. A watery death was a horrible one, yet Lancer did not let go of Cat.

Then he felt an inner peace. It was all right to die, even such a painful death as this. There was something within like a burning ember, a white hot spark that warmed him now. It was growing larger and brighter, washing away all sensations of pain and struggle. He opened his eyes and saw its warm light suffusing everything, his limbs, the limbs of Cat, the ocean waters. It was all miraculous, after all. The molecules of the water, photons of dancing light, tiny crystalline castles of salt, thought and being, what a glorious trick!

My Lord, what a master! The light was growing brighter, warmer, burning to silhouettes and then fading away the traces of the natural world, revealing the essences. Lancer felt the presence of Cat. He turned and saw her true face, smiling in his embrace.

"Cat!" Lancer exclaimed. "See! We beat the world and the other world, both in one day! Come on! We're still together."

Cat's soul smiled, her happiness merging with Lancer's happiness. He understood her better now. He knew why he had loved her. He could feel her feeling him as they turned their attention to the glorious source of the light.

Ecstatic majesty! In the one moment when they left the domain of time and space, in the moment of their entrance into eternity, they felt themselves merging with a glorious perfection, knowing, being and understanding all things. Individual, yet joined in perfect union, they exited into another secret realm.

36

The evil current seemed to release Mike McCullough from its slippery grasp. Suddenly buoyant, he began to rise toward the surface. He fought the compulsion to gulp for air. His chest was tortured with the need to breathe. Yet, the surface remained distant. He could make out the flames on the surface. Remembering his training years ago in survival swimming, Mike raised his hands above his head, thrashed wildly, throwing aside the fuel and flames and heat, and made a momentary gap large enough for his head to break the surface so that he could gasp in noxious air, before he fought to sink again as fiercely as he had fought to rise.

Under the water, he looked for a gap in the burning oil. One, impossibly distant, appeared off to his right. Mike swam in that direction. Only a third of the way to the gap, his lungs began to ache. Mike raised his hands above his head, thrashed wildly, broke the surface and sucked air, this time hotter and more polluted than before. He convulsed, fighting to regain the depths. For a moment, he was disoriented, but then he saw the gap, which was marked by a broad shaft of pure sunlight streaking through it. With limbs as heavy and as dead-feeling as iron, he tried to resume swimming in that direction. He was beginning to believe that he wouldn't make it, when the winds moved the gap closer to him. Mike fought to make it on the last evil lungful of poisoned air. He passed the perimeter of the gap and swam two more strokes until he decided he could swim no more.

Mike McCullough broke the surface. He needed the air, whether it was life-giving or death-dealing. He gasped in lungful after lungful. He struggled to see through sheets of flames and was rewarded with the horrendous sight of the bow of the *Lincoln* towering straight up. It twisted, its huge anchors scraping against the underside of the flight deck. A lone sailor threw himself from the catwalk, plummeting, to be lost in the flames. The hellish magnificence of his ship's death astounded Mike, but as the bow began to settle deeper into the water, he realized that he had to gain as much distance from the sinking ship as possible. The suction caused by such a huge section submerging could drag him back under the surface.

Striking out to the south, Mike was able to swim a few dozen meters through a corridor walled with flames. Fortunately, the sea state was calm, but even so, waves that he had ignored from the safety of the ship now seemed huge and malevolent, intent on pitching him back into the flames or submerging him so that he would drown. Mike struggled against the waves. He saw the gap opening to his right, angling further away from the ship. He struck out in that direction, trying to make as much distance as possible above water.

Some trick of currents and waves caught him and bore him further away from the wreck. His water-clogged, noise-deafened ears hardly heard the final groanings as the *Lincoln* sunk beneath the waves. He continued to swim for twenty minutes. When he finally looked back, all he could see, when the waves carried him to their crest, was a black pall of smoke underlit by intermittently visible flames.

Mike trod water. He knew that he did not have the strength to swim to the nearest land. In his mind's eye, he recalled the position of the *Lincoln*, east of the Bashi Channel, more than ninety miles from Batan Island. He would die unless someone arrived to rescue him.

After five minutes, he began to swim back in the direction of the flames. Topping one crest, he thought he saw a vessel between himself and the datum of the *Lincoln*'s death. With increasingly heavy limbs, he thrashed through the rollers toward this apparition of a vessel. Atop another crest, he wiped his eyes and peered until he recognized the vessel: it was a Japanese command-and-control submarine.

Bagged, and not even by a seventh generation nuke attack boat. By a stinking submersible flagship . . . you'd have thought after the war of '12 that we would have gotten rid of all our carriers. Dinosaurs. Had to keep them for someone to sink . . .

Mike tried to decide whether he should swim toward the *Uzushio*. Although it seemed like his only chance for survival, he resisted the notion that he should become a prisoner twice in one day, the same day his ship had sunk beneath his feet. Finally, the heaviness of his limbs convinced him that he had to swim for the *Uzushio*. he knew from several reports that the Japanese were making only sketchy attempts to rescue survivors, and that these attempts were made only because of the heavy penalties they had paid for their war atrocities in the twentieth century. He couldn't rely on the *Uzushio* remaining surfaced for more than ten minutes.

Several hundred meters from the surfaced submarine, Mike was surprised by the roar of outboard motors. Looking around for the source of the noise, he saw a Zodiac boat leaping toward him. For a moment Mike had the irrational idea that an American force had come to rescue him. He raised his arm. A loop

thrown over him hauled him out of the water and pivoted him
into the rear of the Zodiac. Wiping the salt water from his eyes,
Mike saw that the naval ensign at the rear of the Zodiac was the
rising sun.

Several Zodiacs were bounding across the water, snatching
survivors out of the water. Several minutes later, a whistle blew.
Turning with survivors still ahead of them, the Zodiacs headed
back toward the *Uzushio*. Mike found himself in the boat well
atop the huge submarine. Strong hands pulled him up onto the
landing. A hand pressed the crown of his head, forcing him to
duck as he was hustled through a hatch.

Salt water splashed on a steel deck. The air stunk of lye, the
chemical trace of air scrubbing. Momentarily blinded by the
sudden dimness of the submarine's interior, Mike stumbled forward, guided and hustled by a succession of uniformed Japanese. Eagerly looking about him, he ignored whatever he could
have learned from a glimpse of the interior of an imperial
command-and-control ship. He sought out the faces of the
other survivors. He knew that the beginning of a capture or
rescue was always the most disorganized phase. He had a responsibility to see who else had been saved. Their later disappearance would have to be explained.

A dozen American sailors and marines were lined along the
corridor. Mike peered at their faces. He didn't recognize anyone. *Lincoln* had been a big ship; not all of the two thousand
crew and troops knew each other. Mike's life in the ship had
been unusually sequestered.

The Japanese were attempting to separate the officers from
the enlisted. The deck began to tilt downwards as the submarine began its dive. Guttural Japanese sounded over the ship-
wide address system. Mike caught a glimpse of a face he
recognized. Resisting his handlers, Mike drew up short and
wrenched free, turning around to find himself face-to-face with
Trickster.

Before, the intense look had blazed with the violence of desperation. Now Mike saw the heavy black power of fatalism.

Hard hands were grabbing for Mike's arms.

Trickster accelerated. He smashed the nearest Japanese in the temple, breaking the thinnest part of the skull. In the cramped quarters of the submarine passageway, Trickster advanced in the style of the monkey king, attacking the Japanese guards. He disabled four Japanese before anyone could understand what was happening. The American marines perceived the tumult as an attempt to escape. Shouting their battle cry "uhruh!," Turkish for "kill!," the marines assaulted the remaining Japanese guards. A brief staccato of automatic weapons fire sounded impossibly loud in the cramped steel space.

Trickster disappeared down the corridor. Watching him, Mike caught a glimpse of a naked member of the tribe running after Trickster, but the glimpse was so brief that Mike was unsure of even the sex.

"To me, marines!" Mike shouted. He scooped up a submachine gun and began to plunge down the slanting passageway, following Trickster.

Ahead of him, Trickster and Crush ran at top speed. Japanese crewmen appeared everywhere, confronted them or slowly attempted to throw themselves down cross passageways, seeking cover. Armed with a submachine gun and an automatic pistol, Trickster dropped the Japanese as soon as he glimpsed them. Crush, who had snatched up two weapons, ran sideways, directing most of his attention and fire backwards, covering their rear as Trickster plunged deeper into the submarine.

They arrived at the first water-tight hatch, dogged shut. A klaxon was sounding throughout the submarine.

Trickster swore, naming evil smells and substances. "They've gone into full security alert!" he shouted at Crush.

"Did you see Sly?" Crush shouted.

"No."

"He was ahead of us. The boat before mine, two before yours. Taken up ahead. I think Dreamer was with him."

"Anyone else?"

"Not that I saw."

Mike McCullough and five marines arrived. Trickster and Crush kept their weapons trained away from the Americans, even though the marines were drawing down on them. Mike saw the look in Trickster's eye. He observed the alert relaxation of Trickster's musculature. Mike understood that if he gave the order to fire, the first shots fired would be Trickster's and the other's killing the marines.

"What's happening?" Mike shouted. "What are you doing?"

"Taking the submarine," Trickster answered. "Do you know the layout of this class?"

"In a . . . in a general way," Mike said. "They're based on the American *Swordfish* class."

"Where's damage control central?" Trickster asked.

Mike thought. He tried to understand what role Trickster had played in the sinking of his ship. Ignorant of the fact that Trickster had implanted the location report, Mike had only his suspicions that Trickster had contributed to the death of the *Lincoln*. He knew, however, that the Japanese had sunk her. Although he believed that the enemy of his enemy was also possibly his enemy, Mike decided that he would collaborate with anyone who was working evil against the Japanese. "Somewhere on the fourth deck, two decks down and farther forward," he answered. "Near the combat command center."

A loud metal clanging sounded from the far side of the shut hatch. Trickster recognized the pattern. He rapped on the hatch in an answering pattern. Immediately, the dogs eased away, allowing the hatch to swing inwards. Sly stood there.

"Dreamer's forward," he said. "She got through to the next water-tight compartment."

Trickster and Crush streaked through the hatch. Mike and the marines followed.

"Can we get to damage control central from here?" Trickster asked Mike.

"Yeah, I think so . . . if we can break the hatch to the next deck down."

Emphatic Japanese continued to blare from the ship-wide address system. Trickster and Crush led the way down the passageway. They passed two hatches to the next deck down, but they were closed and dogged shut. As they were approaching the third hatch downwards, Trickster saw that the dogs were sliding away from the hatch frame. He shouted to Crush. Crush motioned to Mike and the marines. They set themselves against the right-side bulkhead, where they could not be seen easily from the opening hatch.

A Japanese security team began to emerge from the hatch. As soon as the first one turned enough so that he could glimpse the intruders, Crush shot away the top of his skull. The marines opened fire. Bullets ricocheted throughout the passageway. The hatch slammed downwards, but caught on the corpse of a Japanese. Trickster and Crush inserted their weapons through the crack between the hatch and the deck. They emptied their magazines. Stepping back, they waved the marines forward.

Throwing back the hatch, the marines leapt down into the body-strewn, smoky ladderway. Gunfire erupted. Trickster and Crush collected fresh magazines from the fallen Japanese. After the fire died down, Trickster waved Crush forward. Crush leapt down into the void. He was firing before he hit the bottom of the ladderwell. He waved Trickster down. Trickster and Mike descended to the command-and-control deck.

Down on the third deck, the marines lay strewn, dead, their bodies intermingled with a dozen Japanese troops. The intruders continued forward. The submarine had finished its dive; now the deck was level. Trickster moved forward, shooting crewmen as they appeared.

They investigated spaces that looked increasingly like command-and-control centers. Trickster and Crush began to shoot only those Japanese who were armed, which was increasingly rare. They had penetrated the security defenses of the *Uzushio*; sailors at sea, even in wartime, even when prisoners were aboard, were rarely armed.

Trickster recognized the damage control central from the large displays of the interior of the *Uzushio*, showing the layout of the entire vessel, including all the hatches, passageways, communications conduits, ballast tanks, pipes . . . the entire anatomy of the submarine.

Using his still-smoking weapon, Trickster waved the watch-standers away from their stations. He sat down at the central console and began to investigate the human-computer interface. Despite his lack of Japanese, within minutes, he was able to understand the workings of the damage control watch.

"How do you want to take it?" he asked Crush.

"We could flood . . ."

"We don't know where Dreamer is or whether there are any more of us aboard."

"Lock open the hatches," Crush suggested. "Take down all the power. That'll leave the battle lanterns. They run on battery. We'll go through the entire ship. Take the rest of the crew."

"Not bad," Trickster said. "But even though these wimps are slow and soft, their weapons are quick and hard. Everyone is out except you and me and Sly and maybe Dreamer and . . . maybe no one else. Just the four of us left. Maybe three. And if Dreamer is out, this gambit is a loser."

"I'm here," Dreamer said.

Trickster looked over his shoulder. Nude, submachine gun in hand, Dreamer stood inside the doorway.

"Are you all right?" he asked.

"Yes."

"Did you see any of us—"

"No. It's us four. The rest are out."

"Cat took it in the head on the ship," Trickster said. "I saw Lancer go down after her."

"I saw Cut-Back get it when the ship blew," Dreamer said.

"You put down Snake yourself," Crush said heavily. "That drops us eight down to four."

"They've moved on," Trickster said. "And we're not far behind unless we finish taking this ship. For this gambit to succeed, we need two to survive. That's me and Dreamer. You, Sly, and you, Crush, you're the soldiers. I'm going to flood these compartments. The others can't be flooded. I'll open the hatches when you need them, close them when you don't. I'll take down all power except battle lanterns. Use the darkness. Go through the rest of the ship and neutralize the crew."

"The Americans?" Sly asked.

"Leave this one with me. Drop the others if they draw down on you. Don't let them back into the command-and-control part of the vessel."

"Right, Hero," Sly said.

"We'll do it," Crush said.

Crush and Sly departed. Moments later, a single shot volleyed from the distances of the passageway. Trickster slammed shut the hatch, dogging it closed. He returned and sat down on the console chair. Turning to Mike, he said, "We are living by your rules. We are acting as you would act."

"I don't know about that."

"Today I have killed two thousand in order to save four million," Trickster said. "Four million, perhaps one billion. That conforms to your moral calculus, correct? I haven't made a mistake, have I?"

"What are you about, Trickster?"

"I am largely as I was made," Trickster said. "They wanted to make us into the perfect forebrains of generals. Cold calculating killing machines. Our brains, weapons. Tools of directors of battle. Maybe I could have been free . . . gone with Cat, es-

caped, been something greater, better . . . but I saw this gambit, such a beautiful gambit. I am as they made me, finally. A
warrior. At least I am choosing my own enemies. I am choosing my fight."

Trickster lapsed into a deep silence. For a long minute, he
seemed unable to move. Dreamer spoke to him in rapid-fire
tribal Mandarin. Trickster stirred and manipulated the damage
control system, flooding compartments and killing the generators.

Periodically, Crush and Sly used the damage control circuits to call from various water-tight hatches. Trickster un-
locked the hatches so that they were able to finish their sweep
of the submarine.

Forty minutes later, Crush and Sly returned to the damage
control center.

"The submarine is ours," Crush said.

"We damaged all of the weapons except ours," Sly said.
"About half of the Japanese crew is dead. There's at least fifty
Americans, most of them sailors. Most of the marines are dead.
We pushed the Americans forward, into that compartment
there. That one. Most of the off-duty Japanese, we pushed aft,
into that compartment."

"Let's go check the command-and-control, then," Trickster
said.

Trickster led the way into the bridge. Most of the watch
team, including the captain and the admiral, were dead. Lieutenant Takahashi stood among the few survivors.

"Who speaks Mandarin?" Trickster demanded.

Lieutenant Takahashi's face twitched. Trickster pointed his
submachine gun at him.

"You are my prisoner," Trickster said. "This vessel is my
prize. I'm going to take this vessel to my home port, where you
and my other prisoners will be treated as prisoners of war under
the Geneva conventions. According to these conventions and
the practices of naval prizes, you are allowed, with all military

honor, to render the assistance necessary to conduct this vessel and her surviving crew to safety."

Takahashi nodded. Trickster's speech had provided the means for him to collaborate without losing face.

"Familiarize me with the workings of your command-and-control interface," Trickster said.

While Dreamer and Trickster learned about the command and control of the *Uzushio*, Crush and Sly checked the prisoners, many of whom were attempting to escape or to subvert control. Working as a pair, Crush and Sly were able to hog-tie and lock up all of the surviving Japanese.

Trickster's first order of business was to check the communications logs. He verified that *Uzushio* had not been able to send any distress signals during its capture. While submerged, the *Uzushio* had no low-probability-of-intercept circuits, only one high-frequency circuit that would have broadcast to the entire globe its general location. Trickster felt a rush of relief that he had succeeded in taking the *Uzushio* without Tokyo discovering. A single short message would have checked the gambit. *Cat's death . . . her exit from this realm would have been wasted,* he thought. *We still have a chance to make it count.*

"Take me to the computer room," Trickster commanded Takahashi.

On their way down, Trickster asked, "Do you have a Mitsubishi holographic cell reader?"

"No," Takahashi said.

Trickster refused to believe that his gambit would fail.

"You must. You must have a holographic cell reader."

"Ah . . . we have Haitachi readers, yes," Takahashi said. "I believe they are compatible with the Mitsubishi equipment."

"That is good."

In the computer center, Trickster shed the marine's flight suit. He unstrapped the holographic cell case from his lower back. He removed the cells, which were undamaged, washed them in the cleansing equipment and then inserted one into the Haitachi reader. While waiting for the petabytes of information about the world to be downloaded onto high-speed optical readers, Trickster studied the computer infrastructure of the *Uzushio*. He was pleased that there were a series of Fujitsu S-7 supercomputers. *I won't have to reengineer the world modelers*, he thought. *Just run them on the S-7s as if we were in backup mode.* After launching his doppelgangers, which began to infect and take control of the entire computer infrastructure of the submarine, Trickster turned his attention to communications hardware.

"Take me to the communications center," he told Takahashi.

In the submarine's radio shack, Trickster rooted around for an appropriate radio. Nothing was readily available. Finally, he decided to strap together several components, which were not designed for his purpose, but which served it nonetheless: a fiberoptic cable compatible with the Fujitsu S-7; a general purpose digital data switch; a portable extreme high frequency radio and a long strip of pure copper for the antennae. He carried the communications gear to the computer room, strapped them together and tested the apparatus. After some nasty problems with electromagnetic interference, Trickster determined that it should work.

His doppelgangers had spun up the world. Trickster called Dreamer and explained the communications apparatus.

"Our energy sumps are nearing depletion now," he said. "We can just let that happen. Become meat puppets. Or we could take a chance and light up this gear. It might kill us. What do you think?"

"Go for it, Hero," Dreamer said.

"All right."

Video cameras trained on him allowed his doppelgangers to see his gestures. Trickster made the hand commands that caused the world modelers to begin to generate signals for Dreamer.

Dreamer grimaced but then slowly smiled.

"I'm back in my personal realm," she said. "It's perfect. Nothing has changed."

"All right, I'm going to try it," Trickster said. He commanded the broadcast of the signal that reinitiated the radios of his interface wafers. He experienced a long period of serious disorientation. His guts writhed. He smelled copper, lilacs, burning rubber, wet wood. Pains radiated, jumped randomly from spot to region, streaked through his limbs. Proprioceptors scrambled, he felt as if his thumbs were connected to his forehead, then his upper back. He saw swirls of colors, bright explosions, radiations of dancing lights. Trickster's instincts screamed for him to stop this horrendous experience, but he reasoned that if his radios were working at all, it was possible that they would begin to work correctly, once their energy sumps were replenished. He concentrated on breathing normally and remaining calm, telling himself that his heart was beating normally, even as he experienced it tripping wildly and exploding with pain.

Slowly his senses began to perceive cleanly. Part by part, his personal domain began to form around him. His heart was beating strongly, but not wildly. He had mastered himself.

The presence of his personal realm comforted him. He sent a request-to-enter to the Realm of Night. Wearing her default avatar, Dreamer received him with great ceremony.

"How is it with you, Hero?"

"The world without Cat is not the world."

"No . . . but . . . I am here with you still."

Dreamer shifted into an avatar patterned after her body. She opened her arms, lifting her palms toward her wild skies.

"You loved Cat," she said. "You loved her more than you loved me. I always knew that. But I maintained, Trickster. Because I knew that I loved you more than she loved you. And I knew that someday that you would know it."

"I think I didn't really understand that."

"To be loved more than you love . . ." Dreamer said. "What is that like?"

"It is more comfortable than loving more than you are loved," Trickster said.

Dreamer laughed. "Yes, I would imagine so."

"We'll . . . have a long time together, Dreamer," Trickster said. "I can't rush after Cat, because I'm not sure that she still exists anywhere . . . except in my memory. So I have to keep that part of her here, in this realm. A long time . . . maybe long enough that I'll grow enough, learn to love enough . . . that I can teach you what it feels like to be loved more than you love."

"I doubt you'll ever love me more than I love you," Dreamer said. "I don't think you can. But I'm willing to let you try. And you can keep me company when I'm tired with the infinite."

"The infinite?"

"Yes. The other world has beautiful patterns. Some violent, gross, others very fine, subtle. Overlaid. Reinforcing, canceling. I look at the patterns here and I glimpse the next world, I think. I realize now that it was patterns in the world that allowed me to know the other world. Staring at the brush strokes so that I could know the artist."

"So now . . . my friend . . . are you ready to finish this gambit?"

"I feel tired, but I think I can do it," Dreamer answered.

"Then," Trickster said, "let's throw fire into the face of the enemy."

37

Exiting the world, Trickster briefed Crush and Sly, warning them about the pain of the reinitiation of their interface wafers. Without hesitation, Crush and Sly elected to run the risk. Minutes later, the four survivors of the tribe were gathered atop War Council Rock.

"Battle!" Trickster cried.

As the battle problem erupted from the valley, Trickster shivered with an exquisite sensation of power. He ordered the *Uzushio* to climb to periscope depth. He deployed the communications van and initiated extreme high frequency communications. The battle problem shifted and crystallized. The Japanese forces abandoned their uncertain, foggy forms and assumed the clarity of truth. By commandeering the *Uzushio*, Trickster had intruded profoundly into Japanese command-and-control. Many secrets were revealed. The true face of his enemy appeared from the fog of war.

Dreamer scouted ahead. She busted encrypted signals. She expanded their range of knowledge to ever greater regions.

Trickster unleashed doppelgangers that infected other command-and-control nodes. By subverting switching centers, he managed to link ever greater networks together. Since they already had the keys to Chinese command-and-control, they were able to bridge over to the Chinese side. Eventually, Trickster was able to monitor and intrude in every important circuit on both sides of the conflict. Their power overshadowed all of Asia and the western Pacific.

Then the moment of greatest clarity arrived. They sighted their target.

"The emperor," Dreamer signaled. "There. In that train-borne command post. He's moving from that deep shelter toward the other. We have a window of opportunity."

"Emperor," Trickster acknowledged.

Through six relays, he opened a circuit that narrowcasted to Beijing. Masquerading as a Chinese intelligence node, he informed the Chinese of the position, course and speed of the emperor of Japan.

"Now," Trickster said to Dreamer. "Prepare for confusion to the enemies."

The four survivors prepared hundreds of reports. They prepared cease-fire commands from the emperor of Japan and from the high command in Beijing. They manufactured scholarly articles from influential intellectuals. They robbed from the most secret archives of Beijing and Tokyo, preparing memoranda that would destroy careers of high-ranking politicians and generals. They isolated and targeted the Imperial Party's mobile headquarters.

When the Chinese supersonic, terrain-hugging cruise missiles obliterated the train-borne command post of the emperor of Japan, Trickster triggered the program that controlled the scheduled release of the hundreds of reports. Warfare continued in Asia for another two hours, but the targets were not the combatants, but the political and military leadership on each side. The survivors of the tribe facilitated the desire of Beijing and Tokyo to decapitate each other's national command authority. When the mutual slaughter had progressed far enough that the two sides lacked national direction, Trickster assumed it. While his other informational warfare tricks created a political dynamic more conducive to war termination, he continued to direct hot steel. Surgically he destroyed more and more of the Chinese and Japanese ability to wage war, while sparing the civilian populations, the cities and the economic infrastructures.

"It's like playing chess when you can move both side's pieces," Trickster remarked to Dreamer. "I can create any position I want."

"I'm . . . losing it," Dreamer said.

"Hold on. We're almost done."

Finally, he allowed the orders for cease-fire to be transmitted. Across the eastern hemisphere, the flames of war died, the smoke of war moved away before the breeze. Trickster flipped through the dozens of channels of public information that he had manipulated.

". . . his last words, the last desire of our great emperor, was for peace. For lasting peace for his beloved people . . ."

". . . since all strategic objectives have been met, hostilities have ceased . . ."

". . . political opponents pursued this course of action, this madness, this stupid and unnecessary war, remains a mystery, but it is for us who opposed it from the beginning to take up the burden of rebuilding our great nation . . ."

". . . cowardly enemy capitulated. We have won!"

". . . battled the perfidious enemy to a standstill. Our brave men and women in uniform have saved us from imperial aggression. We are safe. Thank the heavens, the war is over!"

Trickster looked out over the battle problem. He knew his doppelgangers would continue to spread, infecting more and more of both Chinese and Japanese computer systems. Even if either side attempted to reinitiate hostilities, it would have to attack with bayonets. *And the Sea of Japan is deep*, he thought.

Trickster slashed his hands before his face. He stood in the computer room of *Uzushio*. Dreamer lay in the corner, collapsed from exhaustion. Crush and Sly stood, respectfully waiting for orders.

"Let's put the prisoners ashore," Trickster said.

38

To Mike McCullough, the broad light of tropical day seemed superreal. The absolute reality of the sunlight, the pure royal blue of the sea, the perfect azure of the sky, and the shock of the vibrant green of the vegetation of Batan Island washed away optical memories of computer-generated environments. *Survived,* he thought. *I survived. This day is mine.* He smelled the sea, the scent of sunlight on a world of salt water. They were close enough to the island that he could also whiff the shore, with its notes of the rottenness of beach-wrecked organisms. Upon his skin the tropical sunlight was warm, reassuring, raising a healthy sweat from his skin, too long sweatless below refrigerated decks.

He watched as one of the Zodiac boats bounded over the surf, kicking up a rooster tail as it sped toward him, high in the tower of the surfaced submarine. Mike noticed the excitement rising in this strange creature who called himself Trickster. It seemed strange to Mike that this cold-blooded killer could react with so much emotion. Looking out at the returning Zodiac,

Mike could see it contained two of the tribe: the one called Crush and the one that moved so strangely. He supposed Trickster was evacuating the one who moved strangely, gathering together what was left of the tribe into the submarine. The other Zodiacs, carrying American and Japanese survivors toward the shore, bounded in the other direction.

"Now we're five again," Trickster muttered. "Six, in the world."

The returning Zodiac roared into the boatwell. Trickster turned to Mike.

"This will be the last boat," he said. "You can stay with us, if you want."

Mike shook his head. "Don't think so. Thanks."

"All right. Go."

Mike turned to descend from the tower. Trickster grabbed his elbow with surprising force.

"Tell me. What do you think of my gambit?"

Fighting to keep his emotions under control, Mike answered, "You killed my admiral. My friends. You sank my ship."

Trickster's expression did not change. "I saved many cities. What do you think of your moral calculus now?"

"It sucks."

"What?"

"It's no good."

Trickster released Mike's elbow. "Then you are wearing the wrong uniform. Good-bye."

Mike glanced at his uniform, the black blood-stained flight suit of the United States Marine Corps. He remembered his duty.

"Where are you going?"

"What?"

"Where are you going?"

Trickster smiled. "That would be telling."

"I mean, why not give yourselves . . . why not join—"

"Part of the beauty of this gambit is how neatly it sets me up for pawn advance to the final rank," Trickster said. "Having sacrificed my queen, I must now advance my pawns. This ship has stores and fuel for the five of us to live submerged for many years. We'll come ashore, maybe next week, maybe five years from now. None of you will know when or where. If you want to find us, look for us in civilization."

Trickster tossed back his head and laughed, as if he had made a joke. Then he turned his back to Mike. He watched Sly help Barker/Dummy climb out of the boatwell. They disappeared into the skin of the ship. Impatiently, Trickster waited for the last American to depart the ship. Finally, Mike appeared, climbing into the Zodiac. After fumbling with the outboard's controls, he managed to cast off and roar toward Batan Island. The last that Trickster saw of him, he was turned back, staring at the submarine. Trickster raised his palm in the universal gesture for peace. Mike's hand lifted from the outboard yoke, but then it settled back. Trickster grunted and descended into his ship. He dogged the hatch and shouted, "Dive."

The deck was already sloping as he entered the command center. Dreamer lay curled in a corner, still asleep, resting from the exhaustion of the long battle. Crush and Sly were directing the operations of the great vessel. Trickster jumped into the world, then skipped to the command interface they had created for direction of the submarine. They were descending below a thermocline eighty fathoms deep. Under the cover of this acoustic layer, their course crept slowly, silently, out into the deep Pacific, into regions far from shipping lanes and far from acoustic sensors and far from any submarine operating areas, far from anyone who could find them.

A hand rested on his shoulder. He returned to his natural senses. Dreamer was looking at him, her eyes peering with watchful concern. Trickster reached up and placed his hand over hers. A long profound wave of inattention, of exhaustion, swept through his brain.

"You did well, Trickster," Dreamer said.

Trickster made a gesture. He catapulted Dreamer and himself into his personal realm. Atop the same grassy knoll where he had conversed with Iva, he pulled her onto his lap. He buried his face in her hair, which stank of smoke. Her skin was silken. Remembering the rich feel of Cat's skin, he began to sob.

"It's all right now," Dreamer said. Her voice was low and musical. It had taken on a new assurance that reminded him of Cat's voice when she had spoken to him privately. The memory caused him to sob more wrackingly.

"It's all right now," Dreamer repeated. The touch of her hand, as she stroked the back of his head, smoothing his hair, was beyond his imagination.